THE CROSSING

eMotions Magazine

Inspired by Mrs. Serita A. Jakes, *eMotions* magazine is an informative and inspirational digital publication for today's Christian woman. Each issue is filled with: heartwarming stories, encouraging testimonies, fabulous recipes, lifestyle features and much, much more!

Mission Statement

The magazine represents our desire to inspire women to move forward with a personal relationship with the Lord in every area of their lives…and to motivate each woman to:

- *embrace* her true identity in Jesus Christ as she invites others to follow in the righteousness of our Heavenly Father

- *empower* her to love abundantly so that she can make a meaningful difference in the lives of others

- *engage* her heart to celebrate the treasure she truly is as she inspires others to honor their own self worth

- *encourage* her to dare to dream for his best so she can awaken aspiration in others

- *educate* her to create an inspired life for herself as she influences others to achieve greatness

Visit *eMotions* at www.emotionsmag.com and find out what the excitement is all about!

Praise for
The Crossing

"Serita Jakes has created a rich story about confronting the debilitating wounds of one's past and standing at a crossroads of hope and healing—or ongoing suffering. Her characters take meaningful and relatable journeys, and they will serve as an inspiration for many to find the path toward wholeness."

—DR. FRANK LAWLIS, best-selling author, consultant to the *Dr. Phil* show, and author of the revolutionary program PTSD Breakthrough

"An amazing story of hope, loss, and the unconditional love that brings us back to God. Serita Jakes has created a meaningful novel that tears at your heart while mending your brokenness at the same time. *The Crossing* is powerful storytelling."

—PAT SMITH, founder and CEO of Treasure You and president of Pat & Emmitt Smith Charities

"*The Crossing* is captivating from page 1—a remarkable tale of betrayal, pain, and spiritual anguish. Her writing uncovers an important core message: how to find freedom from past hurts and wounds and move toward a life of forgiveness, healing, and Divine wholeness."

—DR. TIM CLINTON, president, American Association of Christian Counselors

"Serita Jakes's *The Crossing* is so much more than you expect. She's a brilliant woman of God, and this stirring novel will reach so many hearts and lives with its message of grace and healing."

—LISA OSTEEN COMES, associate pastor, Lakewood Church in Houston, Texas, and author of *You Are Made for More!*

"First Lady Serita Jakes is a unique lady with a big heart. She has experienced hurt in her life; therefore, *The Crossing* is a perfect novel for her to write. She is a woman who loves much and wants to help others. This book will impact, and may even save, your life. I salute Serita and consider her one of my children."

—DODIE OSTEEN, cofounder of Lakewood Church
    and author of *Choosing Life*

"I hope whoever reads this book never has had to go through loss and suffering. But should you be faced with one or the other or both, Mrs. Jakes's powerful words will help you through it because this story demonstrates God's forgiveness, powerful healing, and unconditional love for us all."

—JAMIE FOSTER BROWN, publisher, *Sister 2 Sister* magazine

"Serita Jakes has captured the true meaning of what it means to "wear the mask." And the phrase 'cover your sins and keep up appearances' penned in *The Crossing* says it all. The depiction of the novel's main character, Claudia, reveals the devastating and irreversible effects of untreated trauma and the dire consequences if left undiagnosed and untreated—as it does all too often. *The Crossing* hits home on these important issues in a down-to-earth and entertaining way."

—TERRIE M. WILLIAMS, author of *Black Pain*

"A meaningful novel about loss, forgiveness, suffering, and God's healing, unconditional love. A perfect read for women who have seen hard times. I highly recommend it."

—PAULA WHITE, Paula White Ministries/senior pastor,
    Without Walls International Church

THE CROSSING

A NOVEL

SERITA JAKES

WATERBROOK
PRESS

THE CROSSING
PUBLISHED BY WATERBROOK PRESS
12265 Oracle Boulevard, Suite 200
Colorado Springs, Colorado 80921

Scripture paraphrases and quotations are from the following versions: The New American Standard Bible®. © Copyright The Lockman Foundation 1960, 1962, 1963, 1968, 1971, 1972, 1973, 1975, 1977, 1995. Used by permission. (www.Lockman.org). The Holy Bible, New International Version®. NIV®. Copyright © 1973, 1978, 1984, 2011 by Biblica Inc.™ Used by permission of Zondervan. All rights reserved worldwide. www.zondervan.com. The King James Version.

The characters and events in this book are fictional, and any resemblance to actual persons or events is coincidental.

ISBN 978-1-4000-7303-0
ISBN 978-0-307-73034-3

Cover design by Mark Ford; Cover photo of woman: ©JLP/Sylvia Torres/Corbis

Published in the United States by WaterBrook Multnomah, an imprint of the Crown Publishing Group, a division of Random House Inc., New York.

WATERBROOK and its deer colophon are registered trademarks of Random House Inc.

Library of Congress Cataloging-in-Publication Data is on file with the Library of Congress.

Printed in the United States of America
2011—First Edition

10 9 8 7 6 5 4 3 2 1

To all who have been redeemed by His love, recipients of His mercy, and amazed by His grace... Perfect Peace—Perfect Love

Part One

Rock of Ages, cleft for me,
Let me hide myself in thee;
Let the water and the blood,
From thy wounded side which flowed,
Be of sin the double cure;
Save from wrath and make me pure.

Prologue

No one prepares you for this. Parents, teachers, professors.

Preachers, at least, try to make you aware of that final moment, just before your heart stills and breath stops.

If you die tonight, will you be ready? The two-dollar question anyone raised in church has heard a hundred times.

But when the time comes…

After the bullets tear into your body, while your blood spreads out across your new white shirt and your extra large Diet Pepsi splatters to the floor, as the man holding the gun screams at the kids on the bus to shut up or they're next.

…will you be ready?

Now isn't the time to ask why.

My body slumps to the floor like the strings holding me up have suddenly been cut. Somewhere, Claudia is crying. If she's crying, she's alive. *Lord, she's eighteen and searching. She's not ready for life to end.*

He's nudging me with his foot. I pray he doesn't check my pulse.

"Leave her alone!" The voice of a football player coming to my defense. *Don't be my hero, Casio,* I want to say, but I can't move, can't speak. The gun fires.

No, not Casio.

A few students are screaming. Most are crying. But the noise of the passing train is drowning them out. Everyone except Claudia.

One

It's strange. Since childhood, I've believed I would die in my sleep.

Now I lay me down to sleep, I pray the Lord my soul to keep...

In my mind's eye, I picture myself sandwiched between Mama and Daddy as we knelt beside my bed, speaking the prayer together. It always seemed like they were sucking up all the oxygen, leaving me with none. I thought I might suffocate. But I could smell Mama so well. She hadn't had her nightly bath yet, so she still smelled of southern cooking and a hint of Chanel No. 5. The smallest amount behind her ears and inside the crook of her arm was enough for it to linger wherever she wandered in the house. I loved the smell of Mama.

I remember the expression on her face when she opened the box one Christmas morning. By the look of wonder, I knew she loved it. She blushed under Daddy's admiring gaze as she dabbed some on her wrist and lifted her arm to his face. As I watched, a bubble, like the ones I used to blow with those huge pieces of sugar-coated bubble gum, started deep inside me and got bigger and bigger. It was a rare moment of sheer joy in our family.

A few years later, a pin of reality burst the facade, but in that moment...joy. I'm glad my mind took me back to that place, if only for a minute. I can remember Daddy as he was. And forgive what he became.

...and if I die before I wake, I pray the Lord my soul to take.

PRESENT DAY

Claudia

Claudia hated this moment. Stopped at the tracks, watching the lights flash and hearing the bell clang. First in line, as the wall forms in front of her. The whistle growing louder as the engine nears. The rhythm of steel against steel, the train racing by, beating in her ears. Other cars had lined up behind her, hedging her in. Suffocating. Blocking any chance of escape.

Could a heart really pound right out of its chest? She felt her breath coming in short bursts. Her phone beeped, but she couldn't bring herself to look for it. Closing her eyes tight, she gripped the steering wheel.

Her chest hurt, and she could smell the metallic tang of blood. The rest of her senses picked up the sensation. She could taste the iron, way back in her throat, and her ears pounded with the rhythm of her heartbeat. Then her hands felt a sticky warmth—BJ's blood, soaking her cheerleading skirt. The wetness spread over her legs. She gasped and stared down at her lap. Her Diet Coke had spilled on her light tan linen pants. Still, she couldn't move.

No matter that the train had come and gone, still she sat, staring at the bare metal tracks. Her body shook all over. Vehicles sped around her, blaring their horns. People glared at her, some even shouting obscenities at her, but it was no use. She'd become paralyzed. She didn't know how many minutes she sat there while the world swept by her, a still body in a raging storm.

A dull tap registered in her brain. She turned toward the sound and tried to focus on the man outside her window. He reached out and made another clipped, three-rap knock on the glass. Finally, recognition flashed, trying to convince her that everything was okay. She pressed the button and lowered the window for the waiting police officer.

"Claudia?" His voice sent a shiver down her spine. Images sped through her mind, blurring her focus. "Is there something wrong with your car?"

His voice was a little deeper now than it had been ten years ago, but she could still hear it screaming, "Leave her alone!" And then the gunshot. She could feel herself fading again…

"Claude!" He reached in through the window and shook her shoulder. "Come on, girl. I know what this is. I've been there too. But snap out of it. You're in the middle of the street."

She felt herself slowly ascending, as though swimming from the bottom of a deep lake. At the surface, a ragged, cold breath filled her lungs. "Casio." Tears filled her eyes.

"It's okay, baby," he said, his voice soft, taking her back to the days when he was quarterback, she was cheerleader, and everyone said they'd be America's sweethearts. "Can you drive the car into the parking lot?" He pointed to the right where a mom-and-pop café sat practically empty.

She nodded.

"I'll be right behind you."

It took every ounce of willpower to slide the Tahoe into gear and drive toward the parking lot. Once she stopped, her lungs screamed and she could feel the breath-stealing, muscle-seizing horror of hyperventilation coming on. Casio appeared at the passenger side door. Clutching her chest, she pointed toward the glove box. "Bag," she managed to gasp.

"What?"

"A bag. In there!"

"Oh! Okay! Are you okay? Hang on." Casio opened the glove box and pulled out a paper bag, then brought it to her mouth. "Breathe. In-out-in-out."

She did. Her lungs felt like they might burst as the panic spiked. "Oh, God. It's just like that night." A scream vibrated in her throat, and she squelched it before it could pierce the air inside the Tahoe.

"No." Casio's hand pressed against her clammy neck. "Now, listen, Claude. Keep breathing." His smooth-as-silk tone calmed her and evened out her breath. She tried to focus on his tone. "This isn't like that night on the bus. No one is after you. The person with a gun was after BJ. No one else. It wasn't a random act or I wouldn't have just been shot in the arm. Right? If that man was on a killing spree, we'd all be dead right now."

His voice was beginning to soothe her, and slowly, the words sank into her muddled brain. She set the bag in her lap and filled her lungs with a cleansing breath. "Thanks, Casio," she whispered and tried to smile. "You're a hero."

His jaw clenched as he inhaled from a freshly lit cigarette and then passed it to her. "Yep, that's what I am." He expelled a stream of smoke. "A real hero."

At the sarcasm in his tone, Claudia regretted her choice of words. She reached across the seat and took his hand. "We did what we could."

"Too bad that doesn't make the dreams go away."

She stared into the horizon where clouds were beginning to roll their way. Silently, they sat, hand-in-hand, passing the cigarette between them, remembering that they shared a bond of pain and loss.

Somehow, for the moment, it made things calmer.

Victor

Embarrassment wasn't a normal part of Victor Campbell's MO. As a matter of fact, he'd been accused of overconfidence more than once during his rise to ADA. And the talk around town was that he'd be a shoo-in for DA if he chose to run. But as capable and on his toes as he liked to think of himself, he sat in awkward silence across from the clearly irritated event planner named Lindsey and fought an excessive need to squirm.

The twenty-something woman glanced down at an elegant gold watch wrapped around her delicate wrist. She seemed too young to be so put out.

"I'm sure my wife will be here soon," he said, drawing on his lawyer voice.

But even his trust-me smile didn't appear to soften her tough-as-nails demeanor. Rather, she looked across her desk with poorly concealed impatience, breathing in deeply, then giving a controlled exhale. "Mr. Campbell. I have another appointment in twenty minutes. If you'd like to call your wife again, perhaps we can check her schedule against mine and find a more convenient time to meet." She punched in some keys on her computer. "My next available opening is..." She squinted at the screen and punched in another key. "Tuesday."

Retrieving his BlackBerry from the jacket of his black "court" suit, Vic pulled up his own calendar. Claudia was going to hate waiting five more days, but it was her own fault. She'd just have to pull together the anniversary dinner of the year that much quicker. "That might work. I'll call and find out why she's so late. This really isn't like her." Or it hadn't been until lately. He started to place the call, but hesitated, casting a quick glance at the attractive Lindsey.

Exhibiting surprising intuition, the young woman pushed back from her desk and rose. "I'll give you a minute of privacy." A tight skirt hugged her slim figure, and he quickly averted his gaze as he punched in number one on speed dial.

The phone rang four times then moved to voice mail.

He pressed his lips into a tight line. Of course she still wasn't answering. Claudia's erratic behavior had been escalating since suffering a miscarriage two years ago. He'd attributed it to postpartum depression, but lately, instead of getting better, she seemed to be getting worse. Being late for a meeting to plan the thirty-fifth anniversary of her parents in marriage and ministry was definitely over the line. How long would this go on? Part of the reason he'd fallen for her in the first place was her ability to organize and hold things together. Where had that Claudia gone, and good grief, when would she be back?

He ended the call without leaving a message and pressed the number again. Still no answer. Shoving the phone into his pocket, Vic walked to the door.

In the foyer, he looked around, but didn't see Lindsey, so he made the Tuesday appointment with the receptionist in Claudia's name and headed for the elevator. The Lord knows he tried to be understanding, but the incompetence and inconsistencies Claudia was displaying lately were getting old.

Claudia

As Claudia pulled onto the street where her parents lived on the cul-de-sac, she stared straight ahead, her thoughts on the last hour, sitting with Casio, opening up to each other about that night on the bus. It had been almost a relief to rehash that night with someone who truly understood how she felt. Fleetingly, she wondered if she smelled like smoke from the cigarette she'd shared with him. She'd know soon enough. If her mother smelled smoke on her, she definitely wouldn't let it pass. After all, it wouldn't do for the daughter of Pastor and Mrs. King to be seen committing a sin of the flesh, would it?

The thought was so ludicrous she would have laughed if she didn't want to cry. Cover your sins and keep up appearances. The unspoken rule, more sacred than the Golden.

She glanced at the clock. It had been an hour since she'd called her mother to let her know she was running a little late and to ask if she would please pick Emily up from school. She'd tried to get there sooner, but this episode, or flashback, whatever it was, had lasted longer than ever before. She simply hadn't been able to move.

The familiar 1970s-*Knots Landing* homes slipped past her with their perfectly manicured lawns and respectable members of AARP sitting on porches or watering flowers out front. Claudia remembered days and nights when her parents gathered her into the backseat of their car and "took a drive" through streets of these nicer neighborhoods, dreaming of the day when God would "bless" their faithfulness. A house on the good side of town. Their reward on earth.

The smiles and waves she now received from the neighbors as she fifteen-MPHed her way toward her parents' house were a far cry from the reception her parents had received as the first biracial couple in the neighborhood—even after twelve years of ministry to the growing town of Conch Springs. A suburb of Dallas wasn't exactly the most welcoming place on earth to set down roots in the late '70s and early '80s if you weren't white and Republican, but Daddy had a call from God and had no intention of running away from white hoods and backwoods bullies. He was the bravest, smartest, holiest man Claudia knew.

They'd weathered the threats, broken windows, and smashed-up mailboxes. Everything short of burning crosses. And here they were still. Standing proud and strong. Living well. Thirty-five years in this town and in ministry.

Even though Claudia hadn't come along for several years after her parents had arrived in Conch Springs, she had to admit a certain amount of pride when she thought about all the obstacles her parents had faced coming here and refusing to be ashamed of their relationship or Daddy's heritage. Her mother was a paradox. Married to a black man and proud of it, but refusing to be honest about anything else that might draw criticism.

The town had its bigots—some had even left the church after Daddy took over as pastor. But the ones who stayed—even reluctantly—came around pretty quickly. Daddy had a way of winning over skeptics. It was one of his gifts.

Too bad Mother was the one standing on the porch looking like she had something on her mind.

Claudia drew in a breath and prepared herself as she climbed out of the Tahoe and walked toward the porch. She smiled as five-year-old Emily rushed out of the house and skipped toward her. "Hey, sweetie," she said, stopping halfway down the front walk and kneeling. "How was kindergarten today?"

"Fun." Emily shoved her backpack into Claudia's hands. "Miss Grishem sent a note. It's inside."

"Okay, hop in the car and buckle up." Still smiling, she stood and focused on her mother, who stood in the threshold of the front door. "Thanks for picking her up."

"I didn't mind. But Vic has been calling. He said you missed the appointment."

Alarm seized Claudia's stomach. "He didn't tell you what the meeting was about, did he?"

She scowled in the way only Mother could, making Claudia feel small. "No, he didn't. Although I don't see why it's such a secret. Are you pregnant again?"

"No, Mother," she said, wincing at the way her tone dropped, but resolute. "And I can't tell you what the meeting was for. That's between Vic and me."

But Mother would know soon enough. The night of the

anniversary dinner, she would complain and protest as they asked her to trust them and not ask questions on the way to the four-star restaurant. Then she would realize there was a party given in her honor, and for an hour or two, she would smile and be so pleased. Then later, when the two of them were alone, she would pick it apart.

"Did you tell Vic I called?"

"Of course. But you better have a good excuse for missing that meeting—whatever it was about. He's pretty upset."

"I have a good *reason* and that's also between Vic and me."

Her mother gave a shrug of her slim shoulders. "Fine. Keep your secrets. I best get inside and tend to your daddy's dinner. You know he likes it on time." The implication being, of course, that Claudia might not care about her husband, but her mother would not disappoint hers.

Everything in Claudia wanted to blurt out fifteen years' worth of reminders, but instead, she met her mother's gaze with the appropriate amount of humility and bit her tongue.

"Bye, Mama. Thanks again."

Claudia remained where she stood on the walk between the driveway and front porch until the door shut, then with a sigh, turned toward her waiting daughter.

Fat raindrops splattered over the hood of her SUV. Thunder rumbled overhead fifteen minutes later as she pulled into the driveway of the forty-year-old split-level home she and Vic had purchased the year Emily was born. She'd loved it back then, but now, even after her remodel of the kitchen and addition of a master bedroom, it didn't feel like home anymore. She couldn't explain the unrest, just that it felt like her whole body was jittery, tickly, like all she wanted to do was make it stop, but everything she did made it worse.

The sky moved again. Claudia hoped a gentle thunderstorm was on its way. Maybe she'd sleep tonight.

She frowned at the sight of Victor's Camry and shot a glance at the clock. So he'd decided not to go back to work today. That was a surprise, considering how hard he'd been working lately with DA Slattery's pending retirement. She glanced in the rearview mirror. "Looks like Daddy's home early, Emmy."

"Yay!" The little girl's enthusiastic response brought a smile to Claudia's face. If anyone understood daddy hero worship, she did.

Claudia slid the car into park and glanced over her shoulder at Emily. "Don't forget your backpack."

"I won't!" Her tiny body looked even tinier against the massive Tahoe door as she reached for the handle.

"Wait for me to help you out."

Emmy scrunched her nose, looking exactly like Vic when he was trying to form his closing arguments. "I can do it." Before Claudia could stop her, Emmy pushed open the mammoth door with a grunt and slid out.

"Be careful, Emily!" Honestly, sometimes the child's independence nearly gave Claudia a heart attack.

Shaking her head, she grabbed her shoes from the back floorboard and her purse from the seat next to her. Her gaze fell on the Camry as she walked past. She reached out her hand and felt the hood. Still warm. He hadn't been home long. Claudia couldn't remember the last time Vic had come home early.

Guilt slammed across her heart. Would she ever stop letting everyone down?

Casio

"Dear Jesus, please make him stop."

The voice sliced through Casio's rage, and he stopped short, as though something otherworldly stayed his hand, this close to smashing his two-thousand-dollar entertainment system into a million pieces. For the first time, Casio Hightower took stock of his surroundings. The broken glass, destroyed TV—a forty-seven-inch LG flat screen. What the...?

Harper lay curled in a fetal position, her body shaking with silent sobs.

"Oh, my..." He took an engulfing breath. "God, what did I do?"

He swiped a pool of sweat from his forehead with the back of his hand and knelt down beside the woman he loved.

If only she hadn't turned down his proposal.

Her lip was split and bleeding. He was the worst kind of monster.

She put up her hand to shield her face, and a diamond sparkled from the engagement ring he'd forced onto her finger. Slowly he reached out. She gasped and shriveled before him. "Don't...," she pleaded.

"It's okay. I'm done." He lifted her hand and gently removed the ring. "I'm sorry. Honey, I'm so sorry. Forgive me."

"C-can I go?"

Nodding, Casio sat back, knees up, arms and fingers clasped loosely around his legs. Weak, tired...so sorry, he watched her scoot away from him and stand up slowly, painfully. She grabbed her purse from the kitchen counter and stumbled to the door.

Lying back, he closed his eyes, replaying the stupid, mean, vile things he'd said and done to the woman he thought he'd spend the rest of his life loving. Frustration pushed through his throat as a groan. He hadn't had a flashback of the night on the bus in months. But tonight, he couldn't stop seeing the man in the mask, all the blood on the floor of the bus. BJ Remington's death. It had to have been caused by seeing Claudia again. Rehashing those events had triggered this craziness.

Shame washed over him. He knew there was no way to free himself from the guilt that clenched his gut, nauseating him with the memory of his hand slamming into the woman he loved. She'd taken him back before when he'd gotten a little rough, but the fear in her eyes, the blood—no way would she walk through those doors again. Not even to pick up her things.

Weary, he shoved to his feet and started the process of cleaning up the mess. Harper knew how much he loved her. They'd been through too much together for her to just walk away. She'd be back and he would get help this time, so that he could cope with the anger that built up in him.

When the phone rang a few hours later, he'd barely finished the cleanup. "Yeah?"

"Hey, man, it's Bob down at the station."

He sighed, resigned. At least they'd done him the courtesy of not showing up at his door with cuffs and a warrant.

"We have a situation."

"Yeah, I know."

If she'd gone to the hospital and she was pretty beat up, the doctors would have called it in.

"Harper says you raped and beat her. We might not be able to make this go away. They're calling in a special investigator from Dallas to look into her allegations against you."

Rape? That's not the way he remembered their lovemaking. Things had gotten rough later, but he hadn't forced her. The very thought grated on him. He'd never had to force a woman to be with him. He struggled to keep his voice calm.

"When do you want me in?"

"In the morning. Nine o'clock."

After the call, he stood in the middle of the room, feeling it spin around him a million miles an hour. Harper's betrayal smashed against him, harder than any blow he'd landed on her.

His boots crunched over a pile of broken glass he'd forgotten to sweep up, and he made his way to the bathroom. He washed his hands and stopped, staring at himself in the mirror. The memory of her face, already beginning to bruise, shoved into his mind. The scrapes on his knuckles were telltale—open-and-shut case. That couldn't happen. As much as he cared about Harper and hadn't meant to go that far, his job on the force was all he had, and he couldn't let this incident rob him of the rest of his life. He staggered into the kitchen and glanced around.

Victor

A suspicious mind came naturally to Vic. After all, he'd been raised by his mother in a rough part of Dallas, and his job depended upon him being suspicious.

He dumped Emmy's half-full glass of water from dinner and set it in the dishwasher. A rueful smile touched his lips. Half-full. Maybe that was his problem. A suspicious assistant district attorney with optimist tendencies. No wonder he was always in a state of turmoil. At least where Claudia was concerned.

She had looked good coming home a few hours ago when he'd met her and Emmy at the door. Almost too good in her snug jeans and the low-cut blouse he'd never seen before. He tried not to step in on household things. He knew she'd always done well with the budget, but lately new things were showing up all the time. An ADA in the state of Texas didn't make anything close to the six figures he could make in private practice—especially defense.

When Claudia missed appointments like she had today, he couldn't help but worry. He thought back to their predinner conversation, right after she'd sent Emmy to put away her backpack.

"So, where were you?" he'd asked, trying to keep his voice even, unthreatening.

She had glanced at him sharply as though she might snap, but he decided to diffuse the situation before an argument ensued.

"I was worried."

She expelled a heavy breath. "I had another panic attack," she said. "Only this one was really bad. I got stuck at the tracks and then I couldn't move even after the train was gone. Someone called the police, and lucky for me, Casio Hightower was the one who came. He got me off the road and sat with me while I calmed down." Her shaky smile touched his compassion. "I took a few puffs of his cigarette to calm me down."

He shoved down his jealousy at the thought of Claudia and the police officer sharing a cigarette. When he stepped forward, she moved into his arms.

The rest of the evening had gone smoothly, but Victor sensed a deep unsettling in his wife. He hated how helpless he was to do anything about it. How could he be so good at putting away bad guys and so bad at making his wife happy?

"Hey, look at you, cooking and doing the dishes too. How'd I get so lucky?"

Vic looked up to find Claudia standing in the doorway, wearing a pair of yoga pants and a strappy top that hugged her figure and made him want to forget the dishes and carry her upstairs. "Emmy all tucked in?"

She nodded, walking into the kitchen. She plopped her hands onto her curvy hips. "Go relax. You've done enough. I'll finish up here."

"You sure?"

"Positive."

"Thank you, honey." He transferred the dishtowel from his shoulder to hers and pressed a kiss to her cheek. The faint smell of smoke still clung to her hair. "Claude?"

"Yeah?" She angled her gaze to him as she plunged her hands into the soapy water. Her beautiful brown eyes were wide and innocent, but her body had tensed in such a way that he knew, from two years with this virtual stranger, they could easily go from friendly banter to an argument in no time flat.

"Never mind. I'll meet you in the living room when you're finished and we can watch a movie or something. Whatever you want."

"Sounds fine. I won't be long."

The AC kicked on, sending a blast through the vent as he walked by. He stopped and let the semicool air dry the sweat glistening on his skin from the warm kitchen. "Did you call the air-conditioning people?" he asked.

Claudia let out a long breath. "No. I forgot. I'll do it tomorrow."

"It's just that Indian summer is in full swing." He tried to keep his tone light. "The weather guy on Channel Ten said no relief from the heat for at least five days."

"I said I'll call tomorrow. Okay?" She kept her gaze fixed to her task.

"I didn't mean to sound critical." Vic walked back to the sink and slipped his arms around her, unwilling to let go of the ease of the afternoon and evening.

She sighed and set down the baked beans pan she'd been scrubbing. She tilted her head, inviting him. "I know you didn't. I'm sorry, baby. It's just been a rotten day."

He buried his face in her neck.

Turning in his arms, she slid her soapy hands around his neck. Victor leaned his head back and studied her face. The emptiness in her eyes stole his passion. He knew she would do her duty, but her heart and her mind wouldn't be engaged in their lovemaking. Her indifference chafed his ego.

He pressed a kiss to her forehead. "I have some work to do."

Her expression changed only by a fraction, then she turned back to the sink.

Vic wandered into the living room. He missed Claudia. His

Claudia. The funny, sexy partner he'd had for the first five years of his marriage. He caught a glimpse of her every now and then, but eventually that vacant look returned, and his Claudia went away.

As he dropped onto the couch, his mind took him back to the day they'd met. The day his life had gone from empty to full. He had walked into her dad's office to discuss a church robbery case where Pastor King was to testify. Claudia had worked as her dad's assistant back then, and the moment he saw her at the desk, smiling as she spoke on the phone, he was a goner. Her smile still made him weak.

He only wished he could help her find her joy again.

Two

The flashing red glow of the crossing lights reflects off the ceiling of the bus. I hear the kids panicking around me. Oh, how I wish I could make my body move. I'd reassure them that everything will be okay. Claudia is leaning over me. "BJ?" she says, her voice thick, as though she's swallowing back tears. "Don't worry. He's gone. You'll be okay. The ambulance is coming. I hear it. Please hang on."

She's lying next to me. In the blood I feel pumping from my body.

"Who am I going to talk to if you're not here?" she whispers.

"Shh," I say, but the word never quite leaves my lips. Why won't my body do what I tell it? Am I paralyzed or just that close to leaving this body of flesh, bone, and blood?

I'm cold, so cold I should be shivering, but I don't think I am. Claudia is pressed up against me, but I can't feel her body's heat.

I try to focus on the first time I spoke to Claudia—just over two years ago. My first day as the new English teacher. Two minutes past class time, I had rushed into the closest bathroom, my overwrought nerves getting the better of me. I barely noticed her and almost knocked her down in my hurry.

When I exited the stall, Claudia was still there. Her eyes clouded with concern. "Are you okay?"

I nodded, went to the sink, and rinsed my mouth. When I raised up, she pressed some paper towels into my hands.

"I'm sorry. I made you late to class," I said.

She shrugged. "I was late anyway." Her eyes perused me. "You're new, aren't you?"

Then I realized she thought I was a student. My face went hot, and I was too embarrassed by my behavior to tell her I was actually a teacher, so I just nodded.

"If you need directions to your first class, just ask."

"You know what?" I said, dipping into my purse for breath strips, "I actually could use directions. I'm headed to sophomore English Lit. Can you point the way?"

She grinned. "I can do better than that. That's where I'm going too. We're getting a new teacher. The last one didn't get along with the new principal and decided to retire."

She put air quotes around "retire." I wasn't sure why and didn't ask because I realized it was time to pony up. Besides, I didn't think gossiping with a student was very professional. Although over the next two years, Claudia and I shared plenty of gossip.

"Listen, I appreciate your kindness more than I can say." I

swallowed hard as we headed for the door. "I'm actually not a student. I'm the new English teacher."

Her eyes got bigger than they already were. "What are you, one of those geniuses who went to college early?"

I laughed. "No. I'm just short and have a baby face." I reached out my hand. "I'm BJ Remington. I just graduated from college last year, so I'm probably not much older than most of my students, but everyone has to start somewhere, right?"

She shrugged, and I could feel her distance as she mentally separated us into two different teams: student and teacher.

"Well," I said, "we're ten minutes late, but I guess I won't give you a tardy slip." I laughed.

A tentative smile curved her lips. "Thanks."

I learned pretty early on that Claudia King wasn't like other kids her age. Her insights into Emily Dickinson and Robert Frost impressed me. And she was the daughter of an interracial, high-profile couple in a southern town with barely thirty-five thousand residents. That had made her thoughtful, quiet, and responsible, and everything she did, she did with excellence.

She was an old soul and, I realized as we grew to know one another, a kindred spirit as well. The fact that I wasn't much older than she was gave us a camaraderie that perhaps wasn't always as wise on my part as it could have been. But that aside, we became friends. First, Claudia came to me, sharing her life, her heart, her pain and joy. I tried to keep it professional, but little by little, the friendship grew and she became my confidante as well.

So when she whispers, "Who will I talk to?" I understand. If I could, I would weep too.

FRIDAY

Casio

The first thing Casio did after walking into the Conch Springs PD was surrender his firearm. Procedure demanded it, and he was in enough trouble as it was. He wouldn't quibble over the firearm when he'd probably have it back in a week or two.

Toni Blankenship was heading up the investigation. The lady seemed friendly enough, but Casio knew she was most likely good at handling her emotions in cases like these. Wisdom and experience told him that even though she'd been pleasant enough when she shook his hand and thanked him for coming in, she could turn on him in an instant. And would.

They sat in an interrogation room behind a glass where he had questioned too many suspects to keep count. The room smelled like sweat. He'd never noticed that before. Casio tried not to be nervous, but couldn't help wondering who was on the other side watching, listening to every word out of his mouth.

The African American investigator was probably in her midforties, with straight, shoulder-length hair and a white smile. High, exotic cheekbones made her pretty enough to walk the runway if she'd been twenty-five years younger and several pounds lighter. She was a little old for his taste, but that didn't stop him from turning on the charm. After all, she was a woman, wasn't she? And Casio knew how to get around female emotions.

He smiled, extending his hand toward her over the table. "Sorry we had to meet under these unfortunate circumstances," he said.

She stared at his hand until he felt like a jerk and lowered his arm, resting his palm on the table.

"Here's the thing, Officer Hightower," she said, looking him in the eye. "Miss Abbott's face is a mess. There are bruises on her body. Bruises that she says you obliged her with. What do you have to say about that?"

"I don't know what I can say." Shaking his head, Casio kept his tone controlled, but concerned. "She came at me with a knife. I fought her off. She's a tough little cookie."

As the lie rolled off his tongue, the image of her bloody face flashed through his mind, and he had to force himself not to look away from the officer's steady gaze.

The investigator's nostrils flared and she breathed in. Casio could see she was getting angry. Which might work to his advantage if he could keep from responding in kind. She leaned forward, her arms folded and resting on the table. "So you're denying that you beat and raped your girlfriend?"

"I'm denying rape. I'm saying I had no choice but to fight her off when she tried to stab me." He pointed to his arm. "I have a stab wound to prove it."

"You sure you didn't self-inflict?" She gave him a humorless smile.

"Now, why would I do that, officer? I'm not into pain."

"Giving it doesn't seem to be a problem." She drew a breath and looked at his arm. "What hospital did you go to? I'll need to speak with the doctor who tended your wound."

"St. John's. I don't know who the doctor was, but they'll have it on file."

"Fine. In the meantime, let's finish up here. Are you willing to testify against her for the knife wound?"

"No."

"I didn't think so. I'll recommend we don't pursue charges then. Without your testimony, it would do no good."

He nodded. He knew that. He hadn't wanted to get her into trouble, just to cast doubt on her allegations against him. The whole he said/she said in domestic violence cases wearied officers of the court, and more often than not, they were dismissed. That's what he was hoping for.

She opened a manila file and slid several photos across the table with a dramatic flair worthy of *Law and Order*.

The full force of the beating he'd administered stared back at him. A bluish, swollen lump over her right eye, lips swollen and crusted with dried blood. Bruises on her arm. God, what a monster he was.

Still, he couldn't offer himself up like a sacrificial lamb. Pleading guilty meant a conviction for domestic violence, which meant he couldn't serve in a position that required carrying a firearm. He'd even have to surrender his own guns. No. As much as he loved Harper and wanted to sort things out between them, he couldn't admit to something that would cause him to lose his job.

"Is she going to be okay?" he asked. He knew from this point in the interview, he would have to be extremely careful what he said, the looks he gave, the tone of his voice. Right now there could be one of those body-language freaks on the other side of the glass watching every movement and facial expression to determine if he was lying or not.

"Shouldn't you have asked that before you beat and raped her?"

"I didn't rape her." If he had, he'd blocked it out, because he didn't remember forcing her into making love. He'd made a romantic dinner to commemorate their six-month anniversary. Or "six month-a-versary," as Harper called it. Her nose had crinkled when she said it, laughing. After dinner, they'd gotten passionate on the living room floor.

She'd turned down his proposal, but that was after the sex. That's when he'd gotten angry.

"Is it all coming back to you, Officer Hightower?" The investigator's tight tone yanked him out of his confusion.

"Ms. Blankenship...," he began.

"Officer Blankenship."

So she was throwing off all pretense now. Okay. That worked for him. "Sorry. Officer Blankenship." He pushed the photographs back across the table and hardened his expression and his heart. "I've already given my statement. An argument got out of hand. She came at me, I fought her off. Period."

Wordlessly, she gathered the photos—one at a time to give him ample opportunity for one last look—he'd used the tactic himself from time to time.

"I think we're finished here." She closed the folder and stuffed it under her arm as she stood. "You already know, I'm sure, that you're suspended until the matter is cleared up."

He nodded.

"And of course you need to stay away from Miss Abbott."

"I didn't hear anything about a restraining order."

Her eyes glittered hard. "Miss Abbott hasn't requested an order of protection, but I'm saying stay away from her."

Casio grinned. "So you're asking me as a friend?" Relief washed over him. If she hadn't asked for a restraining order, it meant Harper was willing to see him. To try to sort things out.

"I'm advising you as a colleague not to make things worse for yourself."

"I can't tell you how much your concern means to me. I feel like we've bonded in the past few minutes."

She rolled her eyes and headed toward the door.

"Not only are you a rapist and abuser, Hightower," she said, looking back at him, "you're also an idiot." She gave a short laugh. "I won't have to find evidence enough to have you charged; you're going to hang yourself."

Before he could respond, she exited the room and the door banged shut behind her. Casio pushed himself up from his chair, suddenly feeling all the strength go out of him. The photos of Harper were horrifying, brutal. The thought of someone causing her that kind of pain infuriated him, and yet he'd done it himself. He had to see her. To talk to her. To make things right.

Harper

Harper Abbott's face hurt. The doctor had told her she was lucky not to have been injured worse than she was. A lot of bruising and swelling, but no broken bones. *Lucky.* Funny how she didn't feel so lucky.

She'd refused the morning-after pill, even though Casio hadn't bothered to protect them—and hadn't a couple of times lately. That pill felt a little too much like abortion to her, no matter if the doctor called it birth control. Maybe she hadn't made good choices lately, but that didn't mean she was ready to completely throw away everything Pastor King had taught her all her life.

The doorbell rang, and her heart began to thump against her chest. Casio knew where her parents lived. Of course he did. And he was probably angry that she had dared to go to the police.

She shuffled across the living room until she reached the front door and peeked through the little triangle-shaped window. Her stomach sank at the sight of him on her doorstep. She'd ignored all of his calls. How could she not have known he'd show up here?

She held her breath, praying he'd eventually believe she wasn't home and just go away.

"Harper!" he called out. "I know you're here. I see your car in the driveway. Open up and let me talk to you."

"Oh, Casio," she whispered. What was the point of hiding? He'd eventually find her, no matter where she went or how long she hid out. Eventually, she would have to face him. He would make sure of that.

She opened the door, but left the screen door locked. Her stomach jumped and fear washed over her like a wave. "What do you want, Casio?" Her swollen lips distorted the words.

"What do I want?" He smiled, his eyes gentle as they scanned her. "I want to see if you're okay."

"Well, now you see." Her anger filtered into her voice. "Will you please go away? Don't make me call the police."

"I'm not threatening you, sweetheart. Besides, what will you tell them? I haven't done anything."

She glanced at his arm and noted the bandages. "What did you do to your arm?"

"What do you mean what did *I* do?"

Her gaze narrowed. "You told them I did that to you?" A short laugh moved through her lips. "What a creep you are."

"I can't lose my job."

They both knew she hadn't done anything to harm him. She'd hardly even protected herself. He had been too strong, too angry. Sure, he'd hit her before, but never with a closed fist, never raped her, and never, ever left a mark. Now she was a freak show with puffed-out lips, her right eye swollen, and bruised arms and ribs. But worse than a bruised body was her bruised heart. And...the terrible part was she still loved him.

"Don't worry," he said. "I already told them I wouldn't testify against you."

The ludicrous statement left her silent. She couldn't even muster anger.

Apparently, Casio took her silence for acceptance. "Let me in and let's talk about all of this."

If he thought she was letting him in the house, he was crazy. She shook her head. "That's not a good idea, Casio. Not now. My parents made me promise I wouldn't let you in."

He glanced past her into the house. "Are you alone?"

As much as she hated to admit it, she realized she had already all but told him the truth, so she nodded. "Mama had an appointment and Daddy's at work."

"Then let me come in. I won't stay for more than a few minutes."

"No."

His chest rose slowly as he gathered a breath and then released it. "Okay. I guess I don't blame you. But think about giving me a chance to show you I'm sorry."

"It's over, Casio." She shook her head as tears filled her eyes, the right one burning where it was swollen.

"Please, baby. Don't say that." He put his palm gently on the storm door. "I'll get counseling. We can go together even. I just need help to deal with all the stuff from my past. Isn't that what you've been telling me all this time?"

A bitter smile tipped her mouth, pulling and burning her lips. "Now you're willing to get the help?"

"Better late than never. Right?" His cajoling tone sent a shudder of anger through her.

"Get help and don't bother me again."

She slammed the door, her heart racing so fast she thought she might pass out. After a couple of minutes, she summoned the courage to peek out of the triangle of glass. His truck was gone.

She leaned against the door, and as all strength left her legs, she slid down until she met with the cold, tiled floor.

Three

I'm floating. The sky above me is so beautiful I'm afraid to breathe.

"BJ!" I hear Claudia's voice like an echo. "Oh, God. Who knows CPR?"

The sky becomes the bus ceiling again, and Georgie Newman is on her knees over me, her hands shoving against my chest. "One-two-three-four..."

I hear a long, gasping, choking intake of air. Then I realize it's me, and I feel heavy again.

"Thank God, she's back." It's Claudia's voice. I stare up at Georgie, Principal Newman's chubby sixteen-year-old daughter. In her face I see potential for great beauty and I wish I'd told her that. I thought I'd have more time.

I thought I'd have more time for so many things...

SUNDAY

Claudia

Claudia's lungs burned and her legs screamed for relief, but she refused to give in. She pumped her legs harder. The sweat dripped from her forehead into her eyes, but she didn't stop to wipe it away. Too much fried chicken at Mama and Daddy's after church today. Why did Mama insist on cooking that garbage when Daddy had already suffered a heart attack a year ago? Did she want him dead? True, she only allowed the indulgences for Sunday dinner, still...

She glared at her glistening reflection in the wall-length mirror and focused on her own chunky, coffee-colored thighs. She'd always wanted to be either a little darker or a little lighter, with more delicate features. Why couldn't she lose the extra twenty pounds she'd been carrying around since Emmy was born? Lord knew it wasn't from lack of effort.

Her chest tightened as another woman stepped onto the elliptical next to hers. Claudia inadvertently caught her gaze in the mirror. The size-four smiled with lips that had to be fluffed. And if Claudia had to guess, she'd say the woman's lips weren't the only pair of somethings on her anatomy to be enhanced.

Claudia glanced away. How long did she have to stay on the machine next to this woman? If she left too soon, the woman would know Claudia was intimidated. But no way was she going to stick around for much longer and make herself feel worse.

She switched off the elliptical, kept her gaze averted while she grabbed her water bottle, and climbed down.

"Claudia?"

Dread clutched her stomach. The blonde had spoken. Parishioners often recognized her. Another annoying side effect of Mama insisting the entire family sit in the front row. She plastered on her public face—not so easy to do drenched in sweat—and turned. "Yes?"

"It's Georgie… Georgie Newman."

The name didn't ring a bell. Claudia's face must have shown her confusion, because the girl frowned, her expression incredulous.

"You don't remember me?"

"No, uh…"

"My dad was the principal. I was the mascot." She paused, then looked down and frowned. "I gave BJ CPR."

Claudia remembered seeing Georgie's face. But what she mostly remembered about that night were the shots and the blood. The rest of the details were smudged together in a disjointed collage of images that she tried hard to push away most of the time. When they began to surface, her mind overwhelmed her body and panic took over.

"You've lost a lot of weight since then. Of course I remember you now."

Georgie Newman probably wanted an apology, but why should Claudia be sorry? The girl had been fat and two years younger than Claudia's crowd. And she hadn't seen Georgie around town or at church. At least not that she knew of.

Georgie shrugged, her eyes cold. "It doesn't matter. I was pretty forgettable in high school."

"We're all pretty forgettable in high school." Claudia smiled generously.

"Not all of us." She gave a short laugh. "I remembered you. Head cheerleader. Girls' basketball star. For a preacher's daughter, you were quite the popular chick."

"Those were the days." Too bad they were over.

Georgie shrugged, her gaze following Claudia's generous curves, then she looked her in the eye. The accusation flashed, but Claudia had no idea what she was being accused of. "I'm so over high school."

Clearly she wasn't. But that wasn't Claudia's fault or her concern. "Good." She smiled. "It was nice seeing you again, Georgie."

"You too, Claudia." She smiled broadly. "We'll have to have lunch sometime."

"Sure."

Claudia felt Georgie's eyes on her as she headed toward the locker room. When she stepped into the shower, images assaulted her— chubby Georgie pressing down on BJ's chest over and over while Claudia sat back, sniveling, useless, shaking in her teacher's blood. Claudia's body quivered at the memories, and tears mixed with the shower spray.

Twenty minutes later, she averted her gaze as she walked back through the cardio room. The last thing she wanted was to draw Georgie's attention again. This week had been too much. First seeing Casio, and now another student who was on the bus that night. She reached the Tahoe and her breathing sped up. She closed her eyes, forcing calm.

Why couldn't she stop the panic attacks, the nightmares?

Would she ever feel normal again?

Victor

Vic closed the dishwasher and set it to wash. He heard the front door open and close, and he felt a sense of relief—as he always seemed to feel these days when Claudia made it home safely and on time.

Her face showed her dismay as she walked in the door from the gym. "Something happen?" he asked.

She shook her head, but opened the fridge and pulled out a bottle of wine. She poured herself a glass—a telltale sign she needed something to calm her nerves. She almost never drank on workout days. The calories weren't worth the extra effort.

She lifted the bottle toward him. "Want some?"

Why not? After two hours of steady research and pouring over files, he could use a bit of a break. The red liquid flowed into the glass and she slid it across the countertop to him. "Thank you, honey."

She nodded.

"How was your workout?"

"Brutal." She rolled her eyes, but smiled. "What have you been up to?" Her eyebrows rose in question as she sipped from her glass.

"I'm looking over some documents."

Grabbing her glass, she walked past him toward the kitchen door. "Working a little late on a Sunday, aren't you?"

He followed her into the living room and took a seat next to her on the couch. "Just a little project I'm considering, actually. Not a current case." He knew he was hedging, knew she would figure out that he didn't want to tell her about the case. He glanced at the files on the coffee table, hoping she wouldn't open them.

"What do you mean?" She frowned. "Not a current case? Don't you think you have enough to deal with without taking on something else?"

He shrugged. "It's personal." Cringing, he knew he'd said the wrong thing. No self-respecting wife could let something that cryptic go unchallenged. He struggled. Should he tell her he wanted to solve the murder? Or would that send her further into that place where he'd never be able to help her?

"Oh, I see," she said, her attitude rising to her tone. "It's personal. Well, excuse me for moving in on your personal space." She stood. "I'll just take my glass of wine and let you be alone."

Vic took her gently by the forearm and tugged her back to the couch. "Sit down. I'll tell you."

"Well, not if you don't want to."

Vic smiled. It had been awhile since he'd seen a true pout from his lovely wife, and just now the picture she made was incredibly cute.

"I'm looking at BJ Remington's murder."

Instantly her face changed and her guard went up. "Why?"

"I'm curious about a few details I think might have gone overlooked in the investigation."

"Curiosity?" Her tone rose in incredulity and hinged on anger. "That's kind of odd."

"Not the idle kind, but more like trying to fill in the holes that you can't bear to discuss."

She stared at the files on the coffee table. "Did you find what you were looking for?"

Vic adjusted his position on the couch so that he could face her more easily. She ran her manicured finger along the rim of her glass, her expression almost morose. As he watched her, he decided not to venture into the conversation he had planned. Doing so would be more than she was obviously willing to discuss. And as fragile as she'd been lately about the past, he seriously doubted she would be receptive to his plan. Better to move forward without her knowledge.

He reached toward the coffee table where he'd been perusing the documents and lifted the folders.

"I think I understand better now." He shoved the files into a box and closed it. "So maybe I can be more help to you when you're struggling."

"I don't see how you could." She turned toward him and let out a sigh. Her face softened. "I saw another friend from high school tonight at the gym. Well, not a friend really. She was younger. The school mascot. But she was on the bus that night too." She took another sip and swallowed, then met his gaze. "Don't you think that's sort of an odd coincidence that I would see two people from that time in the same week?"

Everything inside of him wanted to remind her of God's sovereignty and guidance, but Claudia's resentment toward her mother had been growing lately along with her panic attacks and nightmares over the murder. All he knew was that if God was leading, he was following. He'd learned to trust God as a kid, and God had never let him down.

For now he was going to look into that old investigation without her knowing. And if anything actually materialized that might lead to an arrest, he'd tell her. Until then, he was going to leave her in ignorance. And peace.

Casio

Casio jolted awake, still hearing the cries and seeing the cold eyes of the gunman. The masked man stormed the bus and shot Hank Montrose, the assistant coach who happened to be driving the bus that night. Then the faceless voice screamed for them to shut up—

Stop screaming, or so help him God, he would shoot every one of them. The bus swayed with the swoosh of bodies hitting the deck as four fast shots slammed into Miss Remington's body and she fell.

"No!" He heard the sound of his own voice, saw himself rush forward to tackle the killer, felt the pain as a bullet tore into his arm. He watched the blood spread across his blue and white football jersey.

The killer stood over him. "You okay, kid?" he whispered. Casio ventured a look up. The gunman stared for a long couple of seconds, turned and fled the bus, leaving behind a comatose bus driver, a half-dead teacher, and him, wounded and wishing to God he'd been braver. What if he had grabbed the man's legs while he was standing over him? Knocked him to the ground and overpowered him. Taken the gun and turned it on the killer. What if he'd been braver?

In his fantasies, that awful night turned out a lot differently.

Sweat beaded Casio's upper lip as the memory replayed itself over and over. Always the same.

He'd learned today from a friend at the PD that Victor Campbell had requested all the documents involved in the ten-year-old case. Casio understood. Claudia's husband probably wanted closure for his wife. He understood wanting to protect the woman he loved. But Victor Campbell's reinvestigation terrified him. As much as he wanted to find the killer and stop his own nightmares, the last thing he wanted to do was look into those eyes again.

He stared, without seeing, at the TV. Some news show. He'd been there for hours, conjuring the memory of that night over and over, not that he had any choice. The images persisted as he tried to remember anything he might have blocked out. Anything that might give him the perp. What if he could remember something new? Something not in the original testimony?

He'd been thinking about getting back to work. Blankenship's investigation should be over soon, and he had no doubt they wouldn't proceed with charges against him. The fastest way to worm his way into the hearts of this town would be to find the man who killed BJ Remington and help the ADA put him away. It couldn't hurt Campbell either. If what Claudia said was true, he planned to run for DA when Slattery retired in the spring.

He was dozing off in the La-Z-Boy when the phone rang.

"Hightower here."

"It's Burt. Gabe needs a ride."

Casio's stomach dropped. "It'll take me thirty minutes to get there," he grumbled and hung up. At least it was Sunday night, lighter traffic.

He headed for his truck. This had to stop. Dad's every-other-night binges were getting old fast now that he was off the wagon. Finding out he had stage-four lung cancer had sent Dad off the deep end barely a month ago. He was meaner than ever, more sarcastic, and a nasty drunk.

But he was still Casio's dad, and who else was there to drag him out of a bar before he passed out? True to his word, Casio pulled into Burt's at 9 p.m., thirty-five minutes after the phone call.

The bar was practically overrun with off-duty cops. Burt had retired from the force the year before Gabe and had bought the bar two months later. It wasn't long before every cop in Dallas County, including those from Conch Springs, found their way here. Most nights were standing room only.

Burt jerked his head toward the end of the bar. Releasing a hot breath, Casio walked over and took the stool next to his dad. He knew it would do no good to try to muscle the old man out. Especially drunk. He'd make a spectacle of himself and blame Casio. Casio had no choice but to sit for a few minutes and suffer through the drunk women, cops, ex-cops, and honky-tonk music.

Burt slid a draft beer toward him and his dad glanced up. "Hey! It's my boy." He grinned, pulling his oxygen tubing from his nose. "Burt call you?"

"What do you think?"

"Watch your mouth with me. You got it?" He threw back the last drop in his mug. "Burt! Gimme another."

"Forget it, Gabe. Go home and sleep it off."

"You refusing a payin' customer?"

Burt placed his beefy hands on the counter and looked Casio's dad in the eye. "The last three were on the house. Now go home with your boy here, before I refuse you service permanently."

"How about it, Pop?" Casio chose his tone and words with the care of a witness for the defense. "I have my new truck. We can come back for yours tomorrow."

His dad scowled and pushed back from the bar. Casio took another swallow of his half-downed beer and wrapped his fingers around his dad's arm to steady him while he stood up. Predictably, the old man jerked away. "Ain't a day yet where I'm too drunk to walk out the door without the help of a punk like you."

They both knew that was bogus, but Casio turned loose anyway. He followed his dad as closely as possible until they stopped outside of the men's room. "You gonna hold my hand?" his dad asked through twisted lips.

"I'll be here when you're done."

Man, he was sick of this. Sick of cleaning up after Pop. Sick of being treated like this. Sick of everything. The dim, smoky bar was filled with more women than men. Any other night, he might have cozied up to one of the desperate women on the prowl for a man in uniform. But now wasn't the time to venture out. Not when he wasn't convinced Harper was through with him for good. No sense in hooking up with someone else yet. He just needed to give her a few more days, maybe a couple of weeks to cool off. Lose the marks that stood out as a reminder of what he'd done.

He shook aside the image that followed. The memory of shoving the ring on her finger, yanking her to him. Tasting her tears.

Mercifully, the door opened and his dad staggered out, wheeling the oxygen tank behind him, walking toward the exit sign. He glanced over his shoulder. "Well? I can't drive myself home in this shape."

The highway was calm and quiet. His dad stared out the window. Casio could only imagine the rush he felt as the lights sped by him.

"So, what happened to the arm?"

"Knifed."

He glanced over, looked impressed. Casio squirmed a little. If only Pop knew, he wouldn't be. It sort of felt like getting an A on a test, only you know you cheated. Pop's pride didn't count unless he came by the A or, in this case, the wound honestly. "Did the guy get it worse than you?"

"Something like that."

The sound of Pop's laugh tightened Casio's grip on the wheel. Great, he'd set him up. "You little woman-beating punk. Lucky for you she got your arm and not your heart."

"So why the setup if you already knew how I got stuck?"

"Just wanted to see if you'd cop to it. I guess not." His sneer was so much more pronounced and cruel when he drank.

"You don't know what you're talking about, Pop." And could he be any more in denial? Casio flashed back to nights at home, listening to his mother scream while Pop slammed her around their bedroom. He'd always despised him for that.

"Yeah, right. I don't, huh?" He shook his head. "So you have some time off. Want to go camping?"

That was Pop. Rip him a new one and then ask him to go on a vacation together. That would be punishment worse than sending a cop to prison. "I can't."

"Why?" His tone mocked. "I hurt your little feelings like a girlie?"

"No." Casio refused to give in to the baiting. Shame and manipulation only went so far. He wasn't a kid anymore. "I heard this morning that the ADA is reopening BJ Remington's case. I want to get in on the investigation." If anyone deserved to help with the case, it was him.

"My case?" Gabe let out a string of curse words that ended in a fit of coughing. "Now they think I didn't do my job?"

Casio handed him a wad of takeout napkins sitting in the seat. "Victor Campbell's wife was one of the cheerleaders on the bus." He turned on his blinker and slowed down for the red light.

"Which cheerleader?"

"Claudia King."

"The preacher's daughter?" He gave a lecherous laugh that made Casio want to puke. "You tapped that for a while, didn't you?"

Casio gripped tighter on the steering wheel and didn't bother to answer. Pop didn't expect him to. He was too drunk to stick with any one emotion for long. Now he was back to indignation.

"At least she wasn't hurt like you were." He cursed again. "Don't they think I did everything I could to find the perp who shot my boy? It's an insult. I should slap them with a lawsuit."

"Sure, Pop. Slap the DA's office with a lawsuit for trying to find the most notorious killer in Conch Springs history."

Pop muttered something unintelligible and reached into his pocket for his flask.

"Don't you think you've had enough?"

"If I did, I wouldn't be drinkin' more."

"Fine, Pop. Drink until you pass out."

"Don't talk to me like that."

"Listen, Dad. I need your help with something."

"With what?" he gruffed out. "You don't come around for two weeks, now you want my help?"

"I showed up to take you home, didn't I?" As he had several times over the last two weeks. But apparently his dad didn't remember the puke he'd cleaned up, the abuse he'd taken, and the bar bill he paid each time.

"I didn't ask you to." Gabe swigged back the flask and turned. "What do you want from me?"

Casio almost told him to forget it, but he would probably get more out of his dad in this condition than he would sober. So he shoved down his anger and went for it. "I need to convince the ADA to let me be part of the investigation into Miss Remington's death."

Casio kept his eyes on the road, but he could feel Gabe's gaze drilling into him. "So ask him."

"I have a possible case pending against me. The ADA isn't going to let me near him until the investigator sends her findings and recommendations."

"You think Harper might testify against you?" A deep cough rendered him speechless for a minute while Casio considered the question.

"I don't think so. I don't know. She's really mad."

"How bad did you beat her up?" Gabe's voice was angry and again Casio wanted to introduce pot to kettle. He knew Gabe had always liked Harper. Who wouldn't? She coddled Gabe, cooked for him, lightly chastised him when he smoked or drank too much. Gabe wanted her for a daughter-in-law. But if anyone had taught him to punch a woman, it was Gabe. His mother's bruised face and body flashed through his mind in an unsettling but familiar way and melted into Harper's image.

"It was bad, okay? It's been bad lately with the flashbacks and nightmares." He expelled a heavy breath and brought his hand across his forehead.

"Excuses," Gabe spat out. "Be man enough to admit she made you mad so you went after her." His words slurred and he slouched.

"Okay, fine. Whatever you say." Gabe was just about done for, but Casio needed him to stay lucid for just a little while more, so he allowed him to semi-win the argument. "What I need to know is whether you can think of one thing I can bring to the table so Campbell will let me join the reinvestigation."

"No." He snarled the word, and Casio knew the conversation was over.

After he pulled up to the house, his dad was nearly passed out. Pain seared Casio's arm from the struggle of getting him out of the truck and inside the house. He felt the wet, telltale sign of the wound reopening, and his shirt was soaked in no time.

As they stumbled into the old man's bedroom, Gabe seemed to perk up. He pointed toward the gun cabinet.

"I'm not getting you a gun, Pop." Casio lowered him onto the bed in a sitting position.

"Idiot." Gabe shoved the oxygen tubes back up his nose and breathed in. When he had enough breath, he pointed again. "Taped behind the cabinet. Get it and take it to the ADA."

"What is it?" Casio walked to the corner and struggled to push the heavy oak cabinet a few inches away from the wall. His arm screamed with pain, but he found a ten-by-thirteen office envelope taped to the back. He looked at his dad, who had closed his eyes, then tore the envelope open. Inside were what appeared to be only a few pages of an autopsy report for BJ Remington.

He skimmed the documents, trying to wrap his head around

what he was reading. Pregnancy? "What is this? And why isn't it with the rest of the documents?"

"The autopsy showed she was pregnant. I had to take those pages."

Casio sucked in a cold breath. His dad was making no sense here. "I don't get it. Why..."

Gabe grunted and stretched out on his bed. His eyes were closed and Casio could see he was about to pass out. "Pop!" He walked back to the bed and bent over his dad. "Don't leave me hanging like this. What am I supposed to tell Campbell?"

"Tell him you found it behind something."

"You want me to lie?"

"I had to let the case go cold. She was pregnant."

"I don't get it. Were you protecting someone?"

Gabe's eyes popped open and his gaze was fierce. "Yes. And I'm only giving you the documents now because we stick together. Family, police, it's all we have. You give that to the ADA and get yourself on the investigation. But leave me out of it. I'm not ratting out a friend."

"You know who killed Miss Remington and shot me?" Casio's brain refused to believe his dad would close the case out of loyalty to the man who had shot his own son. "And you withheld information?"

"I never said that. He was sleeping with her, but he didn't kill her. I would've been forced to bring him in and he would've been the prime suspect. Why ruin his life if he didn't do it?" Gabe shook his head and repeated, "He didn't do it, so why ruin his life?" He closed his eyes again. "You'll never find out who the father was. Because I'm not ratting out a friend and I guarantee there's no DNA on file to match the tissue samples from the baby. My gut says the man who killed BJ is long gone. You and the ADA are spitting in the wind. But if it'll help my son, I'm okay with the autopsy report going public."

Casio knew there was no point in pushing his dad for more information right now, but something didn't add up. What Casio couldn't reconcile was why his dad would have sat on this for so many years when his own son had been shot. How could he be sure the baby's father and the killer weren't the same guy? That wasn't good investigating. His dad should have put this whole thing to bed years ago.

At the sound of Gabe's snoring, Casio sighed. He clutched the envelope and headed toward the door. Whatever his dad knew or didn't know, and regardless whether or not he'd be mad later when he sobered up, it was too late to go back. The document in this envelope was Casio's ticket into the investigation.

Four

Most merciful God, I confess that I have sinned against you in thought, word, and deed, by what I have done, and by what I have left undone...

How long have I been on the floor of the bus? The train is still rolling along the track outside. If I had known how soon my life would end, I might have resisted temptation. I would have focused more on others and less on my needs.

I hear the sound of adult voices. A lot of yelling and ordering this and that as cars have come up behind the bus and realized something is wrong with the kids. Someone is ushering them off the bus. Some have no choice but to step over me as they leave through the emergency exit. I hear them sobbing, begging to know if I'm alive.

I know there isn't much time left for me. Claudia is still weeping, refusing to leave me. So much left undone, Lord.

I never told my mother how much I appreciated the chicken soup she made every time I got a really bad cold—even after I grew up.

Never apologized to Blake Simpson for giving him that F. It made him miss tonight's game, when all of the college recruiters were there. I could have given him a C-, but he mouthed off too many times for me to overlook his poor writing on that last paper. Still, I didn't have to deduct that many points for participation and tardiness. I should have been less stubborn when his dad came to my room and practically ordered me to reconsider. I'm sorry, Blake. You should have been with your team on the field, not in the bleachers with your dad. You still showed your team spirit. You are a better person than I am. I wish I could tell you that.

I never read all the way through the Bible—kept getting hung up on Numbers, Deuteronomy, and Lamentations. I really wish I'd pushed through the boredom. There's a lot to be said for finishing what you start. I just couldn't. Although there were parts of Deuteronomy I did like—chapter 28 in particular.

I never told my dad that I stopped being afraid of storms when I was ten, but faked my terror until I was sixteen. Oh, Dad, the only times I ever felt your unconditional love were those times when the thunder clapped hard, and you waited outside my door for me to run shaking into your waiting arms. Maybe you loved me better than you had the ability to show, but only during those frightening Texas storms did you reassure me that no matter how the storm raged, I was safe as long as your arms were waiting.

If only I could have told you about the storm raging inside of me. Would you have held me or hated me?

TUESDAY

Claudia

Claudia sat in the event planner's office alone—without Vic to help her face the woman whose disapproval raised Claudia's defenses.

Good Lord, one missed meeting. Get over the queen complex already.

But the party was only a month away, so Claudia tried hard not to be offended by the haughty look in Lindsey's too-blue-to-be-real eyes. "My parents have been married for thirty-five years, the same amount of time they've been in ministry together. We want to celebrate that. So I want the party to be special. Elegant, but welcoming."

She nodded, taking notes. "How many guests are you planning for?"

Claudia thought for a minute. She had to invite the family, of course. Then the staff who had been so loyal to her father, and a few friends.

"I'd say between fifty and seventy-five."

Her expression didn't change as she nodded and made a note of it. She passed a menu across the desk and for the next few minutes Claudia made decisions about each course. Shrimp appetizers, two meats, salad, dessert, bread.

Lindsey warmed up midway through the menu selection, and Claudia realized she was likely going way over the budget she and Victor had planned. The thought was confirmed when the numbers were crunched and the price per person was broken down.

"We'll schedule a tasting for next week, and then I'll just need half down."

Claudia gaped. "Half?" Vic was going to kill her. Mentally she calculated how much was left on the Visa and knew with a sinking gut that there wasn't enough on it. As a matter of fact, most were maxed or close to maxed out. And Vic had no idea. She used e-statements and did all the banking online, and he trusted her. That was the part that made her sad. She truly didn't like lying to him. But what other choice did she have at this point? Vic had turned the finances over to her early in their marriage while he was working fifteen-hour days in the DA's office. She'd proven herself capable. So capable that he never even questioned her. This was absolutely the last account she would open. She'd find a way to get balances paid off and he never had to know.

Lindsey's eyebrows rose and Claudia could see she was this close to rolling her eyes. "If that's a problem, Mrs. Campbell, maybe you can cut back on the number of guests and order a less expensive menu. We have a barbecue ribs and chicken buffet that gets high praise each time we serve it for an event such as this one."

Claudia knew that was exactly what she should do. But the thought of her mother's disappointment in seeing chicken and barbecue pork instead of prime rib and lobster tails, or something equally elegant, made her decision for her.

She thought of the new, preapproved Visa she had ordered and tucked away in a drawer. The limit would be more than adequate for the entire meal even if she chose a menu in the most expensive range. *This is the last one,* she promised herself. And she wouldn't be doing it if the anniversary weren't so important. What else could she do?

"Mrs. Campbell?" Lindsey slid another menu across the desk. "Would you like to look over the menu again?"

Claudia looked up with a decisive smile. "No, Lindsey. That won't be necessary. Do you need any payment today? Or shall I pay next week at the tasting?"

Her eyebrows rose as though Claudia had caught her off guard. "Next week is fine."

Standing, Claudia feigned a confidence she was far from feeling. Of course, she'd been feigning her real feelings and hiding her real thoughts her whole life, so she was good at it. "Now, I'd like to see the room, please, so we can discuss seating arrangements."

"Certainly." Lindsey led her to the elevator, and they waited in awkward silence until the bell dinged and the doors swished open.

Lindsey pushed the lighted 3 and the elevator started downward. Her cell phone buzzed in the holder at her waist. She glanced down and pressed a button. "I apologize," Lindsey said. "I meant to leave it in my office."

Claudia waved away her apology. "Don't worry about it. I'm practically surgically connected to mine."

A breath lifted the young woman's slim shoulders and the tension between them lifted as the doors opened. Lindsey motioned toward the right, and they walked a few steps down an elegant hallway to an empty room. "Do you have an idea of how you would like things arranged?"

"I'm thinking one rectangle table at the head of the room with my parents and their top staff members. And round tables for every-one else."

Lindsey's eyebrows went up. "You and your husband won't be at the head table with your parents?"

Claudia smiled ruefully and shook her head. Mother would think her presumptuous. As though she thought she had anything to do with their years of successful ministry.

"No, but I was thinking of inviting God. I'm pretty sure Mother would have no objections with Him at her table."

For the first time Lindsey smiled in a real way that touched her eyes. "I understand. Don't worry, Mrs. Campbell. We'll throw your folks an anniversary dinner that will make you look like one of the apostles, at the very least."

"You can call me Claudia."

Victor

Vic had trouble staying in the same room with Casio Hightower, let alone making small talk. He had seen the photographs of the woman Casio had brutalized, and every time he looked at the offi-cer, he saw Claudia's face instead, bruised, battered, bleeding. Had this jerk ever put his hands on her in that way? His heart hurt at the thought.

He should never have accepted this appointment. But after he'd okayed the meeting, integrity demanded he keep it. He motioned for Casio to sit in the vinyl chair across from his desk. Gathering his most professional voice, he met the officer's gaze. "What can I do for you, Officer Hightower?"

"I understand you are reopening the Remington case."

Vic sat back in his chair. "What makes you think that?"

"Two things. I spoke to Claudia…"

The sound of Claudia's name on those lips sent a jolt through him. "Leave my wife out of this conversation, please."

Casio frowned and confusion clouded his eyes. "Is this because we dated in school?" He put up the hand that wasn't captured in a sling. "Seriously, dude, I helped her out the other day, but that was the first time I've talked to her since graduation."

"This has nothing to do with your childhood romance with my wife. Nor does it have anything to do with you helping her off the road and sharing a cigarette with her." A sense of satisfaction went over him at the surprise in Casio's eyes. "My wife has no idea we're opening the case. I haven't told her."

"She mentioned you were going to run for DA when Slattery retires. I put two and two together."

Claudia shared private details with a stranger? He hadn't even told his own mother yet.

"That remains to be seen. But I don't see how that information has any bearing on why you think I'm opening the ten-year-old case. What's your other reason?"

"Everyone knows I was on the bus that night, and that my dad was the lead investigator on the case ten years ago. Word gets around in these situations. At least three of my friends from the station told me you asked for the files."

"Interesting. We'll probably be conferring with your father, so if you're curious, he'll probably fill you in on all the details. But you can forget about joining my team." His "team" being himself and his sixty-something assistant, Isobel.

"My father wants nothing to do with this case, so good luck even getting an interview with him. But I do want in. I'd like to help try to wrap it up once and for all."

The thought of spending time with this guy made Victor's stomach turn. Victor leaned forward, clasping his fingers on his desk. "Well, I'm of the understanding that you are suspended until the allegations against you are cleared up. Am I wrong?"

Embarrassment flooded Casio's face. "I'm suspended from the force for now. But that wouldn't keep me from helping you on a cold case, if you decide to use me."

"Which I'm not going to do." Vic shook his head. "Look, Hightower. The most despicable kind of person in the world to me is someone preying on anyone weaker. Child molesters, wife or girl-friend beaters, abusers in general. So I can't allow you to work on this case."

Anger deepened the color in Casio's face as his eyes narrowed and glared. "Listen, Campbell. I figured you wouldn't hop to work with me. But if I'm so despicable, why am I still walking around free? You can have me charged and arrested anytime."

"Because, despite my personal opinion, the investigation isn't finished."

He gave a short, humorless laugh. "Wrong. Mainly it's because Harper isn't willing to testify against me."

Vic would have loved nothing more than to shove his fist down this guy's throat. "Did you threaten her?"

"I didn't have to." He pointed to his shoulder. "Did anyone bother to mention that she came after me with a knife first?"

"Yes. And I think that's a lie. I've looked at the doctor's report. They haven't ruled out that the wound was self-inflicted."

"But they can't rule out assault either."

"But you're not willing to testify against Harper, right?"

"Let's put it this way, as long as she doesn't testify against me, I won't testify against her."

"So there's that proverbial crossroads."

Casio shrugged. "I'd have called it an impasse. But you're the educated one."

Vic shoved back from his desk and stood up. "Our meeting is over, Officer Hightower."

"Come on, Campbell. Don't be a spoilsport."

"Get out of my office." Vic dropped back into his seat and opened his laptop.

Casio leaned on the desk. "ADA Campbell, I don't think you want me to do that."

"Clearly you don't know me." The guy just didn't go away. "I always mean what I say."

"I don't want to pop your chain, but I know for a fact you'll change your mind when you hear what I have."

A sigh pushed through Vic's lungs. "Okay, fine. You have two minutes. Convince me why I should allow a bad cop and an even worse human being to help me solve a ten-year-old murder."

Casio sneered. "Either charge me or get over yourself."

Methodically, Vic closed his computer and stood again until he looked Casio in the eye. "Back off, man." No way would he be spoken to in such a manner by a thug with a badge. He was this close to charging him just to run him through the system. "Either tell me what you have that might help find the man who shot you, or get out of my office and don't come back."

Casio lowered his gaze and straightened up. He hesitated, then scowled. "Fine. I found a file that wasn't in the boxes from the original investigation."

"What do you mean it wasn't in the boxes from the original investigation?"

Casio's smirk returned. "Those boxes that you had sent over from the PD? I found a file that should have been with them, but wasn't."

"Are you saying you stole a file out of the evidence so that I'd allow you to join this investigation?" Indignation swarmed over him. "That's low, even for a woman beater."

Vic's cell phone buzzed.

"And that comment is low even for a self-important ADA with no real case against me—no matter how much you dislike me." Casio turned and reached for the door. "Enjoy your pointless reinvestigation."

Victor watched him slam out of the room. On the off chance that the officer actually did have something to add, he came this close to going after him.

Instead, he answered his phone.

Five

The day the bomb went off at the capitol building and rocked Oklahoma City, I was home from school with cramps, watching the soaps and eating everything in the house. The news cut in, and I, along with the rest of the nation, watched the unfolding of a horrendous terror attack on American soil.

I'm not sure why this event slips into my mind right now. My dad watched the scenes replay over and over, and I watched right alongside him, until my mother insisted he "turn it off, for God's sake, and sit down at the table for a decent meal." White-faced, hands shaking, she served slightly burned, fried catfish and slightly lumpy mashed potatoes. She pushed her food around and didn't say a word. I shouldn't have done it, but the silence in the room made those images big and loud in my brain, and even though I was eighteen years old, I needed the kind of answers only a girl's parents can give.

"Why do you think he did it?"

My father's warm hand covered mine. "Not now."

"But didn't he know all those little kids could get killed? Could it have been an accident?" Mama's fork clattered to the table with such force that I jumped as it bounced.

"An accident? Oh, this was no accident. He did it because he is an evil man. He didn't care who he destroyed. He didn't care about the families he was tearing apart." Tears flowed down her cheeks and I stared at her, mouth agape.

"Not now," my dad said firmly, his eyes so intent on my mother that I realized they weren't talking about what was going on in Oklahoma.

My dad should have been proud of me for pressing. He was a successful journalist, so he'd taught me to ask the questions, get the story. "But why are some people born evil and others aren't?"

My mother silently grabbed her plate and removed herself to the kitchen. I turned to my dad, expecting to find a frown. I opened my mouth to apologize, but he silenced me with an under-standing smile. In that moment, I found a spark of camaraderie. For the first time ever, I didn't feel like the extra branch in our family tree.

"Keep watching as his background unfolds, BJ," Dad said. "There's a reason McVeigh believed he was entitled to blow up that building. There's always a reason. It may take a few more weeks to discover, but someone will figure it out."

Later, we discovered he was the product of bullying, and as he grew up he considered authority—particularly the government— to be the ultimate bully.

Psychologists held round-table discussions about him, and everyone tried to blame his childhood. The more I watched, the less I bought into the explanation. Didn't he realize that in killing all those people, he had become the bully?

Once, he stared into the TV camera, and I caught my breath at the coldness in his eyes.

The same coldness I saw moments ago in the eyes of the man with the gun. The iceberg I've felt in my heart since the night I decided to sleep with a married man. Sin is so cold...

I think about the tiny baby inside me losing its life as I lose mine. I would cry if I could. I'd lay my palm over my flat stomach and sing a lullaby—comforting her as her tiny, barely beating heart slows and stops.

Like McVeigh, I was born in sin in an evil world. Did the evil penetrate my soul the way it had his? Maybe I never had a chance to be anything but a liar, adulterer, and now because of my sins, a killer of my own flesh and blood. Am I really any better than the most wicked of men? Who decides?

Claudia

Claudia grunted as she picked up the box and shoved it against the wall. "Ma, why are you cleaning out the attic all of a sudden?"

"All of a sudden?" Her mother laughed. "Look at this place. It's a pigsty."

"You know what I mean. Why now? It's needed it forever." Claudia didn't really need to ask. She knew her mother was always overseeing a project or two—or six.

Her mother lifted her slim shoulders. "It's high time, don't you think?"

"I do. But I think you should hire someone to do it. It's going to take weeks." Claudia wiped a glaze of perspiration from her forehead. Of course there wasn't a drop on Mother. She wouldn't have stood for it.

Her mother frowned, staring as though Claudia had spoken in tongues. "Hire someone to go through our personal things? I couldn't stand to think about that."

"Okay, fine."

"Well, don't think I am going to let you out of it. Many of the things up here are mementoes from your childhood. You can either keep them or throw them out. I couldn't care less."

"Or sell them?"

Mother shrugged. "I doubt you'll find much value in those things. Other than sentimental value." She said it pointedly. Passive-aggression in its finest form. Her words said it would be okay to sell the things. But her message was, "If you don't cherish your childhood and the family in which you were raised, then fine, go ahead and sell these things and break my heart."

Her mother drew in her lip and frowned as she stared at the boxes around her. She picked up an old Bible from one of the boxes. "Do you want this?" she asked, holding it out toward Claudia.

Claudia stared, feeling the blankness in her own expression.

Her mother dropped it back into the box. "Oh, never mind. It was only the Bible your father preached from during the first ten years we were here."

"What do you plan to do with all of these old things?" Claudia lifted another box and set it with the other, the dust lifted into the air, burning her nose. "If you're not going to sell them, there's no point in trying to clean."

"We're giving them to charity, of course."

"Let me get this straight. We can't sell the old furniture and stereos and baby bed because of sentimental reasons, but it's okay to shove nostalgia aside for charity?"

"Yes. It's always more blessed to give than receive."

And what if she needed the money herself? That thought would never occur to her mother. After all, Claudia was married to the ADA, they drove nice cars, and they lived in a nice home. Never mind that the house had been in dire need of updating when they'd bought it. Claudia had done much of the work on their first house herself, though she'd still spent more than they could afford. And yet her mother hadn't complimented any of it.

Vic had been working long, arduous hours in those early years just to make it to where he was now. Guilt plunged into Claudia at the thought of the bill collectors she had been avoiding recently. Just the thought of speaking to them filled her with dread. This week, two checks had been returned insufficient, and the bank had refused to pay them. She had no idea how she would tell Vic. She would have to soon enough. The checks would end up in his office sooner or later if she didn't get them paid quickly, and he would be humiliated.

"Are you okay, Claudia?"

Her mother's voice pulled Claudia from her musing. "I'm fine. Where do you want to start?"

Two hours later, Claudia had gone through boxes of old cards, letters, and books, clearly from church members and former members who had moved away but still loved the church and her parents. Claudia's mother asked her to go through them but fought her over tossing any of them out. Finally, when Claudia could no longer hold in her irritation, her mother grudgingly agreed. "Fine, you'll throw it all out when I die anyway. We should get a head start in case I live another thirty years. Then just think how much you'll have to throw out."

Claudia shuddered at the thought, and if her mother honestly believed that argument would guilt her into keeping the papers and junk, she was sadly mistaken. She had ten bags of garbage and had barely made a dent in anything.

"You may not enjoy doing this, Claudia Elizabeth, but just think how I feel. Thirty-five years of marriage and ministry are packed away up here, and you're acting like it doesn't mean anything." Mother stood up suddenly and walked toward the attic steps. "I'm going down for some tea."

Claudia stared after her, shocked to silence by the quiver of emotion in her mother's tone. She looked at the baby bed and bassinet and baby swing. Her gaze slid across the old pulpit her papa had built when they first came to town and preached so hard he'd broken the original one at the church. Claudia smiled. She hadn't been born yet when that happened, but every time her mother or daddy told the story, their laughter grew and they relived the funny moment. Daddy preaching up a storm, his hand coming down hard, and the old pulpit splintering before the eyes of the entire congregation. It hit her that these things meant something to her parents. This clutter reflected their life, and each item held a memory that defined a brick in the structure of their life together.

She looked at the next box, opening the lid with more care than earlier. She reached inside, ready to savor the cards and letters from parishioners who loved and admired her mother and her dad, but it looked to be her mother's more private things. Not more handmade cards and school crafts from Claudia's childhood either. More like diaries and old Bible lesson notes from teaching at ladies' meetings and conferences.

Claudia was about to put the lid back on and set it aside for her mother's own perusal when a lavender sheet of paper caught her eye. It had slid partway out of one of the leather books. Impulse took over and Claudia snatched it from the journal. She frowned as she recognized her mother's handwriting. Crisp, clear strokes in a fine black ink covered the page.

Claudia's mouth curved as she read the first words,

My darling,

Had she ever heard Mother call her dad "darling"?

It's been two weeks since my husband discovered our plans to leave.

Claudia's eyes skimmed over the letter that was obviously not meant for Daddy. Anger filled her chest and her hands shook with rage.

Her eyes watered and Claudia folded the letter, carefully. She had every intention of shoving it back into the box before her mother returned, but it was too late. Hearing footsteps on the stairs, she tucked it into her jeans pocket instead.

"Goodness," her mother said, breathless from the climb up the steps. "I swear I'll be glad when the weather figures out that it's supposed to be fall. Summer should have been over two weeks ago. I am ready for some cooler weather." She smiled, handing Claudia a drink. "Aren't you?" Claudia stared at the sweat already gathering on the outside of the glass, but didn't reach for it.

"Well? Take it," her mother said. "Don't worry. I didn't give you the kind with sugar. Your daddy uses that pink stuff too since that heart scare we had last year."

Claudia shoved off the floor of the attic, the letter still in her jeans pocket. "I have to pick up Emmy from school." Without bothering to dust herself off, she headed toward the steps.

"Well, good grief, you have a whole hour. Why did you let me bring you some tea if you were getting ready to leave?"

If Claudia stayed until time to get Emmy, she would for sure say something she'd regret. She snatched her purse and keys from the table in the foyer, the realization of her mother's betrayal close on her heels. Had she planned on leaving? And then Daddy caught her? There was a familiar ring to the situation. As though she had sort of known about it, but like an out-of-focus shot, she couldn't make her mind clarify the image.

"Claudia, hold on a minute."

With a deep breath, Claudia whipped around. "What?"

"What on earth is the matter with you, hon? You just up and leave without speaking to me? Not even to say good-bye?"

"Mother," she said, barely able to keep her eyes on her overly made-up, beauty-pageant–beautiful mother, "I have to go."

Claudia left her mother standing at the door, a frown creasing her brow and her hands planted firmly on her hips in a huff.

When Claudia's phone buzzed, she ignored it. She couldn't deal with her mother now, if ever. It was too impossible. But when it buzzed again, she answered.

"Vic. Thank goodness it's you. You will never believe the letter I found in one of my mother's boxes."

"Was it from a bill collector?" The angry bite in his words formed an instant knot in Claudia's gut. Vic never, ever used that tone with her.

"No," she said, reminding herself to speak with extra caution.

"Well, after the day I've had fielding calls and making arrangements to pay four thousand dollars in bills, I can almost believe anything."

Tears blurred her vision as she braked at a stoplight. "I'm sorry. Where did you get the money to pay for it?"

"Where do you think, Claudia?"

Her stomach sank. There was exactly sixty-four hundred dollars in their Europe fund that had been growing steadily for the past seven years. When they got to ten grand, Vic said they were going on vacation. England, Germany, France. He had worked hard to save and keep up with that savings account. It was the only part of their finances he really wanted to be a part of. The last thing she wanted to do was force him to use it to pay off the debts she had foolishly racked up.

"I'm sorry, Vic." She wanted to lay it all out in front of him. Confess, and ask him to please, oh please, help her find a way out of their mess, but she couldn't bear the thought of his disappointment.

A frustrated breath pushed through his lungs. "We'll have to talk about it later. I'm just shocked, Claudia. You've always paid the bills and budgeted to keep us on track. Even when I was barely making enough to pay the mortgage and the car payment and buy groceries. What's happened? Why haven't you told me about this?"

"I don't know what happened. Truly. I don't."

Vic didn't answer for a long moment. "We'll discuss it later. I need to get back to work." His tone still had an edge, but had mellowed considerably since that first couple of minutes of the conversation.

He hung up, and she realized she still hadn't told him about her mother's letter.

Betrayed. That's how she was feeling about her mom. And now Vic was feeling that about Claudia. Maybe she was no better than her mother, after all.

Harper

Each day that passed, Harper grew more hopeful that Casio had given up. He'd stopped calling, and she had attended classes today believing he might actually allow her to live the rest of her life in peace.

The professor dismissed for the day, and the class of thirty-five grad students began to stir. No one seemed to be in any more of a hurry to leave than she was. That was the sign of a successful lecture. Psychology of Violence was a disturbing, fascinating class. For her, in particular, it held dual value. Yes, she wanted to complete her degree so she could begin to practice psychology eventually. But even more so, she wanted to help Casio. If she could get him the help he needed, maybe there could still be some sort of future for them.

She slid her three-inch-thick book inside her frayed, six-year-old book bag. The book itself had cost her three hundred dollars and was more precious than gold. Campus was nearly deserted when she stepped out into the twilight. The only problem with registering so late was that only night classes remained open. To get to her car, she had to either take an underground tunnel walkway or cross an impossibly busy street. In daylight hours, there were enough students coming and going that taking the tunnel wasn't dangerous. But this time of night it would be foolish, though she'd seen plenty of young women who didn't take proper precaution. She pressed the button on the traffic light, hoping to get across to her car before twilight slid into darkness.

Her boots clicked on the parking lot as her heartbeat kept time with her quick steps. Her car came into view and she stopped short, her breath coming in short bursts.

"Casio," she whispered. He leaned against the driver's door, arms folded across his chest.

"Hey, baby," he said as though he had all the time in the world. "You're looking as beautiful as ever."

"Black and blue are my colors," she shot back, then regretted her hasty choice of words as his gaze narrowed and eyes darkened.

"What are you doing here?" Her voice shook. She squeezed her hands into fists and forced herself to breathe slowly in through the nose, out through the mouth. If he'd become this bold, how long would it be before he grew bolder, before he became angry and raised his hand to her? Her legs trembled.

"I miss you. I wanted to see your beautiful face."

"I told you I never wanted to see you again."

"Well," he said, "you could always call 911." He smiled again. "There's a lot of white knights down there just waiting to rescue a damsel in distress."

"Do I need a knight to protect me from you, Casio?" Oh, Lord, she prayed her voice sounded nonchalant.

She stepped forward, toward her car.

"I want to be your Prince Charming, baby. You know that." His voice, smooth, like warm air, floated over her. If only he truly meant that. "Why don't you come home with me? I miss you." His eyes moved over her curves.

She shuddered. "I can't. Not right now." She knew to tread lightly. It wasn't very likely he would harm her in a public place, but there was always a first time. But then she'd never thought he'd do more than slap her. They were above ground, and the parking lot was well lit. The occasional student showed up either to class or from class.

Reaching up, she placed her palm across his shadowed cheek. "Casio, I miss you too. I miss the long talks we used to have. The way you used to bring me Chunky Monkey ice cream while I was studying for finals. I miss lying in bed with you and hearing the sound of your heartbeat in my ear."

"Baby…" He stepped away from the door, opening his arms. Harper took advantage of the movement, dropped her hand, and quickly opened and stepped behind the heavy car door. Her hands shook, her insides tight and knotted.

He frowned and grabbed her wrist. "You're playing me?" Tears burned her eyes as she thought about the good times, and then the bad. "No, Casio, I'm not playing you. God help me, I love you. But you have to let me go."

His eyes glistened in the light overhead, and Harper glimpsed the gentle Casio she had fallen in love with in the first place. The tenderness in his expression gave her the window she needed to get away.

Pulling her wrist from his grip, she slid into the car. He stood like a statue and didn't try to stop her. She trembled as she slid the car into gear, grateful to hear the door lock engage. She drove away, knowing she had angered him and praying that he wasn't so unstable that he would come after her.

Six

Claudia is still on the bus with me—and I think Casio is still on the floor somewhere, but I don't know if he's alive. Someone tells me Georgie is checking on the bus driver who, thankfully, is still breathing. He was a new assistant coach. I never even took time to learn his name. I hear Claudia speaking to her dad. Pastor King is on the bus? Where did he come from?

Someone must have used a cell phone to call him. He must have been at home and not at the church, because the church is on the other side of the train. The train that seems to be going on forever.

Forever. I'm about to embark on eternity. I guess it's natural that I think about Jesus at a time like this. Inwardly, I tremble at the thought of our first face-to-face meeting. Will His eyes look on me with love and welcome, or shame and disappointment? Will He open His arms or turn His back?

I've always been fascinated by the gospel of grace. Jesus came willingly, died willingly, and rose victoriously. I am grateful that *although His standards are high, He isn't without mercy. But how much have I trampled over His grace? Is He finished with me?*

I feel the tender touch of Pastor's hand as he takes mine. He's praying softly. "Lord, nothing is too hard for you." Instinctively, I know he's refraining from saying how bad off I am, even to God, because he knows I'll hear him. Or Claudia will. Either way, I wish I could say to him that I already know my breath is almost gone.

This is what happens when someone leads a secret life. One day, someone has enough of the duplicity and storms a bus of innocents to punish the guilty.

Claudia will not be consoled, and no amount of comfort from her father, whom she loves more than anything, will stop her tears. I wish I could tell her, "Don't cry for me. I'm not worth it. If you only knew how worthless I really am, none of this would even matter to you."

I know I'm guilty. I only hope poor Claudia won't pay the price for my sins.

WEDNESDAY

Victor

Pride puffed Vic's chest as he waited at the gate for his mother to buzz him into the retirement community he had finally been able to afford to help her get into. She stood at the door of her two-bedroom duplex as he pulled the Camry into the parking place in front of the garage she had no need of, since she'd never had the money to buy a car. He'd have been pleased to get her one, but by the time he could have, she wasn't interested. "Start driving at my age? I'd be a danger to society."

Vic waved at her through the windshield as he slid the gearshift into Park and cut the engine. Though her face lit at the sight of him, her years of hard living had taken their toll. She was no older than Claudia's mother, and yet in appearance, she could have been fifteen years Mrs. King's senior.

What she lacked in social grace and breeding, she made up for in wisdom and unconditional love, like any good mother who only wanted better for her child than she had herself.

Vic had grown up in south Dallas in a dingy apartment crawling with roaches, and his mother, Darla, worked two jobs to support him after his dad had gone to prison. Mama insisted Dad was set up, that he hadn't murdered the owner of the liquor store. Dad had gone in for a bottle of wine for them to celebrate their anniversary. When he arrived at the corner store, he hadn't noticed a robbery was in place. Foolishly, he had run as soon as the gunshot rang through the neighborhood. He was seen by several witnesses on the street. They didn't know what had happened, and the real robbers, a pair of brothers well known for dealing drugs and petty crimes, had stuck together and made a deal with the DA. Dad had died in a prison brawl when Vic was twenty-one.

Shaking off the ghosts of his past, Vic locked the car door as he walked toward his mother. She enfolded him with the sort of embrace only a mother's arms could deliver. Warm and soft, scented with cinnamon and spicy beans and rice and corn bread. The embrace felt like coming home. Especially nice since his actual homecoming last night had been tense and silent. Claudia had apologized, her face pale and her eyes watery. Then she had left him to fend for himself for dinner. Emmy had eaten peanut butter. Why was he being punished when he was the one having to clean up her mess?

His mother patted his back and pulled back, holding him at arm's length. Studying his face, she frowned. "You're not sleeping. What's wrong? Are you working too hard, or do you have other troubles?"

Releasing a heavy breath, he nodded toward the front door. "Let's go inside so we can visit for a while."

"I cooked for you, so you're going to stay and have lunch."

He chuckled. "Yes, Ma, I'm staying for lunch."

Inside, she took him straight to her kitchen and sat him down at the table. The duplex was warm. "Why don't you have the air cranked? It's hot in here."

She waved aside his complaint. "Waste electricity when I got a nice cross breeze?"

A nice cross breeze? More like a hot one, but he simply shrugged out of his sport coat, rolled up his sleeves and unbuttoned his top button at his throat.

There was no arguing with a woman who had scrimped and saved her entire life to make ends meet. His mother pinched every penny and clipped every coupon. *Too bad Claudia grew up as an entitled rich girl.* As soon as he had the thought, he wished he could take it back.

Darla set a plate of chicken and dumplings in front of him. "No one makes chicken and dumplings the way you do." She went back to the kitchen counter and returned with a plate of fried okra.

"Don't try to flatter me." She slapped him lightly on the shoulder. "I'm going to pour you a glass of lemonade and then I expect you to tell me what is wrong with you."

Digging into the plate in front of him, Vic let a sense of peace comfort him. The sort of peace that came only from a mother's table.

She poured a glass of lemonade for each of them and sat catty-corner from him. "Now tell me why you're fretting."

"I'm not exactly fretting." He savored a bite of dumplings, sipping his lemonade to wash down the thick, cooked dough.

"Don't tell me that, son. I saw it on your face the minute you drove up. Now, you tell me what's wrong. Is it a case? Or Claudia."

Something in his face must have given it away, because she gave a knowing nod.

"What is wrong between the two of you?" She peered closely, frowning.

Setting his fork back on his plate, Vic released a breath and met his mother's compassionate gaze.

"Tell me." It was the same soothing voice that had calmed him after the bullies teased him for having a murderer for a dad. The same voice that told him he had a whole life to prove them wrong. The voice that told him better to be beaten by the gangs than stoop to their level and join them.

"Ma..." He told her about Claudia's coolness toward him, her panic attacks, and the latest—overspending and not paying the bills. Anger began to build as he told her about dipping into the vacation fund they had been saving for so long. "Just like that, two-thirds of it's gone. And the worst of it is that she lied to me. I had no idea until my clerk brought me the checks that had bounced."

"So you were embarrassed?" She gave him what he thought of as her Maya Angelou stare, the one that peered into his soul to get to the truth.

"Well, yeah. But it's more than that. I don't know how much more I can take."

Darla's head tipped to the side, her face resting on two fingers. "Son, you know the Lord won't give you more than you can bear. So you'll take as much as comes. You've made it through before."

Vic scowled. "I guess so."

They sat in silence for a few minutes. Darla's eyes were closed, and Vic knew she was communing with God. And he knew better than to interrupt. When she opened her eyes, she reached across the table and took his hand in her wrinkled, worn hands. "Poor Claudia. You must be worried sick about her."

"I guess I am."

"Of course. That's why you're so angry. It's not about the money. You have plenty of money squirreled away here and there to pull from if you had to."

"You're excusing her behavior?"

Darla shook her head. "No. But something is eating at her soul, baby. Why else would her personality change so drastically? You used to brag about how good she was at budgeting and stretching those pennies to make your home look elegant and beautiful like her mother's."

"She started changing after the miscarriage." The memories

flooded over him. Claudia, four months pregnant, calling him home from work, panicking by the amount of blood flowing from her body. By the time the ambulance arrived, she had fainted.

And he brought her home two days later, her womb empty, her heart broken, and panic beginning to show in her eyes as they sat at the tracks waiting for the train to pass.

"You have to be patient. Go home to your wife, love her, be kind to her, and pay the bills yourself until she's whole again."

She made it seem so simple.

As though hearing his thoughts, Darla smiled. "It's as simple as that. A woman is healed with kindness and forgiveness from the man she loves. Have you ever read Hosea?"

"Yes, Mama."

She frowned at his tone, and Vic's face warmed as shame flooded over him. "I'm sorry, Mama. I don't mean to be disrespectful."

"You be loving to your wife and let God love her through you. She'll heal eventually, and one day this test will become a testimony God can use to help someone else." She stood. "Now, I'm going to wrap up the rest of that food, and you take dinner home to Claudia and my little Emily."

Thirty minutes later, Vic pulled out of the drive, the smell of chicken and dumplings and coffeecake filling the inside of his car. His mother's words were a challenge. He would love Claudia. He would be kind and understanding and take the checkbook and credit cards until she could be trusted again. But in the meantime, there was something else he had to do. He had to find the man who had murdered BJ Remington.

His thoughts drifted to Casio Hightower. The last thing he

wanted to do was let that man into his life, even in a small capacity. But if Casio truly had information that had been overlooked in the original investigation, maybe he should give it a look.

He supposed he could bully the file from him. But Casio might just do something stupid like burn the file, and it would be his word against the officer's that it even existed.

THURSDAY

Casio

Casio gulped his coffee, cleared his throat, and tried not to look squeamish in front of Vic, who held the autopsy report he'd retrieved from storage. It revealed that BJ Remington had died from blood loss even before the train had passed and the paramedics could cross the tracks.

"Why didn't the paramedics go around and cross the tracks at St. Louis Street?" Vic asked.

Casio looked up. "At the time, there was no St. Louis Street. The tracks only opened at that one spot." He shrugged. "Ten years ago, Conch Springs was even smaller than it is now. The new zoning and your father-in-law going on TV has increased the population from the thirty-five thousand residents we had then to the fifty thousand we currently have. After the murder, the town rallied and demanded another place to cross the tracks. Now there are several places, but back then, it was just the one crossing." He glanced back down at the photographs. "There was even talk of building a second hospital on the side of the tracks without one, just in case something like that ever happened again, but it was shot down in committee."

"The town isn't big enough to support two hospitals, I'm sure." Vic said.

Casio tried not to recall Miss Remington lying on the floor of the bus or see the dark, nearly black blood pooling from her body.

"Claudia wouldn't leave her." He stared as the pictures from the investigation took him back ten years. "Just about everyone else hightailed it off the bus, but she just laid there rubbing Miss Remington's hair. Crying. I thought she'd really lost it."

"Weren't the two of you dating during that time?"

Casio's gaze lifted, defenses rising. "What's your point?"

"You were her boyfriend and she stayed with Miss Remington instead of coming to your side after you were shot?" Vic's eyes held no mockery, so Casio took the comment for what it was: a simple observation.

Casio remembered waiting for Claudia to come to the hospital to see him, but she hadn't. He had lain there, like a chump, assuming that as soon as she left Miss Remington, she'd come to his side. Finally, he'd given up. When he called her house later that night, her mother said she had given Claudia a sleeping pill and put her to bed. "What can I say? We were kids." Although they probably wouldn't have broken up so soon if that night hadn't happened to them. Claudia never did come back to him after the shootings. She never called him and didn't take his calls. Finally he moved on to the next girl and got on with his life.

Vic nodded. "She must have been really close to Miss Remington." He sounded like a guy trying hard to keep his distance from something that clearly hit close to home. Close enough that he was willing to turn back the clock and work to bring his wife closure.

Casio shrugged and cleared his throat. "Yeah, well. It was a pretty close call for all of us."

"Do you mind if I take a look?" Vic reached for the pages Casio had found.

Casio turned the folder around, pointing to the part his dad had hidden for ten years. "Here it is," he said. "Approximately ten weeks pregnant."

Victor shook his head. "I can't believe this was lost this whole time, and your dad didn't follow up trying to find the baby's father."

A shrug lifted Casio's shoulders. "We can get a DNA match. I assume they took tissue samples of the baby."

"They would've thought of that the first time around. The report definitely shows that they took DNA samples of the baby." He skimmed over the newly found pages and sighed. "We'll have to interview the original forensic pathologist who performed the autopsy to find out why he left out information about the pregnancy and baby. When we find the killer, he's going to be charged with more than just the murder of Miss Remington. He'll have to pay for murdering her baby also."

"Like you said before, my dad was lead investigator and never mentioned anything about Miss Remington being pregnant. I never even overheard him talking to anyone else about it. That file was probably misplaced while dad was still investigating. As far as I'm concerned, that's our first good reason for even looking at this case again. I just want to find the guy that shot me and killed Miss Remington."

Vic's hands moved apart. "All right, then. Who was she seeing? We need to find the guy and question him."

"How would I know that?"

"You saw her every day. Went to her class, right? Saw her on the field with the cheerleaders. It's a small school in a small town. Surely you saw her with someone other than students."

"She wasn't my type. I didn't exactly pay that much attention."

He sounded like a jerk, he knew. But he was just sick of the images replaying in his head like a freaky movie he couldn't shut off. Like in a scary B movie where you switch off the set and it comes back on by itself, so you unplug it and it still comes back on, scene after scene.

First the lights flashing, then the train whizzing by. A bunch of teenagers goofing off, pumped about the game they'd just won, and then a guy with a gun storms the bus, shoots the assistant coach who's driving the bus, and turns toward the shocked-still students who barely have time to hit the deck.

He drew a shuddering breath and closed his eyes. "I don't have a clue who she was dating. For all I know it could have been a student. Lots of guys thought she was hot. She wasn't all that much older than us."

Something like a revelation crossed Vic's face. "I wonder if anyone ever questioned the students about their private relationships with her."

"Seriously?" Casio laughed. "Man, listen, I was kidding. I said the guys thought *she* was hot. No way she would have slept with a student. She was like Mother Teresa. Just ask Claudia. She went to church all the time where Claudia's dad preaches. Not like how some people go to church but don't mean it. We're talking the real deal with this girl. Woman, I mean."

"According to the autopsy report," Vic said, "BJ Remington was shot four times. Once in the chest. Once in the left thigh, once in the stomach, and one that grazed her neck but did no damage. Half inch down and it would have hit her jugular and she would have bled out in seconds."

Casio's hands shook as he reached for the report Vic held out to him. He paused a moment, then read aloud, "Number one bullet grazed victim's neck, exited with only minor damage, bullet was not recovered. Second bullet entered chest wall, penetrated fifth rib, collapsing left lung and causing internal bleeding. Third bullet entered lower right torso, penetrating liver. Fourth bullet entered left thigh, shattered femur, but did not damage artery. Cause of death: combination of gunshot wounds two and three."

"The autopsy report sent to the medical examiner confirms his findings about the cause of death," Casio said. "The only difference is in the extra pages I found. 'Victim was approximately ten weeks pregnant. Fetus expired with victim. Fetal tissue sample extracted from uterus for DNA testing.'"

Victor stared at him hard. "Those pages weren't lost. They were hidden. Where did you say you found them?"

"In the evidence room. I was cleaning—have to do something to occupy my time."

"But where, specifically?"

It was time to manufacture a better lie. "Between two of the metal shelves. They sit back to back and boxes are loaded in on either side."

"And you just happened to find a file folder with missing pages from the autopsy report slid between two of them? That had to be intentional. I mean, come on. Don't you find all of this a little coincidental?"

"Are you calling me a liar, Campbell?" Casio knew how to look innocent even when guilty. He wouldn't give his dad up. And he sure wasn't going to admit to his own duplicity in the matter.

"It's our job to find out if someone deliberately hid evidence of a pregnancy." The ADA's eyebrows rose. "Don't you think?"

Casio shrugged. "I'm not convinced those pages were deliberately lost, but I'm willing to look into it."

"Well, for now, let's concentrate on what we have in front of us." He studied Casio's face for a few seconds. "Have you seen any of the photos from the autopsy? It's pretty graphic. You think you want in on this investigation, but it might be more than you can stomach."

"I can handle it."

"Okay. Here you go." The ADA shoved a stack of photographs that had come in the file with the autopsy report.

Casio's limbs weakened as he stared at the photographs. Time fell away and suddenly he was back in the bus, seeing Claudia on her side next to Miss Remington while Georgie Newman did CPR. He sat on the floor, shocked as the blood spread across his football jersey. And then those eyes bored into him. "You okay, kid?" the killer asked. Casio had never told anyone about the encounter. He didn't know why. Maybe if he had, the man wouldn't haunt his sleep every night.

"Hightower!"

Casio jumped as Vic knocked hard on the table to get his attention. "What?"

"You okay?"

"Yeah. Why?"

"Are you sure? Because you spaced out. You weren't even there, man."

"I'm here. I didn't get a lot of sleep last night."

Without sympathy, the ADA shoved a sheet of paper across the table. "Take a look at the list of kids on the bus. Do you know any of them today?"

Casio nodded. He recognized all of the names. Most had graduated and moved away, not that he could blame them. Every day in this town was a reminder of that night. Claudia, of course, was an exception. She'd stayed—and married way too young, in his opinion, but he wouldn't say that to Vic. He didn't think Georgie Newman had ever left. He'd heard she'd attended nursing school in Dallas, then moved back to work in the Conch Springs hospital. Blake Simpson worked at Jesse's Garage, which was owned by Blake's brother Jesse, and had fixed Casio's old truck a few times before Casio had finally bought the new one. Casio knew Blake was three times divorced and was probably still bitter because he'd lost his chance to play that last pivotal game.

He was frowning as he stared at Blake Simpson's name on the page.

"What?" Vic leaned in. "Did you think of something?"

With a shrug, Casio shoved the page back, tapping on Blake's name. "It's probably nothing."

"Okay, let me be the judge of that."

The ADA's superiority complex was starting to get on Casio's nerves big time. But he was glad for the opportunity to finally do something proactive toward finding the guy who shot Miss Remington. He only hoped finding the killer didn't dredge up a whole new kind of nightmare.

"Blake Simpson was a football player until Miss Remington gave him an F for a midterm grade and he got benched. He used to argue with her a lot right in class. Treated her really bad."

"He treated her badly? You mean after she gave him the F, or before?"

Casio frowned, coaxing his mind to remember details that had little or nothing to do with him. "Before."

"Do you know why?" Victor made some notes, then looked up at Casio. "If everyone else thought she was perfect, why didn't Blake care for her?"

"I don't know, man. We weren't really close."

"Two football players? Senior year? I thought you guys banded together in some macho club."

"You sound bitter. Get stuffed in a lot of lockers?" Casio noted with satisfaction that the ADA's face darkened. He'd finally struck a chord.

Vic regained his composure. "So why weren't the two of you close enough for you to know why Blake had a problem with her? You never heard him complaining in the locker room or heard rumors that he said he would 'get her back' or anything?"

He shrugged again and squirmed in his seat. "Honestly, man, I would have been the last person Blake would have confided in." He hated to admit this because it made him look like a jerk. "Blake was dating Claudia when I first asked her out."

Vic scowled and started gathering up the papers and photographs. "So you cut in on another guy's girl?"

Unable to resist, he snickered. "Yeah, but if you're worried about Claude, don't be. I don't do that anymore."

A sneer lifted the edge of Victor's lips as he slid the papers and photos into his briefcase and stood. "I wasn't worried." He grabbed his briefcase by the handle and paused. "Coming?"

"Where are we going?"

"To pay Blake Simpson a visit. Let's see if he had a grudge against her and was mad enough to do something about it."

Seven

Pastor King hasn't let go of my hand since he knelt beside me. He's prayed. Comforted Claudia. He's told me Jesus loves me and, if I can hear him, to seek forgiveness.

I can hear you, Pastor. I didn't know you knew about my sins. I'd cry, if I could. If I'd known you knew my secrets, I would have come to you. It might have saved me.

My parents were part of the foundation of Community Church even before you and Mrs. King arrived. And they lobbied hard for you to be hired on in the first place.

They thought it fabulous that Pastor and Mrs. King would rock the town with their unconventional presence—not only was Pastor the first African American pastor in Conch Springs, but he and Mrs. King had the audacity to be a biracial couple. Always forward-thinking—Dad was a journalist at his core, even before he became a hotshot editor—they embraced the couple from the moment they moved in. And then a few years later, something changed.

My mind won't form the memories correctly right now. I know there's a reason, and I can see myself sitting on my bed, hearing Mama cry and Daddy plead, but I can't remember much else. Except that my parents stopped going to church. I did too, for a while.

After I graduated from high school, though, I started going to Community again. Mama didn't approve. Daddy said it was my decision. He was, after all, the more open-minded of the two.

As I lie here unable to move, unable to speak, and struggling to breathe, I remember how hard I tried to live the way you encouraged us to live, Pastor. I did okay for a while. I stopped partying. Stopped smoking cigarettes. Those weren't that hard. It was the deep-down stuff I couldn't seem to let go. What was that Scripture? Those things I want to do I don't, and the things I don't want to do, I do?

Wretched woman that I am...

I remember now. Vaguely, like trying to find my way out of the woods in a heavy mist. Daddy fell in love with Mrs. King. They were going to go away together. But Mrs. King changed her mind. I heard Mama and Daddy fighting about it. And then it eventually went away, and I guess I put it out of my mind.

Pastor's gentle hand is stroking my hair. I wish I could ask him how he managed it. How he and Mrs. King continued as though nothing had ever happened. My parents stayed together, but all the light left my home that day.

With me gone, what will they have to keep them together?

THURSDAY

Claudia

Claudia knew it was her own fault that Georgie Newman held her all but captive. She never should have indulged her weakness for iced coffee. Claudia had tried to pretend she didn't notice that Georgie Newman's car blocked hers in the packed Starbucks parking lot. She was at the other woman's mercy. With a sigh, she sat back and surrendered to the inevitable.

"Hey, there." Georgie wore blue scrubs and her hair was clipped into a messy ponytail, which Claudia took in with envy. She had pretty much inherited her hair from her dad's African ancestors and couldn't do the messy ponytail without a lot of crazy work to make it look that way. "You on lunch break?"

Embarrassment flooded Claudia as it usually did when working women assumed she too worked outside of her home. She smiled and was about to say, "Something like that," when Georgie tipped her head back and gave a wave of neatly manicured, short, clear-coated nails. "Oh, you get to be a stay-at-home mom, don't you?" She tapped her on the shoulder and winked. "Lucky."

Red-hot anger flashed through Claudia along with several unclean words. Luckily she reined in both, just in time. Still, the unspoken words expressed her sentiments, and she had to force herself to sit there and smile at the flawless face leaning in way too close to her personal space. "How are you today, Georgie?"

The other woman smiled brilliantly. Was there anything about this woman not faked or enhanced? "I'm peachy. On my lunch break. The ER is crazy today. We must be in for a full moon tonight or something. I'm an hour past lunchtime and *starving*. But I only have time for a coffee and I have to rush back. Otherwise we could sit down together and catch up!"

"Yeah. That's a bummer." Claudia marveled at how sincere she sounded to herself. "We'll have to make a point to get together when you're not working," she said and immediately she realized the folly of her olive branch, as Georgie's Mary Kay–shadowed eyes widened. Those sorts of statements weren't meant to be taken literally. It was like saying, "I'll call you sometime and we'll do lunch." It just doesn't happen.

But Georgie obviously didn't understand social cues and insincere efforts to be polite. "I'm off tomorrow. Do you want to do lunch?"

Kicking herself the entire time, Claudia smiled and nodded. "That sounds really great."

"Awesome. How about Olive Garden at noon? My treat." She glanced back at her car as though she just realized she was blocking Claudia in. "Oh shoot. Do you mind waiting just a couple of minutes so I can go in and get a drink to take back to work? I'm going to die if I don't get some calories in my body." She grinned. "Nonfat calories, of course."

"Of course. Um… No, I don't mind. It's not like I have a job to get to."

The facetious comment brought a frown to Georgie's face. Maybe she did have more sense than Claudia gave her credit for. "Hey, you know I didn't mean anything by that, right? Before she died, my mother was always a stay-at-home mom. When I have a baby, I plan to do that. When I said you were lucky, I totally meant it. I really honestly think you're lucky to have a little girl and a home to care for." She smiled, but her eyes seemed hesitant, as though waiting for approval.

The desperation fueled compassion in Claudia. She smiled. "It's okay. Motherhood is supposed to be noble, but just tell someone you're a stay-at-home mom and the nonverbal and sometimes verbal judgment starts to fly. Just wait. You'll find out."

Georgie rolled her eyes. "If I ever find a man who wants to marry me and make babies. Hey, if you want me to move my car before I go in, I really don't mind."

"It's okay. I have a call to make anyway."

"If you're sure." She patted the window frame. "I won't be but a minute."

Nodding, Claudia watched her walk away, looking cute and professional in her dumb nursing scrubs and messy ponytail. Gee, when did fat mascot Georgie Newman get gorgeous and capable when she, Claudia, the head cheerleader and basketball captain got depressed and frumpy? The woman would be an idiot to give up a career for motherhood. Maybe she'd tell her new BFF just what she thought of her wannabe stay-at-home dream over lunch tomorrow.

She lifted her phone and dialed Tara's Tangles Beauty Salon. At least she could have her hair and nails done. The place was typically booked three weeks in advance, but there were certain benefits that came with being the daughter of beloved Pastor King and the wife of ADA Campbell. Sure enough, Tara had an opening in twenty minutes if she didn't mind being shampooed by the new shampoo girl. Which she didn't.

Ten minutes later, Georgie exited carrying a coffee to-go. She smiled and gave a finger-wiggle wave as she passed, saying, "See you tomorrow!"

Claudia pulled out of the parking lot behind her, headed south on Martin Luther King Boulevard, and turned her head sharply as Vic's Camry pulled out of Jesse's Garage. She dialed his number. He answered immediately.

"Hey, beautiful," he said, his voice leaving her breathless— though she knew she didn't deserve his kindness after the money situation. He had come home the night before with a completely different attitude than he'd had the previous night. They'd discussed the situation, and he said he would take over paying the bills, which was a relief to Claudia. One less thing she had to stress over. "I was just about to call you," Vic said. "I saw you pass by. Want to go grab some lunch?"

True regret hit her stomach. Vic rarely asked her to lunch anymore. "Sorry, I can't. I'm headed over to Tara's. Why were you coming out of the garage? Something wrong with your car?"

"No. I was conducting an interview."

"Oh. That's a relief. We don't need another repair bill right now." She could have kicked herself for bringing attention to finances.

"That's for sure." He chuckled. "So, you're going to the salon?"

"Yes." Her defenses rose. "I haven't gone in a while. But I could cancel if you don't think I deserve to go."

He hesitated. "Claudia, honey. Enjoy yourself. We can afford for you to have your hair done. Although"—his tone dropped—"you're already too beautiful as it is. I'm not sure my heart can take you after a salon day."

Claudia's lips curved upward. "You're full of it. But I'll take it."

She was smiling as they hung up, feeling closer to Vic than she'd felt in a really long time. Maybe after her appointment, she'd have time to stop off at Adam and Eve's for some new lingerie. He'd like that and she would apologize for how tense everything had been. Maybe everything would go back to normal.

Tara's was abuzz and Claudia felt a little guilty for forcing her way into an appointment when clearly all the stylists were at or over capacity as it was. Tara sashayed toward her, her wide, toothy grin lighting the room. "Hey!" She gave her an air kiss on the cheek then mulled over her hair. "Can you wait ten minutes? Shawna's shampooing Miz Stokes."

"Sure."

She sat in the waiting chair next to Tara as she worked on coloring the hair of a forty-something white woman. Tara's cell phone buzzed. She removed it from the pocket of her smock and looked down at the caller. Her light skin flushed as she pressed the phone to her ear. "Hey," she said, breathless. "What are you doing?"

Claudia hid a smile. At twenty-seven, Tara had never been married or in a serious relationship as far as Claudia knew. Tara graduated one year after Claudia, went straight to beauty school, and worked for three years in someone else's salon until she could afford to open her own. To see her blushing and breathless over a guy made Claudia happy for her.

Midway through the conversation, Tara glanced over at Claudia and frowned. "Mrs. Campbell is sitting right here in my salon," she said. "Oh, wow. I forgot all about that. I wasn't into sports during school, so I didn't know her that well except for sophomore English."

Blood rushed to Claudia's head as instinct took over. Tara could only be talking about BJ Remington.

She hung up a minute later and slid her phone back into her smock. Her words confirmed Claudia's suspicions. "Did you know they're reopening Miss Remington's case?"

Claudia's spine crawled hot and cold all the way up her neck and around to her jaw. "No. I don't think that's true. It would have to come from the DA's office. My husband would have told me." Her mind shifted back to the evening she had come in from the gym to find him going over files from the ten-year-old investigation. Maybe that's why he was acting so positive today. He thought he was doing something to please her.

Tara slid a cap over the color client's head. "Let's get you under the dryer to process." She glanced at Claudia. "That was Blake Simpson on the phone. He graduated your year."

"I remember him." They had dated briefly, but Claudia saw no reason to point that out as her thoughts shifted to a day during senior year. She and BJ were in the English teacher's classroom, laughing at the way Principal Newman always tripped over himself whenever BJ was nearby. The poor man was hopelessly in love. Claudia frowned as she recalled how their laughter had been cut short as Blake slammed into the room, demanding to know what right she had to take away his whole future. Before either of them knew what was happening, he had grabbed a solid brass statue of Shakespeare from her desk and threw it over BJ's head—or at least that's where it hit—shattering the whiteboard behind her. If he'd hit her, she would have been hurt or killed instantly. He let out a guttural yell, told her next time it would be her head, and stomped out of her office, leaving them both shaken.

Tara shrugged. "Blake said your husband and Casio Hightower came to question him about the case. They said some new information had come up and they were looking into things again. They asked him if they could swab him for DNA."

"DNA?" Then Vic must have figured out about BJ's pregnancy. Claudia's breathing nearly stopped as she watched Tara's mouth moving but barely heard her words. She rose slowly to her feet and grabbed her bag. "I have to go."

"Shawna's ready for you," Tara said.

"I'm sorry, Tara. I have to go." Her chest tightened. She had to get out of that building now, before she suffocated. She stumbled to the Tahoe, reached in, and grabbed her bag out of the glove box. Breathe in. Hold. Breathe out. Breathe in. Hold. Breathe out. She followed the protocol several times until her breathing slowed and her pulse rate stopped racing.

The thought of Vic actually reopening the case sent a wave of dread over her. The nightmares were more than she could bear as it was. To dredge it all up again... She couldn't do it. She fumbled in her purse for her phone and dialed Vic's cell. It went to voice mail.

She had to tell him to forget it. Tears welled up in her eyes. She'd just spoken with him twenty minutes ago. Where could he have gone that necessitated turning off his cell? She punched a button and dialed the office. She was glad now Vic had programmed her speed dial. Off the top of her head, she had no idea what the office number even was.

"Victor Campbell's office."

"This is Mrs. Campbell. I need to speak to my husband, please." Grabbing a tissue from her purse, she swiped at her nose.

"I'm sorry, Mrs. Campbell. He called a while ago and said he wouldn't be in for the rest of the day."

What had changed over the last twenty minutes to make him go from flirting with her to blowing off work the rest of the day? Did it have something to do with BJ's murder case? Her chest tightened again. "Did he say whether or not he was going home?"

"No, hon. I'm sorry." Regret tinged the assistant's tone. Claudia had always liked Isobel. She should have retired five years ago, but Vic had convinced her no one could take her place. He was right, of course, but the woman couldn't work forever.

"Claudia?" the older woman said. "Is something wrong? Maybe I can snoop around on his desk and find out where he is. I'm sure if Vic knew you were this upset, he wouldn't mind."

Claudia thought about it, but shook her head. "No." She was already beginning to breathe normally and the shaking in her hands had slowed to a slight tremble. "I'm just going to go home and wait for him."

"If he calls, I'll let him know you need to speak to him."

"Thanks, Isobel."

Claudia pressed the button to disconnect her call. Detecting movement ahead of her, she looked up. Tara stood in the doorway of the salon. As they made eye contact, the stylist walked toward the Tahoe. Claudia pressed the window button and the glass lowered.

"You okay, Claude?"

Claudia gripped the bag tight in her hand. "Just a little panic attack. Sorry I freaked out. I'm better now."

"You wanna come in? My one-thirty cancelled on me. So I won't have to squeeze you in after all."

It was rare that she didn't feel like spending a couple of hours under Tara's capable care, but now all she wanted to do was find Vic and convince him he didn't need to do this. "I don't know."

"Come on, girl. You can use the pampering and I can use the money."

She glanced at her watch. "I'll need to pick up Emmy at three o'clock."

Tara grinned. "Then we best get started. Time's ticking away."

Time was definitely ticking away. Tara had no idea how right she was about that. It seemed like a countdown had begun the day BJ was murdered. Every day Claudia felt like she was another hour, minute, second closer to following in her teacher's footsteps. She couldn't remember the last time she awoke and didn't wonder, "Will I die today?"

Victor

Vic would have much rather had lunch with Claudia than his current lunch partner, but since he was driving and Casio had heard him get turned down for lunch, the only polite thing to do was to invite the officer to join him.

He'd decided to turn it into a working lunch, so he grabbed his briefcase, notepad, and some of the notes from the senior Officer Hightower—Casio's dad. The little Mexican place served the best, most authentic pork tamales and chili *rellenos* he'd ever had. A semi-regular customer, he had a favorite quiet booth in the corner and had called ahead to ask if it was empty.

"What'd you think of Blake's answers?"

Vic shrugged. "Nothing in his testimony seemed deceitful to me." He sipped a sweet tea, looking at Casio over the rim. "He sure was holding a grudge against you, though." He supposed it would be difficult to stand in a garage, dirt and oil under your nails, knowing you were capable of so much more. Not that there was anything wrong with being a mechanic, but Blake could have been a star, apparently. Instead, he was spending his life working for his brother.

Casio grinned. "I took his girl and got the scholarships he was competing for. I guess he had reason back then to resent me."

Ignoring the comment about stealing Claudia from Blake and the self-satisfied smirk on Casio's face, Vic went over Blake's answers from his notepad. "He admitted to getting upset over the semester grade that kept him from playing that night. He even admitted that he had sort of threatened his teacher."

Lunch came and Casio put on his best Casanova smile, charming the little senorita. He stretched his neck to watch her sashay back to the front of the restaurant. "A little beauty, isn't she?" Casio asked, turning back around.

"Give it a rest, Hightower. Don't you think you should sort out your current woman problems before you get the ball rolling on ruining another woman's life?"

Anger flashed in the officer's eyes. "I thought we agreed to keep Harper and my case out of this."

Victor picked up his fork. "Just remember, we're not friends. I only let you in on this case because you bribed your way in, and if any real evidence presents itself proving Miss Abbott's statement against you, I'll toss you off the case and draw up charges against you in a split second."

"You're not going to get that evidence, Campbell. Harper loves me. It's only a matter of time before I win her back. She's not going to testify."

Vic rolled his eyes. What could he possibly say to this idiot to convince him that he was the lowest piece of garbage on the planet? He should never have agreed to their little partnership in the first place. But the fact was that he had. And BJ Remington's pregnancy revelation is what justified the reopening of the investigation. Otherwise it would have been viewed as a waste of taxpayer money, so he owed Casio.

He glanced at his watch. "We best hurry and eat. I have another appointment this afternoon."

Casio's eyebrows rose as he lifted his fork and tackled a stuffed burrito. "About our case?"

Vic nodded. "The high school principal."

"Newman?" Casio gave a side grin. "He's still the principal?"

"Yep. I want to talk to him about the kids on the list I showed you. And about the teacher. There's nothing in the report from ten years ago that shows he was even interviewed, which I found a little odd."

"Why would he have been? The guy had nothing to do with anything. He wasn't on the bus or even at the game."

"Neither was the killer, most likely."

"You think Newman could be the killer?" Casio chuckled. "Wait until you see him."

Vic sighed. "The point is that as the guy in charge at the high school, he would know everyone who might have had a grudge against Miss Remington. He might know if she was dating or gay."

Casio snorted. "She wasn't gay."

"And you know this how?"

Casio shrugged and scowled. "I don't figure she was."

"Exactly. Maybe it was a hate crime." That was reaching, most likely, but he was trying to establish the fact that every avenue should have been explored ten years ago and that this case was given mediocre attention at best. He didn't understand why.

"She was ten weeks pregnant, though."

"Okay. The point is, Newman might have information that comes to a person who is with someone every day, like he was with Miss Remington."

"Newman was always a nerdy guy. Always trying to be cool, I guess."

Vic's curiosity flared. "How so?"

"He used to try to get us to talk about our dates. Never really busted anyone on the team if we got caught with a girl in places we weren't supposed to be. Like closets or bleachers or making out in the car in the parking lot. Kinda creeped us out." He frowned a little. "Should I come with, or are you too filled with indignation to walk around with the likes of me?"

"Get over it." Vic scowled across the table. "Whatever I think of you, I agreed to your involvement on the case, so if you want to come with me, I'm not going to stop you."

Vic wasn't sure if having Casio there would make things better or worse. The principal might not be inclined to open up if what Casio just said were true. On the other hand, if he still wanted to be in the cool crowd, it might be an asset for Casio to come along.

"Fine. I'm coming then." He swallowed down a bite. "It might be fun to go back to the old stomping ground again."

"Okay, but I do the talking, you hear?"

"Don't talk to me like I'm a lackey, Campbell. You might be a prosecutor, but I'm a cop. I get people to confess for a living, remember?"

"Yeah, well, I'd rather not muscle a confession out of him. Got it?"

"I'll keep quiet as long as you're getting results. But I'm not going to sit back and listen to him jerk you around if it seems like he might know something about the killer." Casio pointed his fork at Vic, his gaze narrowed. "I have a lot at stake with this case. It's been sitting on a shelf for all the adult years of my life, just doing nothing but taunting me. Driving me crazy that some guy could kill a cool chick like that and just walk away from it." He reached forward and grabbed a chip from the basket. "It's time we get him and give him the chair for what he did. Especially now that I know Miss Remington was knocked up."

Vic bristled a little at Casio's crudity, but he had to admit, the guy had a point. He did have a stake in the results of this case—as much as Claudia—and it was also true that the killer had taken more than one life that day. Whether he knew it or not. Although Vic's best guess was that the killer had definitely known about the baby. It was time for this guy to come to justice. And in doing so, maybe Casio and Claudia could find a way to put those demons behind them.

Eight

Why won't I die? Is this part of my penance? Going over the damage I've done?

"When is the train going to be done?" I hear Claudia's tearful query, and inside, I second the question.

Pastor's gentle voice answers. "It's only been a few minutes. It's a long train."

"I wish it would hurry," she whispers back.

"Do you want to go outside with the other kids?"

"I have to stay here with her. She needs me, Daddy."

"BJ will understand, Claude."

He's right, I want to say. Please, Claude, leave this bus. Get out of the blood. Live and breathe and don't grieve for me. I'm not worth it.

But I know Claudia's stubborn loyalty to me. The day I found out I was pregnant, she found me crying after school in my classroom.

She refused to go anywhere until I broke down and shared

my situation with her. All of it—except the name of the
father. And she was okay with that. "We'll get through this
together, Beej," she said. Then she smiled. "Just think, I get to
be an aunt after all." And we had truly become closer than
sisters.

I think in that moment, I knew we'd be friends for life.
How could we have possibly known how short life could truly be?

Victor

Principal Newman was about as stereotypically nerdy a guy as Vic
had ever seen. He fidgeted in his enormous brown leather chair, his
hands resting on the arms of it as he clearly tried to look nonchalant.
"So they're finally reopening BJ Remington's case?" He nodded his
half-bald head. "It's about time you guys tried to get her some
justice."

"I agree." Vic gave him a tight smile and chose to let the veiled
criticism pass. "We've been going through files and old interviews and
the thing that surprised us was that you were never interviewed."

The little man swallowed hard. "Why would they interview me?
I certainly had nothing to do with her death."

Vic leaned forward. "We aren't implying you did."

Newman's face slipped of color. Either the man was guilty, or he
was afraid his words had implicated him. Some people watched too
many legal dramas on TV. He cleared his throat. "What do you
want to know?"

Casio shoved an open file across the table. "This is a list of the
kids on the bus. What do you know about Blake Simpson's relationship with Miss Remington?"

Near-tangible relief passed over Newman's face. "You want to know about Blake?"

"That's right."

Victor allowed him the momentary relief before they asked him about his own relationship with the teacher. That would come soon enough.

Newman shoved out his chest with self-importance. He looked ridiculous in the chair that nearly swallowed him alive. "Blake Simpson was a troubled kid. He came from a divorced home. His father moved out of the home when Blake was about twelve. He was the janitor here, actually."

"He was?"

Mr. Newman nodded. "We almost didn't hire him, but he turned out to be the best janitor this place ever had."

"That's not in the files." Vic scratched the information onto his notepad.

"He worked at the school until two years ago when the emphysema got the better of him. He had to stop working around the chemicals and dust."

"So what if his parents were divorced?" Casio's voice edged with annoyance. "Lots of kids come from divorced homes. Sometimes it's better if parents get divorced than fight in front of the kids all the time."

"I probably shouldn't have combined a rough upbringing and the divorce, but Blake had a chip on his shoulder bigger than Texas."

"Big deal. A lot of us did back then."

Mr. Newman's eyebrows rose. "You don't think his rough background is relevant to his anger issues?"

"I don't remember Blake being that angry, Mr. Newman." Casio crossed his ankle over his knee. "As a matter of fact, I stole his girl and he never even confronted me."

"Miss King?" Newman nodded as though remembering back to the incident ten years ago. "I wondered why one day she was kissing him in the hall and the next I caught the two of you in the parking lot fogging up the windows."

Victor bristled at the grin the two of them shared at his wife's expense. "Can we get back to the topic of Blake Simpson and his relationship with BJ Remington?"

"Of course," the principal said, once more taking on a professional demeanor.

"What about Miss Remington and Blake? Tell us about their relationship those last few weeks before she was murdered."

"Do you think Blake killed BJ?" Was it Vic's imagination or did the principal's small hands shake? Nerves?

Casio must have noticed the same thing. "Look," he said, "we know you had the hots for her. Shoot, you wouldn't have been male and not have had the hots for her. We don't care about that."

"What do you mean I had the…"

"Oh sure, Claudia told me way back then." Casio smirked. "Miss Remington and Claudia were close friends."

Vic's voice was tense as he interjected. "Stop asking questions and answer the one we asked. What do you know about Blake and Miss Remington?"

Sitting forward, Newman pinched the bridge of his nose, elbows resting on the desk. He released a breath and looked up. "There was more to his anger at BJ than just the grade. Blake found out BJ was seeing someone."

"Why would a student care whether or not a teacher had a date?" Vic asked. "Unless Blake and BJ were also seeing each other?"

Newman's eyebrows rose. "No, of course not. BJ wouldn't date a student."

Vic leaned back a little and scrutinized the principal. "Then why did Blake care?"

A shrug lifted the thin shoulders. "I guess he had a crush. He started mouthing off to her in class. Just punk kid stuff to the average bystander, but BJ felt very threatened by it. She came to me when he started using profanities to describe her—if you know what I mean."

"What did you do?"

"I called him into my office, told him he couldn't speak to her that way. And I'd be calling his mother if he did it again."

"And?"

The principal gave a rueful smile that showed off a set of teeth in sore need of a dentist. "He basically told me where to go and left my office. I was about to call his mother, and the next day midterms were posted."

"So that's why Miss Remington failed him." Casio shook his head. "That—"

"Watch it, Hightower."

"Don't you see what she did?" Casio stared sideways at Victor, his eyes narrowed, face reddening. "She dummied his grades to get him put on academic probation just because he wouldn't back down."

Victor looked to the principal for confirmation. "Is that what happened?"

He shrugged, then nodded. "I don't have proof that BJ did such a thing. But I can say that during his high school career, Blake never made below a C in any class but that one. I conferenced with BJ about it. She showed me the grades—and it was only that one paper, but his tardiness and lack of participation lowered his grade enough to keep him from playing. That semester, he just wasn't trying hard enough." Newman leaned back in his chair for a moment. "I suspected something was bothering him, but he wasn't the kind of boy to open up. It's a shame, really. With just a little bit of effort, he could have gotten a scholarship to a university anyway. Football or no football."

"What does that mean exactly, that he made minimum grades?"

Newman leaned forward. "Athletes are required to have a C average. First offense puts them on academic probation until they get their grade back up—they can't play football when they're on probation. The problem with Blake being off the team at that time was that he missed out on the game when recruiters from three major colleges were scouting. We were going into the championships, and Blake and Casio were featured in high school sports highlights on the news almost every Friday all season." His eyes drifted upward as though in memory. "That was an exciting time. The town was behind our boys one hundred percent."

Casio nodded. "We played from our guts that night and slaughtered the other team, even without Blake. I got offered two scholarships from two colleges—the third guy was mainly there for Blake."

Newman continued, "Blake took it hard. He barely came to school the rest of the year. I felt sorry for him for losing those scholarships, so I made allowances and helped him more than I should have probably. I tried to encourage him to try for other scholarships, but he lost heart for it after that."

"This is a fascinating sob story." Casio scowled. "But he didn't exactly lose those scholarships. Just the opportunity to be offered them."

Vic interrupted, "If he'd been able to play, it could have gone either way."

Casio glared. "We won the game that night, even without him. I didn't get those scholarships by default, Campbell, so stop implying I somehow didn't deserve them." He looked back at the principal, then frowned. "But I guess Blake needed the college money more than I did, considering I still got to go to college, even when I couldn't play any more football and after the scholarships were withdrawn because of my injuries. But Blake never did go."

Empathy. Maybe there was hope for Casio after all.

"Are we finished here?" the principal asked. "It's just about time for the bell to ring. I need to be in the hall."

"Just one more thing, Mr. Newman."

"Yes?"

"What is your response to Casio saying everyone knew you had a romantic interest in BJ?"

His face flushed. "That's just ridiculous." His voice had risen in pitch and was just a little too intense to be believed.

"Bull." Once again, Casio had inserted himself into the interview.

"Miss Remington showed Claudia the bracelet you gave her. It was a Celtic love knot. I'm guessing she meant a lot more to you than you did to her."

But whether or not he was obsessed enough to kill over that fact remained to be seen.

"She loved that bracelet." The principal's hazel eyes flashed anger. Vic figured that if he thought he could take Casio, he would have come across the desk, fists blazing. But that would have sort of been like a Chihuahua picking a fight with a Great Dane. "She never took it off."

A shrug lifted Casio's beefy shoulders. "He has a point. She did actually like that thing. It used to dangle on her wrist when she wrote on the board. Hard to miss."

"See? So don't think just because I'm not some *GQ* model, that someone like BJ couldn't care about me."

Victor wasn't sure if he was admitting to a relationship with the teacher or not. But he had to cover all the bases. "So you're the guy Blake found out about? The one she was seeing?"

The fire went visibly out of him. His shoulders stooped. "I would have loved nothing more than to make someone jealous, but she never saw me that way. We had dinner a couple of times, but she never really cared anything about me. Not as anything more than friendship. But if I'd had my way, I would have married her."

"And she led you on? Took gifts from you without giving anything in return?"

He shook his head. "I know what you're implying about her. It's not unusual for beautiful women to take advantage of unattractive men." His face glowed with embarrassment and Vic's heart softened with compassion. "But BJ wasn't one of those women. The day I gave her that bracelet, she made it very clear to me that she valued my friendship, but as far as anything else, she didn't have those sorts of feelings for me. She said she never meant to lead me on. Looking back, I think she was trying to tell me she was seeing someone else. But I couldn't begin to guess who it might have been."

"But she still took the bracelet."

He smiled the sad smile of a man carrying a ten-year-old torch for a dead woman. Vic felt sorry for him. "I insisted she take it. I promised her I would only accept her friendship if she took the bracelet."

Casio snorted. "You drive a hard bargain."

"Mock me if you will."

"I think I just did."

Victor scowled at the officer. "Casio."

"Come on, you're not buying this, are you?" Casio stared at him and Vic frowned.

Was he missing something? The rest of the conversation would need to take place away from the principal. Victor stood and offered his hand.

"Thank you for your time, Mr. Newman."

As their hands clasped, the principal stood. "I hope I answered all of your questions in such a way that you might find the killer. It's time for the man to be caught and punished."

Casio rolled his eyes as he stood.

"One more thing," Vic said, pulling a swab kit from his bag. "Would you submit to us getting a DNA sample?"

Confusion clouded the principal's eyes. "Why would you possibly want my DNA? Am I a suspect?"

"None of your business, Newman," Casio said. "Just give us the sample or we'll take it."

"Hightower, back off." If there were a group of Neanderthals still living somewhere, this guy was definitely descended from them. "We're not going to take a sample of your DNA against your will. But since you admit to your feelings for her and that you gave her the bracelet, it would be helpful to have the sample. But it's your choice."

"For now," Casio glared.

"I have nothing to hide. I certainly didn't kill her."

To his credit, Casio finally kept his mouth shut while Vic grabbed the swab, swiped it along the inside of Newman's cheek, and slid it into the plastic bag.

When they reached the outside steps, he turned to Vic. "You aren't buying that guy's I-loved-her-so-much-I-was-willing-to-let-her-go crap, are you?"

Irritation lit up inside of Vic. "Don't judge everyone by your lack of standards, Hightower."

"Come off it, Vic. Mr. Nerdy principal, madly in love with a gorgeous, smart teacher who was way too young for him and way too beautiful anyway."

Vic shrugged. "That doesn't mean he killed her. He actually seemed sincere to me, and he gave us a sample of his DNA more freely than anyone I've ever seen." He started down the steps. "And you might not agree, but I'm actually a pretty good judge of character," he said over his shoulder.

Casio grunted and followed him to the car without saying any-thing. But once they pulled out of the parking lot, he started his pitch again. "Blake was at the game. He couldn't have killed Miss Remington."

Victor frowned. "He wasn't on the bus, though."

"No. He could have and just not played. But he didn't ride with us. Can't say I blame him."

"Then he could have driven behind you. Saw the bus was stopped by a train and decided to take advantage of the opportunity."

"Look, I'm telling you he didn't do it. Okay? I would know. I was there."

"So were a busload of other kids. Everyone who was interviewed ten years ago said the gunman wore a mask."

From the corner of Vic's eye, he could see a rapid rise and fall of the officer's chest.

Casio breathed out and turned to Vic. "There's something I left out of my testimony back then. It's relevant, I think."

Victor parallel parked outside the courthouse where Casio had left his truck that morning. "Okay, what?"

"I never thought it would make a difference, but if you're looking at Blake, you can stop right now. Because he's innocent."

"You keep saying that, but how do you know?"

"Because after I was shot, and I was on the floor of the bus. The guy walked over to me and said, 'You okay, kid?'"

"And you didn't think that might be some important information?"

"I was cowering on the floor like a baby. I couldn't tell my dad that."

"You'd just been shot. I think your dad would have understood."

"No. I was shot in the arm." He let out a short laugh. "You want to know what my dad said to me when he came to see me in the hospital?"

"What?" Vic asked.

"He said, 'You mean to tell me, all you got was a bullet in the arm and you couldn't take down a lone gunman? What kind of pantywaist am I raising here? Thanks to you, a girl is dead and the killer got away.'"

"Sounds like a real candidate for father of the year." But at least he wasn't in the pen for armed robbery and murder. Maybe an unsympathetic dad was better than no dad. Who knew?

"I was used to it. It's the way he was. He fed me, clothed me, all of that after Mom walked out on us. So I could handle a little tough love." Casio shrugged. "I know how it sounds. But he was okay. Just didn't take anything less than the best from me."

"So you didn't recognize the killer's voice."

"No. But it wasn't Blake, and it wasn't Newman. Not that Newman couldn't have hired someone." He reached for the door handle. "Who are you going to talk to next?"

"Probably Blake's dad."

Casio's eyes widened. "Unbelievable! I just told you it couldn't have been Blake."

Vic stared at Casio, who in this minute seemed more like an eighteen-year-old high school kid than a grown man. He refused to be intimidated by the officer's quick temper. "You're probably right. And thanks for coming clean about the details you left out, but just because Blake didn't commit the murder doesn't mean the dad wasn't holding a grudge. His boy lost out on a scholarship. It would explain you getting shot too."

"Yeah, but why would he make sure I was okay?"

"He didn't want you dead, just shot you in the throwing arm to ruin your chance to accept a scholarship."

Clearly two and two were adding up in Casio's brain. Then he frowned again. "Yeah, but I don't see why. Taking me out wouldn't get Blake in. At that point the damage was done."

"People don't usually take time to rationalize when they're so angry and hurt they're willing to kill for revenge. His dad was bitter about the fact that you were getting a scholarship but his son wasn't. He told us he wrote a letter to BJ telling her off and that she should watch her back, but never sent it to her."

Casio rolled his eyes. "Whatever. When are you going to see him?"

"I'll set it up and let you know."

Casio opened the door, then hesitated. "Give Claudia my best."

"Sure."

"Hey, does she still have that tattoo on her back just above her—"

"Watch it, Hightower."

"That used to drive me crazy." He laughed and slid out. "I'm kidding, man." He shut the door and pulled the keys from his pocket, walking toward his truck.

Vic gripped the steering wheel tightly with his left hand as he slid the car in reverse and pulled out of the parking lot. He grabbed his phone and dialed the office. "Isobel," he said, relieved she hadn't taken him up on his suggestion to knock off early.

"Where are you, Mr. Campbell? That interview at Jesse's Garage should have been over hours ago. Your wife called, and she seemed very upset. Have you checked your cell phone messages?"

Inwardly, he gave a groan. He'd seen Claudia's number on caller ID. "I'll call her the second we get off the phone."

"Good. Why are you calling me? You must need some information."

He couldn't help but grin. "You're right. I need the name and number of Blake Simpson's dad. Might be easiest to reach him at Jesse's Garage. Actually, could you call and set up an interview with him? He can come to the office or I can meet him. Either way."

"Okay, I can do that." She paused as though writing down his instructions. "When do you want the meeting for?"

"The sooner the better."

"Can't be tomorrow. You have court on the Benray case."

"I forgot all about it." Dread shuffled through him. He was barely prepared for the case. "Thanks for looking out for me, Izzy."

"You know I hate that name," she huffed. "And I'm looking out for the citizens of this town, not you."

Vic chuckled as he flipped on his blinker and pulled into the flower shop. "This weekend or as soon as court is dismissed. I'll concentrate completely on getting justice for my client."

"Good. Then I'll schedule your interview with Mr. Simpson for Monday if he's available."

"Sounds good. Oh, another thing. Round up the number of James Farraday."

"You mean Dr. James Farraday, the pathologist who did the autopsy?

He should have known Izzy would know exactly who he meant. "Yeah, that's the one. There was a little bit of a discrepancy in the autopsy report. I just need to verify something with him."

"I can get that number. Do you want a sit-down interview or is the phone okay?"

"Sit-down, so we can go over his report."

"Okay, I'll get on it."

"Thanks, Izzy."

"And don't forget to stop and get Claudia some flowers. From the sound of her voice earlier, you better get some really good ones. No carnations."

"What do you suggest?"

"No roses. They're romantic, but typical. I'd go with orchids."

Vic chuckled. "You got it. Thanks again, Izzy."

"Stop calling me that or I'm quitting."

"Sure you are. You only have an hour and a half if you're going to go home early like I told you to."

"I'm going as soon as I get that number and give Mr. Simpson a call."

Nine

My friend Kelley had an older brother who was blind. As fascinated as I was by his Braille books and audio learning devices, I couldn't help but fear that I would wake up and be like him, finding myself in darkness. As he felt his way around the house, unaware sometimes that I watched, I wondered what it would be like to be at the mercy of creatures that existed only in shadows.

But now that my eyes have suddenly gone dim, I find myself more terrified of the light. The moment I face eternity for my crimes against the blood of Jesus. Oh, how my heart breaks. What if I could do it over? What if I had never met the man I so freely betrayed my faith to pursue?

Am I overreaching to say I wonder if this is how Peter felt when the rooster crowed? Or Judas… when he flung the money into the potter's field and hung himself? Did he know that only death could erase such putrid guilt from a broken heart?

Claudia's sobbing has quieted. Maybe Pastor King has been

able to calm her. I can still sense her next to me. She won't leave
until I do. I know that. I guess Pastor does too, and that's why he
isn't forcing her off the bus.

I wish I could tell her how foolish I've been. She is the only one
who knows about him and the baby. But she's never said a word,
and I doubt she ever will. I pray she doesn't. Because if he would
kill me, he wouldn't hesitate to kill her too.

THURSDAY EVENING

Claudia

Claudia was glad Emmy had asked to spend the night with Vic's
mom. With school closed for teachers' meetings tomorrow, she could
think of no good reason to refuse. Nor would she have wanted to.

After the news that Vic had opened BJ's case, Claudia had become a basket case. She knew he only wanted to give her closure.
And she loved him for it, but her nerves couldn't take it.

Especially not now. She'd almost hurt Vic's credit and reputa-
tion by her stupid buying and spending. And if that wasn't bad
enough, she'd discovered a letter from her mother to someone who
had obviously been a lover. Her mother had actually been involved
in an illicit love affair. It would have been funny if not so tragic and
pathetic.

She had been lying on the bed for the past hour, and like some
sort of sick punishment, she'd pulled out the letter, reading it over
and over, each time not quite believing the truth staring at her in
black ink.

My darling,

It's been two weeks since my husband discovered our plans to leave. What you didn't know at the time was that I am the reason he discovered the plans. I confessed everything. I don't believe you could have left your wife and child any more than I could have left the ministry, my husband, my daughter.

Each time Claudia came to this part in the letter she had to stop and give a rueful laugh. Ministry, husband, daughter. Claudia, her mother's afterthought.

I realized we could never be happy causing so much suffering. At some point, love must take a backseat to doing what is right. To live out the rest of our lives with dignity and good conscience. If we had followed through with our plans, we might have had days, possibly weeks, of happiness, but ultimately, the pain would have caught up to us and we would have ended up resenting each other. My life is for a bigger purpose than just to fulfill my own happiness. I couldn't bear the thought of leading anyone astray, darling. And there are those in my congregation who would never forgive me or, I fear, God. And while I could suffer the consequences for my own sin, I could never stand before God and try to explain those dear sheep I lost.

So, dear one, we'll never again speak of this. And you

will never see this letter. I am writing it for closure at my
therapist's suggestion.

I pray it makes me forget your arms, your lips, your
gentle voice, speaking my name.

I will miss you always,
Liz

Liz? Elizabeth King had allowed someone to call her Liz? It
seemed so beneath her. The revelation that her mother had not only
had an affair, but had clearly loved another man, came as the kind of
shock that shoots through paddles on the chest. The kind her dad
had experienced a year ago when he collapsed before his congregation, his heart stopping three times before he reached the hospital.

Mother had been strong. She never shed a tear, never showed one
second of weakness or fatigue, though she stayed at the hospital the
whole time he was in there. When he returned home, she had nursed
him with Nightingale-esque diligence. The woman had truly been
amazing. She had fielded calls, arranged for guest speakers, and fed
Daddy a bland diet, except for Sunday dinner, all with a beautiful
hairdo and perfect makeup.

What a fraud.

And Claudia was going to have to actually host this fraud party
for her and pretend she believed her parents had the perfect marriage
and ministry. And had for thirty-five years.

Poor Daddy must have been so wounded.

Tears were beginning to stream again when Claudia's phone
rang. She rolled her eyes, as she recognized her mother's number.

There was no point in letting the call go to voice mail. Mother wouldn't leave a message and she'd keep calling until Claudia either turned off her phone, which she wouldn't do with Emmy gone, or gave in and answered.

"Yes, Mother?" She knew her voice was hostile. But how could she pretend? The betrayal was still too fresh.

"You sound upset. Is something wrong?"

Yeah, a whole lot of something was wrong. Her mother had the morals of Rahab before the scarlet cord. "I'm fine. What's up?"

"Your daddy asked me to call. Velma is going to have to step down from her position at the office and he would like you to come back for a few weeks until he finds a replacement."

"I haven't worked in a long time."

"I know that, Claudia, but this is a favor for him. You'll fall right back into the routine. Not much has changed."

"I'll have to talk it over with Vic." Claudia released a breath. "When does Daddy need me to start?"

"As soon as possible."

"I'll let you know." Would she ever be able to look her mother in the eye without wanting to slap her across the face? "Is that all? I think I hear Vic coming in downstairs."

"Downstairs? What are you doing upstairs this time of day? Shouldn't you be helping Emily with her homework and fixing dinner?"

"Emmy's at Darla's for the night and I didn't feel like cooking. We'll probably either order pizza or open a can of soup."

Mother's hesitation gave her a tiny sense of satisfaction. She hated it when Emily spent time with her other grandmother, "Mimi," as Emmy called her.

She heard footsteps on the stairs. "I have to go. I'll discuss the job with Vic and let you know in a day or two."

She disconnected the call without saying good-bye. Passive-aggression might be childish, but it helped her cope where her mother was concerned and when she had been raised to honor her parents. She was an obedient daughter, perhaps because she'd learned long ago that she couldn't confront her mother in any way that was meaningful. Their relationship just wasn't conducive to that sort of honesty.

"Claude?" The soft sound of Vic's voice preceded him into the room.

She glanced up to the sight of roses. "Beautiful," she breathed as he set them in her lap. "Thank you."

"Izzy said you'd rather have orchids." He sat next to her on the edge of the mattress and leaned over, dropping a quick kiss on her lips.

She smiled. "I like roses best. Did she tell you to get me flowers?" Disappointed, she looked down.

"After you called the office looking for me? Of course she did." He grinned, stealing her heart. "But I was already at the flower shop, on the phone with her when she mentioned it. The flowers were be-cause I love you, not because my assistant was trying to manipulate you into forgiving me."

Ashamed of herself, Claudia pressed her nose to the soft red pet-als. "Mmm. I'm glad."

"I'm sorry I got busy this afternoon and didn't get back to you." His soft brown eyes searched hers. "Are you feeling okay?"

"Yeah, why wouldn't I be?" Her face warmed. "Oh, I'm in bed. I'm fine, I just decided to take a short nap after I got back from dropping Emmy at your mom's."

"Why did you need me? Izzy said you sounded upset."

Glancing at the letter on the bed, Claudia froze. She wasn't ready to share her discovery with anyone, not even Vic. And as much as she wanted to ask him about reopening BJ's case, she didn't want to take a chance that he might see the letter and start asking questions.

His gaze followed her and her heart skipped a beat. "Honey," she said quickly, "why don't you get your shower and we can go out to dinner? It's been a long time since we had a date night without Emmy."

Loosening his tie, he stood. "That sounds like a great idea. Olive Garden?"

She sighed. "I got suckered into having lunch there tomorrow with Georgie Newman. How about Mexican?"

"Had that with Casio Hightower today."

"Casio?" Claudia realized that could only mean that Tara had been right. Vic had reopened the case. He must have been interviewing the officer because he was on the bus that night. Although if Casio were with him while he interviewed Blake, it probably meant Casio was helping out with the investigation.

Vic nodded, sliding his tie from his collar and beginning the process of undressing. Claudia watched, trying not to overreact and ruin the moment, but just the thought of what Vic was attempting numbed her hands and sent a tingle to her jaw—both quick signs she was beginning to hyperventilate.

"I'm going to shower," Vic said. "I'll be quick about it so we can get going. Since you're having Italian tomorrow and I had Mexican at lunch, how about a nice seafood and steak place?"

Nodding, Claudia fought to keep from showing Vic her situation. "Sounds good," she said, her voice strained.

Thankfully, Vic seemed not to notice as he padded into the bathroom. "You could join me, you know," he called.

"Nice try. I'm not getting my hair wet."

She heard him laugh, and relief flooded over her that he didn't push to get her in there. She heard the shower turn on and set the flowers aside. Reaching over with numbed fingers, she took a bag from her nightstand drawer and began to breathe deeply.

She would confront him later about it. Dread filled her at the very thought. They had to move on. She had to move on. And dredging up the case would make everything real again.

With a weary push, she sat up, breathing deeply into the bag until thankfully, the episode passed quicker than usual. On the dresser, Vic's phone rang. The caller ID said MOM, so she answered.

"Darla?" she said. "Everything okay with Emmy?"

"Mommy?" Her heart lurched at the sound of Emily's tiny voice.

"Honey? What's wrong?"

"Mimi won't wake up."

"What do you mean? Did she fall? Where is she?"

"On the floor in the kitchen." Her voice caught. "She has blood, Mommy."

Oh, dear God. "Okay, Emmy, listen to Mommy. I want you to go sit in the living room and get ready to open the door when the ambulance comes, okay? Stay on the phone with me."

She rushed to where she'd dropped her purse on the floor next to the bed. Rummaging inside, she found her phone. "I'm going to call 911 from my phone, so you might hear Mommy talking to someone, okay?"

"Okay, Mommy."

She dialed 911 while rushing across the room and into the bathroom. She flung open the shower door. Vic spun around, surprise flashing in his face, then a grin. "Change your mind?"

"Get out. Your mom collapsed."

Victor

Vic and Claudia rushed into the ER. The nurse behind the counter seemed to recognize Claudia. "Hi!" she said. "What are you doing here?" She frowned. "Everything okay?"

"Georgie," Claudia said, her words coming out around deep gulps. "Thank God it's someone we know. Vic's mother was brought in. Darla Campbell. The paramedics brought my daughter with them."

"Oh, Emily is your little girl." The nurse turned. "Bring Emily out, would you? Her parents are here."

Another nurse came through the door, holding Emily's hand. The little girl broke free and ran to Claudia, who scooped her up, holding tightly. "You were so brave. I am very proud of you."

"What's wrong with Mimi?" she asked.

"We don't know yet," Claudia said. "The doctors are very smart and they're doing everything they can to make her better."

Relieved that one worry was over, Vic took over the questioning. "What's going on with my mother?"

"Why don't you two have a seat?" the nurse at the counter said. "I'll see what I can find out and whether or not you can come back and be with her."

"Thank you, Georgie," Claudia said.

"A friend of yours?" Vic asked, more to have something to say than curiosity.

"Not really. We went to school together. She's the principal's daughter."

"Newman?" There was nothing about a daughter in the case files. He couldn't help but wonder if she were another lead.

Claudia nodded. "She was a little younger than we were."

By the past tense reference, he wondered if she were going back to high school in her mind. He filed the information about the nurse in his memory, where the investigation never seemed far from pushing its way to the foreground.

Before they had time to find a seat, the door opened and Georgie came out. Her smile eased the tension some even before she spoke. "Your mom is awake and lucid. She's getting oxygen and they've taken her to get some tests run. A heart attack is suspected but we won't know for sure until after the EKG and chest x-ray."

"When can we see her?" Vic asked.

"As soon as she gets back to her room from the tests. We're a little backed up, so it could take awhile."

"You're working long hours," Claudia said. "Weren't you on lunch break when we saw each other at the coffee shop earlier?"

Georgie's face lit up as though she were happy Claudia remembered. "One of the girls got sick, so I took her shift." She shrugged. "It's not like I have a life outside of this place anyway."

"I'm glad you were here," Claudia said warmly. This was the side of Claudia that had drawn Vic. Competent, kind, able to make people feel valued in the midst of crises. It came out on occasion. Those times when she had others to concentrate on. "Will you keep us posted on my mother-in-law's progress?"

"Of course. I best get back to my patients. You two have a seat. There's fresh coffee over there in the corner. Or there are vending machines around the corner if your daughter is hungry."

Vic turned to Claudia as Georgie left them. "Do you want to call your mom to get Emily? We could be here awhile."

Claudia stiffened her shoulders at the mention of her mother.

"Everything okay?"

"Is everything ever okay between her and me?"

"Good point." He placed his hand on the small of her back and led her to the chairs in the packed waiting room.

A soft sigh escaped Claudia's lips. "I suppose I'd better call them." She shifted Emily to Vic's lap and pulled out her phone. Her side of the conversation was tense, extremely polite, and even more strained than normal. She hung up without saying good-bye.

"Mama is sending Daddy over so he can go back and pray with your mom."

"I appreciate it. If God hears anyone's prayers, it's his."

She gave a short laugh. "Definitely not my mother's, that's for sure."

Vic frowned. This was more than the usual disdain she had for her mother. "Did you and your mom fight?"

Claudia shook her head. "I'm just so sick of her hypocrisy."

"That's a little harsh, don't you think?" Vic knew he was risking Claudia's anger. Anything that smacked of taking Mrs. King's side was seen as betrayal, but *hypocrite* wasn't a fitting description for his mother-in-law. And he didn't like when Claudia forgot Emmy was within listening range.

She opened her mouth, then glanced at the little girl in his lap and clamped her lips tightly. She shrugged instead.

Pastor King showed up thirty minutes later, absent Mrs. King. Vic was relieved. At least they wouldn't have to endure the tension between the two women. They sat for another hour before Georgie returned to the waiting room and said they could go back and sit with his mother. Vic and Pastor King stood.

"Follow me," she said.

"Is she going to be okay?" Vic asked, following the nurse.

"The test results are still pending. The doctor will come and speak with you as soon as they're ready."

She opened a curtain and escorted them into a tiny room where his mother lay looking frail and old in the bed. She smiled as soon as she saw him.

Vic frowned at a bandage across her forehead. "Did you hit your head when you fell?"

She waved her hands in dismissal. "Yes. And I'm embarrassed as all get-out. All this fuss about nothing."

"I don't think your fainting is nothing, Mom."

"I'm sorry it was in front of Emmy. How is she?"

"Claudia kept her in the waiting room until Pastor King finishes praying with you."

Darla smiled weakly at the pastor. "Thank you for coming."

He took her hands. "It's my pleasure, Darla. May I pray for you?"

"Yes, Pastor, thank you."

His simple prayer of petition for healing and many more years brought a mist to Vic's eyes. He wasn't ready to say good-bye to his mother.

When they opened their eyes, Georgie was standing at the edge of the room, her head down reverently. Another woman stood with her. "I don't mean to interrupt. But this is Dr. Bakker."

Pastor King patted Vic's shoulder. "I'll go so I can get Emmy home. Call me if you need me for anything."

When he left, the doctor stepped forward. "Mrs. Campbell, I'm Dr. Bakker and I studied your test results. I don't find anything of real concern at this time."

"Then why did she pass out?" Vic said, ready to have his mother moved to a Dallas hospital and get more tests run.

"I don't believe she did." The doctor glanced down at Darla again. "Can you tell us what happened?"

Darla looked up at Vic. "She's right, hon. I was getting Emmy a cookie and just stumbled a little. I lost my balance and hit my head."

The doctor nodded. "Which is likely what knocked you out. We did a CT of her head and found no damage other than the cut that we had to stitch up."

"So she's good to go?"

"I'd like to admit her overnight just to keep an eye on her. But I don't really think there's much cause for alarm." She smiled at his mother. "I'll be in to check on you in the morning."

And just like that she was gone. Assembly-line medicine.

Georgie Newman appeared a few minutes later. "They'll be coming to take her to a room in just a couple of minutes. They just called down that they're on their way. She'll be on the fifth floor if you want to go out and get Claudia and head on up." She smiled, a kind, competent smile. "Unless you don't want to leave her alone. In which case, I'll go get Claudia and you can go up with your mom."

"Don't be silly," Darla said. "Let me get settled into my bed and then you can come and kiss me goodnight and be on your way. I don't want you baby-sitting me all night."

"Too bad. I'm not leaving you."

"She's probably right, Mr. Campbell," Georgie said. "We gave her some pain medication for her head and she'll probably be asleep soon."

When the nurse's assistant arrived to take his mother upstairs, he walked back into the lobby. Claudia looked up from the magazine on her lap. "How is she?"

"They're taking her upstairs. We can meet her up there."

Setting the magazine aside, Claudia stood just as the doors to the ER swished open. A woman doubled over and alone shuffled to the nurse's station. She held her stomach. The nurse at the desk picked up her phone and called for a wheelchair. "Hold my hand," the nurse said. "Someone will be here in just a minute."

The poor woman's face was bruised, but it didn't look fresh. Her cheeks were damp with tears. "I think I'm having a miscarriage."

Claudia drew a sharp breath. Vic turned and saw her gaze resting on the new patient, pain flooding her eyes. "You okay, sweetheart?" he whispered.

She nodded, but her face had drained of color. Vic slipped his arm around her waist and drew her close. This was the first time Claudia had been in the hospital since her father's heart attack. One of the nurses hurried around with a wheelchair. Georgie followed with a clipboard. "What's your name, honey?"

"Harper Abbott."

Ten

In Mary Oliver's poem, "When Death Comes," the narrator first sees death as a doorway of wonder.

I once did as well. It's like that when you see it far off. Now I see it as that iceberg between the shoulder blades she so deftly described. I'm dying, and here I am without a legacy of hope. Escaping from a world of lies, knowing darned well that nothing dark stays hidden from light. So while I may have carried my secrets in life, death will eventually reveal all of my truth. I am dying, and I've been nothing more than an unwelcome visitor to this world.

I hear someone entering the bus. Pastor King is leaving my side and someone else kneels beside me. I know by the way my hand is suddenly brought to a warm chest that my mother has learned that I am on the bus. I don't know where Daddy is, but as my mother whispers words of love and comfort, I wish I could speak to her. If I could, I would tell her this:

I understand now why you loved Daddy so much that you

*stayed with him even after he did what he did. After his affair
with Mrs. King. Because sometimes love is stronger than betrayal,
Mama.*

*I was going to give you a grandbaby finally. I suppose you'll
find out. They'll do an autopsy and the knowledge that your
daughter's killer was also your grandchild's killer will bring you
more pain than I can even bear to think about.*

*Death is ever so much like an iceberg between my shoulder
blades.*

FRIDAY

Claudia

Claudia sat across from Georgie Newman, feeling ridiculous and
awkward. She was grateful that Georgie had been at the hospital last
night, but still, she barely knew the woman. And while she had to
admit maybe Georgie wasn't as bad as Claudia had originally believed, lunch with a semi-stranger was just uncomfortable.

"Vic wanted me to thank you for being so great with his mom
last night," she said, scanning the menu for the cheapest meal she
could find. Georgie had insisted upon the lunch being "her treat,"
which also made Claudia uncomfortable. She'd rather eat a seafood
alfredo, but didn't want to appear nervy.

Looking up from her menu, Georgie waved away the gratitude.
"Oh, listen. I'm glad I was there. The ER can get crazy, but of all the
places I've worked, I have to say I love it most."

Claudia took a sip of her water. "I—um. I noticed a young

woman come in just as we were going upstairs. I've been worried about her ever since." That was something of an understatement. She had wanted to stay and check on the woman, but knew Vic would worry if she attempted it.

Georgie frowned. "There are so many. Can you be more specific?"

"She thought she might be having a miscarriage." She drew a breath and rushed on. "I hope I don't sound nosy. It's just that I had a miscarriage two years ago and that sort of thing touches my heart." After seeing the woman, Claudia had struggled to keep from hyperventilating again. Thankfully, Vic had comforted her and refocused her attention on his mother.

Vic had also let her sleep in this morning since her mother had Emmy. She hadn't spoken with him all day, but Claudia's first order of business was to tell Vic just what she thought about reopening BJ's case.

Georgie nodded. "I remember who you mean. She looked beat-up too."

"Did she lose the baby?" Claudia held her breath.

Georgie shook her head, a smile curving her mouth. "She probably just ate something spicy that didn't agree with her, which felt like cramps, and she was spotting, which happens a lot in early pregnancy. We did an ultrasound. She's two months pregnant and scared to death."

"Why was she scared to death?"

"The bruises?" Georgie's eyebrows rose. "The man who beat her is the baby's daddy. They're separated, but he won't leave her alone.

She's afraid once he finds out she's going to have a baby, he'll really come after her." She shook her head, disgust sneering her plumped-up lips. "She wouldn't name the creep, and the bruises are a couple of weeks old. So all we could do was reassure her the baby is okay and send her home."

Claudia settled on lasagna and closed the menu. "Do you get a lot of that?"

"More than we'd like. Of course, even one case is more than we'd like." She shrugged. "Anyway, she was a bit dehydrated, which might have contributed to cramps, so we got her fluids up and watched her for a couple of hours and sent her home."

They ordered, and Georgie carried the conversation, which mostly revolved around nursing, the ER, and why she couldn't find a decent man. When Georgie finally paid the bill, Claudia had never been more relieved to see a meal come to an end.

Victor

It was midafternoon before Claudia finally answered her phone. Vic was glad to hear her voice, especially after last night's ordeal.

"Did you get your mother home?" she asked him before he could say anything.

"Yes. I hired a nurse's aide to come and stay with her this week. She's not happy about it."

"Well, did you expect her to be?"

"No, I guess not. How was your lunch with the nurse?"

"I had lasagna. We talked about nursing, mostly. The woman we saw last night didn't lose the baby."

Vic felt his stomach tighten. If that woman was Harper Abbott, then Casio was going to be a father. And not under very good circumstances. He had a feeling Casio didn't know about it. Casio wasn't one to keep his mouth shut, so Vic was sure he would have mentioned it if he knew. "She talked about her patient?"

"Not by name or anything like that. But I asked her about the baby and she said it was okay. The pains were just gas or something like that."

"Sounds like you didn't have a very good time."

"It wasn't too bad."

Her voice sounded strained, almost like she was angry.

"Is everything okay, Claude?"

"Not really."

"What's wrong, honey?

"When were you planning to tell me you had opened the Remington case and were working on it with Casio?"

Vic drew in a breath. "How did you find out?" No way she could have learned all that at lunch. The nurse couldn't have known about Casio.

"The girl who does my hair happens to be dating Blake and she told me. She said Casio and you questioned Blake. I was going to discuss it with you at dinner last night. But then your mom got hurt."

"Claude, let's talk about this when we get home."

"When I get home, I'm packing my things and moving out."

Vic's heart picked up speed. "What do you mean? Isn't that a little excessive for the crime?" He'd kept the truth from her to protect her from going completely ballistic. He had tried to spare her the emotional trauma of knowing he was working on the case. This didn't make sense.

"Do you mean the fact that I can't stand the thought of sleeping next to you every night, knowing you've reopened a case that gives me panic attacks and nightmares? Or that you didn't respect me enough to tell me yourself instead of making me look like a fool? I had a panic attack right in the parking lot at Tara's."

"Honey, I'm sorry." When Claudia didn't respond, he said, "Please don't do this."

"I have to." Her voice broke, but Vic recognized that she was resolute in her decision.

"Where will you go?"

"As much as I hate to do it, I'll have to stay at my parents' house."

"You don't have to do this, Claude. Come on."

"You didn't have to open BJ's case. It's been this long and no one else has been murdered. So it's not like we're talking about a serial killer. BJ must have ticked off the wrong person, or maybe it was random and she was just unlucky. Either way, why put the town through another dead-end investigation just so you can be elected DA?"

Her words hit hard, stealing a bit of his breath. Was that what she thought? That he just wanted to be elected? An uncomfortable knot formed in his stomach. It wouldn't hurt for him to solve the case. That was certain. But that wasn't his reason. "It's too late to stop it now. We've already started looking into a couple of leads. Just trust me."

"Don't expect any help from me."

"O-kay," he said tentatively. "Claudia, I have a good feeling that we're going to find this guy. Don't be upset."

"Don't tell me not to be upset, Vic. You hear me? Not until you've lain in the blood of your best friend while she slowly stops breathing."

"Claudia, sweetheart." Vic wished they weren't having this conversation over the phone. He wanted to hold her, comfort her through this.

"When you've stood in the shower and the blood won't come off. No matter how you scrub and scrub and it won't wash off. Then, you can tell me not to be upset." Her voice broke. "I have to go, Vic. I can't talk to you anymore."

MONDAY

Victor

Three days later Vic walked into the dimly lit cop bar, allowing his eyes to adjust before venturing more than a couple of steps inside. When he was reasonably sure he wouldn't fall flat on his face, he headed for the bar and waited for the older guy behind the counter to notice him. The man looked familiar, but Vic couldn't place him. Maybe if he were more illuminated.

"Be right with you."

Vic nodded. "Take your time." He watched as the bartender slid a drink across the bar to an older man who was surrounded by a group of younger men and women.

The bartender turned back to Vic and shook his head. He jerked his thumb toward the guy. "The life of the party, ain't he? Give him another hour and he'll be too drunk to know his own name. I guarantee you, none of those rookies will be around to help him get home." He tossed his towel over his left shoulder and placed his hands on the counter—looking a lot like a professional wrestler. "What can I get you?"

"Nothing to drink. I'm supposed to meet a man named Gabriel Hightower. Do you know him?"

The bartender frowned and peered closer. "I've seen you somewhere before."

Vic held out his hand. "Victor Campbell."

Recognition registered in the bartender's eyes. "The Assistant DA. What do you want with Gabe?"

"We have a meeting. And since you know him, think you could point him out?"

The bartender shrugged and pointed at Mr. Popularity. "Good luck prying him away from his fans."

"Thanks." Vic moved toward the group of six or seven admirers and elbowed his way through. "Excuse me, Mr. Hightower?"

The man had silver hair and straight shoulders. He stood and, even retired, would have been a force to be reckoned with if not for the tubing stuck in his nose. Taller than Vic's six feet by at least three inches, he seemed more powerful than a man of sixty should—especially one carrying around an oxygen tank. "You ADA Campbell?"

"Yes sir." Victor held out his hand and tried not to wince as he felt it being crushed beneath the former detective's bruising grip. This guy would never respect a sign of weakness. "You mind if we find a private corner somewhere?"

"Okay by me." Hightower glanced back at his entourage. "Sorry, boys and girls, duty calls." Vic watched the group scatter like roaches. Gabe downed his bourbon and set the glass on the bar. "Burt, give me another and one for my friend here. And a draft."

"Club soda is good for me," Vic said quickly.

"What? Can't hold your liquor?"

Vic gave him a tight smile. "I wouldn't know. I don't drink liquor."

The older man scowled, clearly unimpressed with any so-called man who didn't throw back a few with the boys. He grabbed his fresh drink in one hand and the beer in the other. Vic took his club soda and paid for all three drinks. "Thanks," he told the bartender and followed Gabe to an empty corner table.

Gabe stumbled a bit as he walked. "You're lucky it's dinnertime. Couple more hours and this place will be standing room only."

"I appreciate you taking time to see me, Mr. Hightower."

"Mr. Hightower was my old man. Call me Gabe." Gabe took the chair by the wall—Vic assumed so he could keep an eye on the room. Typical of someone in law enforcement. He needed to make sure no one could sneak up on him. Vic didn't mind. The place was full of cops and retired cops. He felt about as safe as he could possibly feel in a bar.

"So." Gabe tapped on the table and squinted at Vic as though trying to read him. "What do you want with me?"

"We're reinvestigating the murder of BJ Remington, the high school teacher shot to death ten years ago."

"You don't need to remind me of that case. I was in charge of that one. My boy got himself shot. Lucky he didn't get killed."

"Yes sir. That's why I'm coming to you." More out of professional courtesy and a respect for Mr. Hightower's years of service than an actual desire for assistance, but there might be pieces of information he remembered that didn't make it into any of his reports. From what Vic had observed, the man was better at grunt work than paperwork anyway. He got the job done; he just didn't document it well.

"So, what do you want to know?" He drank down his bourbon and chased it with a swig of his beer. The bartender had been right. The way this guy was drinking, he'd be worthless in less than an hour.

"There were a couple of questions that came up while we were looking through files."

He coughed deeply and wiped his mouth. The napkin came away spotted red. "Like what, for instance?"

"For instance, why didn't you interview the high school principal?"

Hightower's eyes narrowed. "That little gnat? What could he have told us? He wasn't even there that night."

"True, but he knew about Miss Remington's relationships with students and teachers. He might have been able to point you toward a reliable witness at least."

The former cop gave a snort and held up his glass toward the bar. "Burt! Another boilermaker."

Trying not to show his irritation, Vic purposely kept his voice amiable. "Mr. Hightower, would you mind holding off on the booze for just a few more minutes so we can talk?"

He released a profanity. "Don't tell me not to drink, boy."

This was getting him nowhere but angry. Vic stood and glanced down at the man. "I'm sorry I wasted your time, Mr. Hightower. If you'll excuse me."

"Oh now, don't get mad. Sit down, I'll hold off for a while."

Surprised, Vic took his seat. "Thank you. I appreciate it. So?"

"Okay, so why didn't I interview the little creep? I didn't see anything relevant he could tell me. He wasn't even at the game that night."

"But you were?"

"Yeah, my son was quarterback. Best quarterback that team had before or since. He should have gone all the way." Vic noted that Gabe was out of breath.

"Except he was shot."

"That's right."

"Now he's following your footsteps. That should make you proud."

His meaty shoulders lifted. "Sure. I guess. He's good at what he does. But he could have gone all the way to the NFL. But he couldn't stay out of the line of fire."

Vic frowned at the tone. Did Gabe blame his son for his own injury? "I heard he got shot trying to save Miss Remington."

"That's right." Gabe sipped his beer. At least he wasn't slugging it down now.

"That must have made you proud. No one else raised a hand to help."

"Yeah, that's my boy. The hero." He sipped again, then leveled his gaze at Vic. "Like I said, the reason I didn't interview the principal is because I didn't think he had anything relevant to add. If he knew something he would have come forward."

So the old man didn't want to talk about Casio's shooting. Vic could understand that. And nothing he could say about that could help, so he allowed the former cop to steer the conversation in a different direction.

"Are you sure Mr. Newman couldn't have helped light up any of your gray areas?"

"Yeah, real sure." The older man's demeanor was becoming bristled as his defenses rose. Clearly, this wasn't the kind of man who enjoyed having his judgment questioned. "Otherwise, I'd have interviewed him."

"Mr. Hightower, I'm not questioning whether you did your job right or not. It was a rough time back then and it would have been hard to know who to interview. Especially when you had your boy to worry about."

Gabe nodded. He seemed mollified by Vic's speech, so Vic continued.

"Just wondering…"

"Yeah?"

"Where was Casio's mother? He doesn't talk about her and you haven't mentioned anything about her. If a boy is in the hospital, seems like his mom would be there."

A scowl twisted the former detective's lips. "She was no good. Left us a month before the shooting and never even sent him a balloon when he was in the hospital."

Vic filed away this information. "Some women aren't the motherly type, I guess."

"That's putting it mildly." He sipped his beer. "She was some piece of work, that one."

Vic cleared his throat and shifted in his seat. "I was thinking if we could put our heads together…maybe you know something I don't know or maybe I've discovered something you overlooked."

The former detective's eyes darted back to Vic. "What'd I overlook?"

Definitely didn't like being second-guessed.

Vic sipped his club soda and swallowed, setting his glass back on the table. "Well, the principal, for instance."

"I told you there was no good reason to waste taxpayer dollars and my time."

This guy's insecurity was beginning to grate. "Did you know he was in love with BJ Remington?"

From the rise of silvery eyebrows, Vic guessed the answer was no. Anger flashed in Gabe's eyes. "That little runt in love with Miss Remington?" He gave a humorless laugh. "No way. The guy swings the other way, if you get my meaning."

Vic narrowed his gaze and studied Gabe. Something definitely bothered him about the idea of Newman being in love with BJ. Vic decided to press a little. "Maybe he swung both ways."

"What's that supposed to mean?"

"The two of them went out to dinner several times, and he even gave her a bracelet she hardly ever took off."

"You mean the one with the knot?"

"You know it?"

Gabe shrugged. "Sounds familiar. The girl must have been wearing it when we found her."

"Probably." Vic nodded. "Anyway, Newman loved her. Or was at least obsessed with her, so he's a possible suspect."

"Are you pursuing him as a suspect?"

"I almost have to. But there's another lead we're also pursuing."

Vic noted with satisfaction that he had Mr. Hightower's full attention now. His hand was no longer even on his mug of beer. "Do you remember another football player named Blake Simpson? He was one of Casio's teammates."

Gabe nodded once. "Sure. That kid could have gone all the way, too. He had the same colleges interested in him as my son did."

"Did you know that he threatened Miss Remington a week before she was killed?"

The blood drained from Gabe's sallow cheeks. He shook his head. "I had no idea."

"You might have if you'd bothered to investigate Newman."

"Okay, so I should have questioned the little fairy."

"You know, Mr. Hightower, I'm beginning to take offense to your hate references."

"Did I touch a nerve?"

"All prejudice touches a nerve with me."

"Sorry. I didn't know you were such a bleeding heart."

Vic forced back a retort. This guy was worse than Casio—by a lot. He leveled his gaze at Gabe, determined to stay professional. "Back to Blake Simpson. You were at the game that night, so you must have seen him in the stands, right?"

"I never paid attention. I was too busy watching my own kid play."

"You didn't notice the star running back was missing?"

He shrugged. "They won without the Simpson boy. I just never thought about it."

"Well, Blake thought about it plenty. Miss Remington gave him a low grade that forced him onto academic probation. That's the reason he didn't get to play."

Only the slightest rise in his eyebrows showed the older man's reaction. "So he should have studied." Gabe went back to his beer and swallowed a mouthful. "So you're looking at two suspects I never even thought of. I guess that makes you the man."

"Casio's helping me too."

"Yeah, he told me. Thought the old man might have some advice." He gave an unpleasant laugh. "I told him to duck if he sees a man with a gun."

"You know, Mr. Hightower," Vic said, rising from his seat. He'd had about all he could take of this guy. No wonder Casio was such an emotional wreck. "Your son was pretty darned heroic that night. There aren't many kids who would have tried to tackle a man with a gun."

"Not that it did BJ any good."

"It wouldn't have mattered anyway. The fatal shots had already been fired, and with the delay in getting paramedics to the bus, nothing Casio or anyone else did would have made a difference."

The former detective raised his glass toward the bar again, and this time Vic didn't stop him. He'd had pretty much all he could stomach of this guy anyway. It was becoming more and more clear where Casio got his rough edges. What a waste of time.

"Don't drive home, Mr. Hightower."

"Don't worry. My boy'll come get me."

Vic walked outside into the welcome fresh air. He clicked the button on his key ring and unlocked the Camry. He couldn't help but feel a little sorry for Casio after meeting his old man. Not that bad DNA excused Casio's actions. Still, Vic could understand a little better why he was damaged.

He lifted his phone and pressed speed dial one. Predictably, it went to Claudia's voice mail. "Hi, Claude. It's me again. I miss you and Emmy. It's been three days. Please give me a call."

He knew he sounded lovesick and lonesome, and that pretty much summed up the way he felt. If he wanted to play hardball, he could insist on a visitation with Emmy, and there was really nothing Claudia could do about it. He'd do it if this continued more than another day or two, but he wanted to give Claudia the space she needed to sort through her feelings and realize that he was only investigating the case for her.

He couldn't just open and close investigations at will and on a whim. Now that they had started this process, they had to exhaust every lead before they sealed it up again. Besides, he had a feeling about this. Something in his gut that told him he was going to solve this thing, and the man who killed BJ and shot Casio and the bus driver would finally be put away. He was getting close to being on the right track.

He only prayed that once it was all over, Claude would forgive him for standing his ground this time. He knew that ground was soft and precarious. If he didn't find this killer, Claudia would never be better, and he was likely to lose his marriage. What twisted his gut was that even if he did find the killer, there was still no guarantee she would return home. But at least it would begin to close the gaping wound inside of her. The best he could do was try to focus on the case and find this guy as quickly as possible before he lost Claudia for good.

Part Two

Not the labors of my hands
Could fulfill thy law's commands;
Could my zeal no respite know
Could my tears forever flow,
All for sin could not atone;
Thou must save, and thou alone.

Eleven

Mama's wearing Chanel No. 5. I'm glad my sense of smell is still with me—it's the most comforting thing. My sight is gone, though my eyes are open. My chest rises slowly. I fight for each breath. Now that Mama is here, I don't want to go. I want to feel her warmth. She's singing to me, the familiar, sweet songs of my childhood—it almost makes this worth it to be in her arms listening to the sounds of her mildly off-key expression of love.

> *Too-ra-loo-ra-loo-ral, Too-ra-loo-ra-li,*
> *Too-ra-loo-ra-loo-ral, hush now, don't you cry*
> *Too-ra-loo-ra-loo-ral, Too-ra-loo-ra-li,*
> *Too-ra-loo-ra-loo-ral, that's an Irish lullaby.*

Inside I'm smiling. I wish Mama knew I could hear her. We are not Irish—not according to my dad. But Mama's grandmother was, and Mama has always loved the culture. I grew up on Irish lullabies. I would have raised my baby on the same songs and old

*classic musicals and corned beef and cabbage on St. Patrick's Day.
Mama would have been the best grandmother. But now she'll
never have a grandchild.*

*"Where is she?" I hear my dad's voice, strong and steady, as
though his very presence will cause me to stand up and walk away
from this mess. He probably thinks that's exactly what will happen. He'll find out soon enough, though. He thinks he fixes things,
but really he destroys.*

*Lord, Daddy. You broke Mama's heart when you cheated on
her. She died a little back then and you never even noticed. You're
a killer, Daddy. And you've made me into one too.*

FRIDAY

Claudia

Claudia lay curled in her childhood bed. Her head itched and her
stomach growled from neglect, but she didn't care. Tears slowly made
their way to the pillow. It seemed like all she could do these days was
cry. She missed Vic, but she knew more than anything that she was
no good for him right now. Not until this thing about BJ was over.
She didn't want to get into bed next to him every night, knowing
that her nightmares were coming as she visualized the crime over
and over, felt the warm, sticky blood seeping through her clothes.

A shudder slid up her spine and vibrated her body. She pulled the
covers higher around her shoulders and slid down into the sheets,
hoping to fade into sleep. A tap at the door elicited a groan from her
throat. *Please, Mother, leave me alone.*

"Come in," she mumbled.

The door opened, and as she'd expected, her mother entered. "Vic called again."

Claudia didn't respond. She couldn't even open her eyes. Had no desire to.

"Did you hear me, Claudia?" Elizabeth King was not the timid sort of mother who would be easily put off by a sullen daughter. No matter how grown that daughter might be.

"Yes, Mother. I hear you."

"Well, you don't have to use that tone."

Oh, yes, she did. She did have to use that tone. It was the only one available to her when her mother walked into the room. "Sorry, Mother."

The bed moved as her mother sat. She reached forward and smoothed Claudia's hair as she used to when Claudia was still a child. At one time she craved that touch more than anything. Now all she wanted to do was jerk away and order this stranger-woman out of her room. But of course she wouldn't.

"Honey," Elizabeth said, "don't you think you ought to return your husband's call?"

"If I did, I would."

"Tone, Claudia."

Sitting up, Claudia leaned back against the headboard and pulled her knees to her chest. "I'm not ready to go home. I can't while he's working on BJ's murder case." And even then, she didn't know if she'd ever go back. "It's too much, Mother. Please try to understand."

"I'm not the one you need to convince." Elizabeth crossed her slim legs. "You do not just walk away from a good man like Victor. He loves you and Emily so much."

"Oh, Mother, please. You are not going to lecture me about staying with a good man. Not after what you did, *Liz*."

Her mother's face drained of color. "What are you referring to, Claudia?"

"I think you know. The day we started cleaning out the attic, I found a letter to your 'darling.'"

"That was many years ago, Claudia, and I've paid for my sins many times over. It took years for your father to truly forgive me and trust me again. And it took many tears before I felt like God truly forgave me as well. It's the most painful thing anyone can do to a spouse. Perhaps I'm trying to spare you and your family the same pain I caused."

"And perhaps you are trying to spare yourself the embarrassment of the town bringing up your past because your daughter has left her husband the same way you almost did." The words flew out of her mouth, and Claudia didn't try to stop them. "Only I didn't leave Vic for another man like you almost did." She knew she was causing the sort of harm that comes from only spiteful, cruel words, but she suddenly didn't care. Years of pent-up frustration with her mother's drive for perfection were finally being released. "So there really isn't much of a comparison. And if anyone asks, you can be sure I'll inform them of that fact."

Elizabeth stood up, her chin raised, shoulders back. Claudia held her breath for a moment. "Well, I'm pleased to hear you intend to get out of that bed eventually. Be sure to shower before you leave the house; you're not pleasant to be around. Your father and I are taking Emily out to dinner. I've invited Victor to join us. We'll bring you some dinner from the restaurant."

Claudia watched her mother leave the room. Elizabeth King had once again gotten the upper hand. Even when she should be hanging her head in shame, she still managed to emerge the victor. For the first time in her life, Claudia wished she had inherited at least that one trait from her mother. Resiliency that refused to be destroyed.

Hearing the front door close, Claudia glanced at the clock. Almost six. She'd been listening to the high school band practice for the past hour. That meant there was a home football game tonight. Her mother was right. It was time to get out of this house.

Casio

Casio stood on the sidelines watching the cheerleaders try to muster up some team spirit for a bunch of guys that hadn't won a single game all year. In the past five years, they'd been lucky to walk away with two wins each season. The new coach was barely out of college and definitely didn't have the chops to turn this team into winners. Whiners was more like it.

"They're nothing like the team we had when we were here, are they?"

Casio was accustomed to girls approaching him, but he never expected to find Claudia at a game. She looked good too, her head wrapped in a turban and wearing jeans and a tight sweater. "Hey, baby. What are you doing out and about?"

"Same as you, from the looks of it. Killing time."

"I was about to head to the concession stand," Casio said. "Can I buy you some nachos?"

Claudia grinned and Casio grinned back. Her favorite snack had always been the nachos. "I don't do those anymore," she said. "But I'll take hot chocolate."

"Deal." Casio took her elbow and guided her toward the booth. Amazing how familiar it felt even after ten years. "Where's Vic?"

"Come on. You two are working together. He didn't tell you I left him?"

"For real?" Casio frowned and stopped, turning her to face him. "Vic never said a word. How long's it been?"

"A week."

"Poor Vic. You know that guy is crazy about you. Almost too crazy." He shrugged. "I think you and Vic are the real deal. It's none of my business, but he might be worth hanging on to and working out the issues."

She averted her gaze, but not before Casio recognized a flash of pain. "He didn't hurt you, did he?"

She gave him a rueful smile. "No, Vic is too much man to raise his hand to a woman. I left because of the investigation." She glanced up at him. "I can't stop the nightmares and this makes things worse."

"Yeah, I know what you mean. But he's doing it for you, you know."

"Hey, do we have to talk about him?" Claudia's smile didn't come close to her eyes.

Casio shrugged. "Fine by me. I'm not exactly the relationship expert." He shoved his hands into the front pockets of his jeans and shifted his feet. "Hey, do you want to go get a drink? For old times' sake? No strings."

She hesitated, then shrugged. "Sure. I guess there's no good reason not to."

"Look at the two of you cozying up just like old times." Casio didn't recognize the woman who nudged her way into their conversation, but apparently she knew him. He glanced at Claudia for support.

She picked up on the cue. "Hey, Georgie," she said. "How's your dad? I think he's the only adult left at the high school that was there when we were there." She gave a fake laugh. "I guess being the principal, he has more longevity than a regular teacher."

Okay, now he knew and he needed to say something to counteract Claudia's awkward moment there. "Wow, Georgie. I never would have recognized you. You look really good."

The young woman looked pleased. "Thanks, Casio." She pressed her manicured fingers to his bicep. "Although I guess I should be a little insulted that you thought I looked so bad during high school."

"It's not that."

"Oh, I'm kidding." She giggled. "I know I was a chunk back then. I'm over all that."

Casio had no idea what she was talking about. His deer-in-the-headlights look must have raised Claudia's sympathy. She tagged in. "Casio and I were just going to get a drink. Want to join us?"

He'd actually just wanted to share some old times with Claude and maybe talk about the stuff she'd been going through. Maybe make some sense of his own issues. Maybe they could help each other out.

But now Georgie "Fat Face" Newman was going to charge her way in like the rhino she once was. He could tell by her stupid grin. "That sounds great. I saw Blake and Tara about to leave the game too. Want me to invite them?"

Claudia shrugged. "Sure, the more the merrier. It'll be like old times, right, Casio?"

Forcing a polite smile, Casio nodded. Although it wouldn't be like old times at all. He and Blake had never been friends, he barely knew Tara or Georgie, and all he'd really wanted was to try to figure out why he couldn't stop hurting the woman he loved. Clearly, this wouldn't be a night for reflection and answers. "We'll meet you at Burt's in the city, sound good?"

Georgie laughed. "Isn't that a cop bar?"

"Yeah. And I'm a cop."

"True. I'll ask them and we'll meet you there."

"You want to ride with me?" Casio asked Claudia after Georgie left them in the midst of laughing kids and parents on their way to the concession stand. "I'll bring you back to your car."

"I have a better idea. How about if you follow me and I'll drop it off at my mom's house. I want to go in and change my shoes anyway. These are appropriate for a ball game, but I need something a little more girlie to wear out."

"Obviously you've never been to Burt's."

"You only make a first impression once."

"True."

Summer heat had finally given way to cooler fall air. Not cold or midwestern fall air by any stretch of the imagination, but it was nice to smell bonfire smoke and eat caramel apples and sip warm drinks at a football game. Too bad the current team couldn't get a ball into the end zone without fumbling.

He led Claudia through the parking lot to her Tahoe and opened the door for her. "Thanks, Casio," she said softly. "I hope I didn't overstep my invitation from you by asking Georgie to come along. We've sort of become friends lately."

The uncertainty in her eyes touched him. "It's okay. Probably better if we're chaperoned anyway. I'd hate for Vic to hear about us being together and get the wrong idea."

"Me too." She climbed up into the Tahoe and Casio shut the door. He followed her to Pastor King's house and parked alongside the curb while he waited for her to go inside and change her shoes. When she returned, her arms were loaded down with photo albums and yearbooks.

"What's this?" he asked.

"My mother has been forcing me to clean out the attic—as my keep, you might say." She shrugged. "I found these and thought it might be fun to look through them. Georgie will be on cloud nine."

Casio gave a short laugh. It didn't make sense to want a trip down memory lane. "Are you sure you want to go there?"

"Why not?" she said recklessly. "It doesn't all have to be about that one bad night."

The one bad night that she couldn't even describe as the night Miss Remington died, or the night on the bus when everything changed, or the night that he lost his chance to get out of this town and away from his overbearing dad and prove to his mom he could be a somebody worth loving. The night that changed them forever. He seriously doubted a bunch of photos and teen memories of football and cheerleading were going to fix what had broken in them all that night.

But clearly, Claudia was going to do her best to deflect conversation. Two hours later, her plan had succeeded as the waitress in a pair of tight Levis, a short vest, and a cowboy hat brought them their fourth pitcher of beer. Georgie opened the last photo album in the stack Claudia had brought from her parent's house. "Oh, here are some pictures you didn't put in albums." She held up an envelope filled with photographs.

Claudia shrugged. "Probably from graduation. My mother never was one to keep up with scrapbooks and albums." She smiled at the waitress and poured herself another glass of beer.

"I don't think so." Georgie held up a picture. "Look, it's Miss Remington. Oh my gosh. It's from the game that night." Georgie's eyes studied Claudia, and Casio was a bit surprised to see the compassion. "Should I put these back? We don't have to look at them."

Claudia shook her head. "I-I want to." Claudia's face grew pale as she took the photograph. After Georgie looked at each one, she handed it over to Claudia, but Claudia barely glanced at it before setting it on the table.

Casio reached for the stack. "You mind?"

She gave a little wave of her slender hand. "You may as well."

There were photos of the field and the players, of the cheerleaders. Claudia obviously hadn't taken these. "Where'd they come from?"

She swallowed down the last of her glass. And Casio deftly took the pitcher before she could refill.

She turned and caught his gaze. "BJ had a disposable camera that night, and on the way home, she asked me to put it in my purse. My mother must have been snooping through my bag and found it. I didn't get them developed."

"Sounds like she didn't show them to you because she knew it would upset you." Georgie's soft tone was gentle and filled with understanding. Again, that impressed Casio. Maybe she was the friend Claudia needed to help her through this while he and Vic finished up with the investigation.

"Either that or she didn't want me to know she was snooping in my purse."

Casio's eyes caught the last photograph in the set. Someone had taken a photo of Claudia with Miss Remington in the bus after the game.

In the window, behind them, Casio noted the stadium lights and other cars, so it was just after they had filed onto the bus. Just before they pulled out, went to Pizza Hut for a victory meal, and headed home. The teacher's arm was slung over Claude's shoulder, drawing her close. They were both laughing, and Claudia was sticking out her tongue. Miss Remington's arm was in plain sight up to her elbow. The bracelet Mr. Newman had spoken of dangled from her wrist, the love knot resting over the back of her hand.

So why hadn't the bracelet shown up in Miss Remington's

personal effects? If the case had been solved, her parents would have received all of her things, but since the case never closed, the item should have been in the bags of evidence. But he hadn't seen it.

"Do you mind if I keep these photographs, Claude? There might be something here that could help the investigation."

Claudia shrugged. "I don't care."

He excused himself, glanced at Georgie, and pointed to Claudia over her head. Georgie nodded, thankfully understanding that he was asking her to take care of the increasingly intoxicated ex-cheerleader.

Grabbing his phone from his pocket, he dialed Vic. They may have just gotten a viable lead.

Twelve

There are times, though they may be few and far between, when all of the elements of a person's life come together and form that one perfect moment. It's surreal and so unimaginably sad that our family moment has come at this time.

My mother's hand is holding mine, but I know my dad has taken her in his arms. He holds her, and they weep together. I am back suddenly to the nightly prayers that stopped before I was eight. Those times when I cuddled between them and felt the hand of God.

I experience that now. The hand of God. I think I do. And then my guilty heart shoves the hand away, and my mind replays the nights in the arms of the man who doesn't belong to me. The father of my child—the poor baby who will never draw a sweet, innocent breath.

I want to ask for Pastor King to come back to me. To hold my hand and tell me that God loves me, that He forgives me in spite of all my sins. I am so sorry. So sorry. If I could take it all back, I would. I would leave married men to their wives and not glory in the attention I receive from men of all ages, backgrounds, races, and marital statuses.

"Claudia," Pastor King says, his tone harsher than I've ever heard, "I can't stay in here with this man. Let's go."

My mother's gasp echoes off the walls. "Not now, Pastor, please."

"For God's sake," my father says. "It ended twelve years ago. Aren't preachers supposed to turn the other cheek?"

"You're an evil man," Pastor responds. "When you die, the devils will rejoice to have you in their grasp."

"Daddy"—Claudia's voice shakes with tears—"why are you speaking to Mr. and Mrs. Remington this way?"

The silence that follows seems to linger forever. But I've lost all sense of time, so I can't be certain. Finally, Pastor speaks, and when he does, his tone is once more the gentle, kind shepherd's voice. "Claudia, let's leave here and let the Remingtons be alone with their daughter."

"No!" My heart breaks at her loyalty to me. "I won't leave her."

"It's okay," my mother says. "She can stay." She hesitates, then she speaks in an even, controlled tone. "But please, I think it's best if you go."

"Not without my daughter."

"Daddy!" Claudia cries.

He releases a breath. "All right, sweetheart. I'll go."

His steps are heavy as he walks away. Heavier than anything

*I've heard before. Almost as though someone is beating a bass drum
in my ear, amplified by my impending death.*

*"I'm so sorry," Claudia whispers. "I've never seen him act like
that."*

*"Don't judge him too harshly, Claudia," my mother says.
"People who have suffered great loss tend to lash out in moments
of crisis."*

Poor Pastor King. He's never given up the pain of that time.

O Death, this is your sting. Grave...your victory.

Victor

At first, the call had just ticked him off. He figured Casio was trying
to rub his nose in the fact that Claudia was out drinking with her
high school chums. But as he calmed himself down, he realized
Casio wasn't putting the moves on Claudia. In fact, he was doing his
best to keep her from doing something stupid. And Vic actually
owed him for that.

They met at Vic's house. With Emmy and Claudia gone, there
was no point in hiding the investigation. Vic had decided to bring all
the evidence and files from the office, and boxes now covered the
dining room floor and table.

Casio rummaged through the evidence box—not that there was
much to go on. Clothing, a watch, earrings, a necklace. All the con-
tents of her handbag were still in evidence; but there was no bracelet.
He dropped into a kitchen chair, shaking his head. "It's not here. If
she'd been wearing it when she got to the ER, they would have removed it and stashed it with the rest of the evidence. She was DOA.

They didn't even work on her. Nurses called the doc and the doc declared her dead."

Vic stared at the photograph once more. The sight of Claudia so carefree and happy sent a wave of longing through him. She hadn't been much older than this when they started dating. He was determined to find that girl again. For her sake, for Emmy's sake.

He shoved away the emotions and glanced up at Casio. "And you're sure this is the same night? No way it was a different game?"

"Nope. This was the only game we played against the Panthers that year."

"Could the film be older than Claudia thinks? Maybe this was the year before the shooting?"

Again, Casio shook his head. "Miss Remington wasn't coaching cheerleaders the year before. Look, face it. That picture was taken after the game, when we were about to head home. Miss Remington had the bracelet on."

If that were the case, there was no doubt that she had either lost the bracelet between the time this photo was taken and two hours later when the gunman boarded the bus, or someone snatched it from her wrist after she was on the floor. It didn't make sense that Newman had done it. He freely admitted giving the gift to Miss Remington. That didn't mean he hadn't paid someone to commit the killing. But he seemed sincere enough in his admission that he'd cared for her. Maybe too sincere?

He dropped to the chair opposite Casio. "All right, let's think about who could have taken the bracelet."

"If it didn't fall off."

"It's a long shot, but it could have happened. So, we need to talk to the cleanup crew from the bus."

Casio made a few scratches in his notebook. "This might not be comfortable for you, but Claudia never left Miss Remington's side. So we need to ask her about the bracelet too."

The thought of actually confronting Claudia about the bracelet tightened Vic's gut. He had promised her she wouldn't have to answer any more questions. "I don't think she'll discuss it. She left me because she can't handle us opening up the investigation." He breathed out heavily. "Besides, I promised her I wouldn't need to interview her."

"Kind of unrealistic, don't you think? The people who were on the bus that night were Claudia, me, Georgie Newman—she gave Miss Remington CPR at some point before the ambulance arrived. Let's see…the bus driver, but he was unconscious the whole time. Claudia's dad showed up, he left for a few minutes when Miss Remington's parents arrived, but came back and stayed there until the paramedics arrived, and, like I said, Miss Remington's parents. And that's it—except for my dad. Once the paramedics arrived, everyone was asked to leave, even her parents."

"Okay, so list anyone on the bus between the time the shooter showed up until Miss Remington ended up in the morgue."

Casio nodded. "Top of the list. Claudia… "

Vic had a feeling the way he kept bringing her up that Casio was testing him. To what end, he wasn't sure. But he had no choice but to agree. Everyone had to be questioned. Even Claude. She was going to hate him.

But he had a job to do. Vic motioned to the notebook. "Okay, top of the list: Claudia. You're next."

Casio nodded and wrote down his own name on the list of those who could have taken the bracelet. "Georgie Newman," he said, "which makes sense if Principal Newman is involved."

It was a long shot, but Vic nodded. "So at what point did Pastor King show up and the other kids get off the bus?"

"It seemed like forever, but was actually just a few minutes."

"How many?"

Casio shrugged. "Five, maybe?"

"Okay, so in that five minutes, Claudia was lying in Miss Remington's blood, Georgie Newman performed CPR, and you did what?"

"At first, I had other kids forcing me down, putting pressure on my bullet wound, but the adults started showing up and all the kids except for me, Georgie Newman, and Claude got off the bus. Their statements are already in the original police report."

"Okay. So the next person in contact with Miss Remington after Georgie was…"

"Pastor King. He sat on one side of her and Claude was on the other."

"How long?"

"Another five minutes maybe?" He frowned in thought. "Could have been a little longer. I don't know for sure. Mostly I was hearing it happen."

"Then who came in?"

He closed his eyes as though trying to see it all happen. "Okay,

Pastor King showed up, and the kids were told to leave. I stayed on the bus because I was injured and no one wanted to move me in case it was worse than it looked."

"So Pastor King left you by yourself while he tended to the teacher?"

"No, come to think of it, there was someone with me."

"Can you remember who?"

"A girl." He snapped. "It was Georgie. How could I have forgotten that—especially after last night at the bar? She was taking a first-aid class, and Claudia told the pastor she should stay in case they needed someone to do CPR on Miss Remington again. I remember Georgie saying she'd look after me, and if BJ needed her, she'd be close by. So Pastor let her stay with me."

"Okay, so Georgie Newman stayed on board the entire time."

"Yes."

"So between ten and twelve minutes have passed between the time the shooter left and Miss Remington's parents showed up."

"Just Mrs. Remington."

"I thought you said her parents were there."

"Yes, but Mrs. Remington arrived a few minutes before her husband."

Why would they have come separately? Vic wrote a note to himself.

"We have a list of the paramedics on call that night as well as nurses in the ER when she arrived, the doctor who called her death, and the forensic pathologist after they took her to the morgue. We'll need to question all of them and show them that photograph of

Miss Remington and Claudia with the bracelet. We'll start with the paramedics, then move to the nurses in the ER—if we can find them, and we should find the medical examiner from the case."

"What about Georgie and Claudia? Don't you think we should go sequentially? They were close to Miss Remington before the paramedics arrived, and for that matter, what about Pastor King and the Remingtons?"

Casio was most likely correct, but for now, he didn't want his first meeting with his wife in a week to be official business. "We can come back to them. After ten years, does it really matter? If we question the medical staff first and someone saw the bracelet, then there's no reason to barge in on her grieving folks or anyone else."

"You mean Claudia."

"I don't want to upset her unnecessarily."

Casio shrugged. "Whatever you say. Want to do this together or separately?"

"What are you thinking?"

"Good cop, bad cop works pretty well."

"On the other hand, we could cover more territory if we split the list."

"You're in charge." Casio gave him that grin that Vic never quite believed.

Vic rolled his eyes. "Fine. Good cop, bad cop."

"Which one of us is the bad cop?" That grin again.

Casio

Casio hated the smell of hospitals. The sterile, glossy surfaces, like everything was clean and pretty. That might fool most people, but he knew what was hiding beneath all that antiseptic—pain, blood, disease, people in beds dying of all kinds of horrible things. And below their feet, the place those people went after the monitor screeched that flat line—the morgue. He hadn't been to a hospital more than twice since the shooting, and only in the line of duty. He wouldn't be here now if he'd had much of a choice.

But both of the paramedics from ten years ago were now employees at St. John's, and no way was he going to tell Campbell that he was too much of a pansy to walk into a hospital without feeling the blood rush to his head and his arm start to ache all over again.

His legs turned weak as his soft soles squeaked along the waxed floor. The hospital directory personnel had sent them up to the eighth floor, maternity ward. Amy Cole. She had been the first paramedic through the door, and though she couldn't have been more than twenty-two or twenty-three at the time—around Miss Remington's age—she seemed to be leading the team.

Casio remembered the young African American man who knelt over him, asking his name, starting an IV. "How's Miss Remington?" he'd said, barely recognizing the sound of his own hollow voice.

"Don't you worry none," the paramedic had told him. "Amy's a firecracker. She's the best of the best. Your teacher's in good hands with her."

But she hadn't been. He could still remember Amy's voice. "There's nothing we can do." Her voice had broken around her words.

"Miss Cole?" Vic spoke to the girl behind the desk, pulling Casio from his thoughts.

The pretty redhead looked up from the computer. She looked at Vic, then settled her focus on Casio.

"She's with a patient."

Casio grinned. "Thanks. I'll wait."

Victor fished out a business card. "She's expecting us. Will you please page her?"

The cutesy nurse's demeanor went all serious. "I'll call her, Mr. Campbell."

Casio flashed his shield. If Vic was going pro on the poor little candy striper, he might as well get some brownie points out of the deal too—girls loved cops. All those cop shows on TV were very good for his sex appeal.

But this one must not have gotten the memo. The badge had the opposite effect, and her face wiped of color in three seconds flat, leaving only a smattering of freckles on a vampire-white face. Sort of made him wonder if she had something to hide. Like swiping drugs from the locked closet.

She slid a cell phone from her pocket and pressed the buttons. "Amy, the ADA and a cop are here to see you."

Pause.

"Okay."

She looked up at Vic. "She says she'll be out when she's finished with her patient. Fourteen-year-old kid in labor six weeks early. Scared to death." She gave a heavy sigh. "I feel so sorry for her. I mean, no mama to hold her hand, and who knows who the baby's daddy is." She shook her head. "So sad."

"Is she keeping the baby?" Campbell asked, his voice smooth

with sympathy. His eyes were so earnest it was hard not to believe he truly cared. But Casio knew the act came with the job, though why Vic was wasting it here, he couldn't guess.

The redhead nodded. "That's the most tragic part of the whole thing. She's determined to keep it."

"You say she has no mother?"

The nurse shrugged. "Not that we've seen. But a mother could be working or something. The girl came in just two hours ago. Amy's been with her ever since."

Her cell phone buzzed. "Excuse me." She answered and flashed a glance to Casio and the ADA.

"Okay. I'll be there in a sec." The candy striper stood and punched a button on the computer, presumably locking them out in case they wanted to go snooping. "I'm going to sit with the patient while Amy talks to you guys." She gave Casio a shy smile as she passed. Casio grinned as he watched her go. So she wasn't immune after all.

"A little young, don't you think?" Vic said.

"Probably, but no harm in looking."

They waited another couple of minutes until a medium-build, dark-haired woman in scrubs strode down the hall. "Amy Cole?" Vic said, stepping forward.

"Yes." She extended her hand. "What can I do for you, Mr. Campbell?"

"Is there someplace we can talk?"

"I have a patient room open at the end of the hall," she said. "We can go in there."

Casio hated to admit it, but the sound of her voice slammed him back in time to the bus. He was lying on the floor, feeling the ridges of the aisle floor through his football jersey, smelling the feet of a thousand football players tromping up and down the aisle. His blood was staining the ground and Miss Remington was dying just a few feet away. There was nothing he could do to save her. Nothing he did that made any difference.

"Hightower!" Vic's voice brought him back to the sterile hallway. By the ADA's tone, it was pretty obvious this wasn't the first time he'd said his name.

"Yeah?"

"Do you need to go get some air?"

"I'm good. Let's follow the pretty nurse to the end of the hall."

"Fine." He dropped his volume and leaned closer so that only Casio could hear his words. "But if you space out again, this is the last of the interviews you get to come along."

"Oh, gee, Mom, I promise I won't ask for anything else."

Vic scowled at him as they entered the room behind the nurse. "Just take it easy and don't blow this."

The nurse walked to the window and turned, folding her arms over her chest. "Now, what can I do for you two?"

"We're investigating the murder of BJ Remington ten years ago. You were on call that night."

"Yeah," she said, shaking her head. "That was horrible."

"I need you to identify a bracelet the victim was wearing earlier that evening."

Now that Casio heard the words spoken aloud, he could see why

Miss Cole's mouth dropped open. "You're kidding, right? That was ten years ago. I was trying to save that woman's life. The last thing on my mind was her taste in jewelry."

"I understand it might be difficult to remember."

She gave him an incredulous look. "Try impossible, Mr. Campbell."

Casio shoved the photograph forward. "Nothing ventured, nothing gained. Let's give it a shot—oops, how insensitive of me."

"Wow, you're a real jerk, aren't you?" She glanced at the photo, but focused her attention on Casio. "And you look familiar."

"I'm touched you recognize me."

Vic cleared his throat. "Detective Hightower was shot at the scene."

She nodded. "The football player."

"How about that bracelet?" Casio asked, his voice impassive.

The nurse took the photograph. "The younger girl was there. We had to pry her away from the other woman."

Vic tensed. "Yes. But we already know that. Could you concentrate on the bracelet the victim is wearing, right there?"

She looked hard for several seconds and then shook her head, handing the photo back to Casio. "I'm sorry, guys. All I remember about that night is how desperate we felt sitting on the other side of those tracks for over twenty minutes while Miss Remington bled out. I've never felt so helpless in my life."

"Is that why you quit the ambulance and went to nursing school?"

She gave Vic a frank nod and leveled her gaze. This woman's

eyes were filled with compassion and earnest assessment. Casio doubted she was hiding anything. "I never rode the ambulance again. I just couldn't."

"Is there anything else you can tell us about that night? Did anyone on the bus say anything that might be relevant here?" He was beginning to feel at loose ends here.

She shook her head. "I'm sorry. I wish I could be more help." The phone at her hip buzzed. She lifted it from the clip and glanced down. "I have to go."

Vic flashed his boy-next-door smile and handed her a business card. "If you think of anything else, please give me a call." He opened the door and waited.

Predictably, she responded with a my-teeth-are-pretty smile and preceded him out the door.

"How do you do that?" Casio asked as they walked toward the elevators.

"Do what? Open a door and walk down a hall?"

Wise guy. "Make a perfectly capable, mature, and really tough woman turn to mush?"

Vic rolled his eyes as the elevator dinged and the doors swooshed open. "Jealous?"

"In your dreams."

They reached the second floor where the other paramedic now worked as an anesthesiologist. Hopefully, he was out of surgery now so they could get the interview over with.

They found the doctor almost immediately. When Casio recognized him, his stomach started to quiver and his hands shook. He shoved them inside his jacket pockets.

The African American man stood nose to nose with Vic. In his memory, Casio was lying down, looking up at the version of this guy ten years younger. He hadn't seemed that big. Back then, his head had been shaved, and he wore a close-clipped beard. Now, he wore long dreds and clearly worked out on a regular basis. The guy should be an NFL linebacker instead of a smooth-handed anesthesiologist.

He grinned when he saw Casio. "Hey, I remember you. So, you made it through and turned into a cop. I guess getting shot gave you the edge you needed to catch bad guys." He raised his hand and clasped Casio above the shoulder. The guy was cool too.

Casio felt himself growing stronger under this guy's familiarity. "Yeah. Good to see you, man."

"So, what's all this about?" Dr. Michael Banes dropped a chart onto the counter and slipped his pen inside his pocket.

Casio looked at Vic, but the ADA hung back, clearly allowing Casio to capitalize on the camaraderie between himself and the other man.

Casio showed him the photograph. "The older woman in the photograph is the victim in the bus shooting that night."

Recognition flashed in the anesthesiologist's eyes. "Oh, yeah. That was a bad deal."

"Detective Hightower says you were working on his arm that night," Vic said. "But we wondered if you could take a look at the bracelet on Miss Remington's wrist and see if it's familiar to you."

"I really didn't get that good a look at her," he said. His eyes roved the photograph. He shook his head and handed it back to Casio. "Sorry, man. The only thing I recognize in that photo is the pretty girl with her. Can't remember her name."

"Claudia," Casio offered. "She was the girl who wouldn't leave our teacher's side."

He nodded. "That must be it. Sorry I can't be more help. That was a bad night."

Casio drew in a breath. "Let's get out of here," he said.

A bad night? That's what that guy thought? For Casio, that bad night had lasted ten years. Would he ever be able to go on with his life?

Thirteen

"Come to Me, all who are weary and heavy-laden, and I will give you rest."

I'm so tired now. So many lives lay wasted in my wake, and all I want to do is close my eyes and let the burden of all my guilt wash away in the light. It looms before me, the light. It's just as so many people describe. Bright, beautiful, beckoning. If only I could reach out for it, I know He would reach back and take me in.

"Draw nigh unto me, and I'll draw nigh unto you."

My parents haven't spoken in the eternity it's been since Pastor King left the bus.

Claudia is quiet, her head resting on my shoulder.

"I don't think you should be lying there," my dad says. He can only be talking to Claudia. She doesn't respond, but I know she heard because she snuggles in tighter. Leave her alone, Daddy, I want to say. Even if my brain would allow the signal to reach my mouth, my lack of breath wouldn't allow it. My lungs must be filling with blood or other fluid because something is choking off my air. It won't be long now.

"Did you hear me?"

"Leave her alone!"

Good for you, Mama. *"Haven't you done enough to that poor child?"*

"Now isn't the time, Sara."

"Isn't it? Can't you be honest even now? While your daughter is dying? Surely you can feel angels here. Would you sit here and condemn yourself in the presence of God?"

She's right about the angels. I can see two of them standing in different corners of the bus. Big, strong, smiling at me as though to assure me that I am almost above this earth's pain and struggle.

I'm ready to surrender, but Claudia is crying again. Mama's words must have crushed her heart. *"Don't go, BJ. The train can't last forever. Daddy always said as long as it's moving, it'll eventually get to the caboose."*

I'd smile if I could. Pastor has used his train analogy for as long as I've known him. It goes something like this: *"God knows how things are going to end. You just have to take it one car at a time and eventually it'll be done. You'll finish this race. You just got to keep on the right track."* Everyone knows the analogy is a bit off, the metaphor mixed, but Pastor King is so beloved, it doesn't matter. Besides, the truth of his words hits the mark nine times out of ten.

"I mean it, little girl, leave me to my child."

I guess he's yanked her up, because she gives a yelp, and she's suddenly gone.

"Let her go!" I've rarely heard my mother raise her voice. And I've never once seen her get physically violent. She never even raised a hand to me. But I can sense her practically tackling my dad.

"Have you gone crazy?" he says, but he's turned loose of Claude, because she's right back at my side.

"You. Leave. This. Baby. Girl. Alone," she says, one emphasized word at a time.

"Doesn't a father have the right to tell his child good-bye?" His voice is choked and I'm moved. I wonder what the angels are thinking of this strife between one flesh. I know it must be grieving them, and I don't have the heart to look. Perhaps I'm growing closer to the spirit world and farther from this body of decay.

"You have no rights here, Nathan. Claudia King loves Belinda Jean more than you could even imagine. Look at her! She's lying in our daughter's blood, willing her to stay alive, while you stand there, pompous in your so-called fatherhood, a man who has betrayed us over and over. How does it feel?"

"Beej?" Claude whispers. "You have such a good mom. I can't stand to be around mine."

I know deep down Claudia loves her mom. It's just this earth. These bodies of sin. My eyes are beginning to see again. Or are they my flesh eyes? Everything is crisper, sharper. This earth Almighty God has created is beautiful, and I can almost hear the trees clapping their hands in praise.

Oh, Mama, Daddy, darling Claudia. Stop. Incline your ears. Hear the sounds of heaven.

And there's a sharp sound that pulls me from my awe. Mother
has slapped my daddy and he's turned to walk away.
The angels share an expression of pain.
I can feel their grief.

Claudia

Emily jumped on Claudia's bed at seven thirty to wake her. "Grandma said you were taking me to school today."

Claudia moaned. Insomnia had tormented her until the wee hours of the morning, and she had no idea what time she'd actually drifted into sleep. "Tell Grandma I'm not feeling well and ask her to drive you."

"I can't. She left." Emily bounced and the bed moved without mercy. "We have to leave, Mommy. If I get to school before Jarrod, I can get the sprinkly crayons."

"I thought I bought you some sprinkly crayons. What'd you do with them?" The ones with the glitter that Emmy couldn't live without. They had driven to three different stores before actually finding them.

"Those are the ones I want to get before Jarrod."

Claudia buried her face in the pillow, desperate for a few extra minutes of sleep. "Well, tell Jarrod he can't have your crayons. I'm sure the teacher will back you up on that one."

Emmy released a sweet little-girl breath that expressed frustration with Claudia's inability to understand the simplest of her concerns. "Mommy. We share in our class."

Surrender seemed inevitable. Rising to lean on her elbow, Claudia rested her ear on her palm and leveled her gaze at her daughter. "Well, sharing is good. But if the crayons are yours..."

"Miss Taylor put all the crayons in the bin." She tugged at Claudia's covers. "Are you getting up now?"

"Sure, I'd hate for you not to get your own crayons." Grudgingly, she swung her legs over the side of the bed. "And why is a little boy wanting glitter crayons anyway?"

"Because his Mommy couldn't afford any."

Claudia carefully weighed her words. "That's sad, honey. But your Mommy and Daddy work hard to give you nice things. You should be able to have your own crayons if you want them."

When Emmy didn't respond, Claudia glanced at the little girl. "Right?"

"Grandma says when we share with poor people, God gets the glory."

The last thing Claudia wanted was her daughter to become her mother. And of course, the little girl couldn't possibly understand what it meant for God to get the glory. Why couldn't Mother talk like a normal person instead of in Christianese all the time? She smiled. "So you think if you share your crayons with Jarrod, God will get glory?"

Guilt flashed in Emily's eyes. "I think so."

"Then why do you want to go to school early to beat him to the punch, little miss?" She grinned and tweaked Emmy's nose.

Emmy averted her pretty brown eyes to the floor. "He got to use them yesterday," she mumbled.

"Then we better get crackin' so you can get there first."

Claudia dropped her off at school a few minutes later and turned her Tahoe toward her own house. She had left so quickly that she had left several items she needed behind. She could pick them up while Vic was at work. That might be the coward's way out, but she couldn't face him. Not now, when she'd made her decision to get her own apartment. They'd been apart for two weeks. Her heart felt so numb.

She pulled into the driveway and sat for a minute looking at her comfortable, split-level home. Fall had painted a breathtaking tapestry of reds and golds on the lawn, and Vic hadn't raked up a single leaf.

The house seemed closed-up and musty as she unlocked the door and stepped inside. She had only planned to climb the steps to her bedroom, pack up some more undies and a few more outfits. But she couldn't resist walking into the kitchen. Her heart swelled with love for the house. This now-elegant kitchen had once been covered in ugly, duck-pattern wallpaper. She'd scraped and scraped until her back and arms ached. Vic had massaged her every night after she finished working. She'd painted walls and sanded and stained wood, just for starters—it was her pride and joy.

Claudia slid her fingertips over the counter. Closing her eyes, she caressed the length of the smooth surface. She loved this counter— every inch of it. A beautiful combination of deep greens and browns, granite and wood that had kept the cost lower than the all-granite she'd originally wanted, it had given them a final product of beauty that sent a thrill down her spine whenever she walked into the room. Of course, they'd still gone over budget.

She couldn't resist tiptoeing deeper into the house, feeling almost guilty—like an intruder. Light streamed through the split in the drapes behind the couch, and she glimpsed a thin layer of dust covering the sleek wood coffee table. Figures he wouldn't dust. But then, to be fair, he'd never had to.

Shaking off the sudden attack of compassion, she trailed her finger through the dust. With a sigh, she moved toward the dining room. Boxes and files cluttered the table and the floor. A frown creased her brow.

A hand touched her shoulder. She screamed, whipped around, and prepared for a fight until she looked up into the beautiful brown eyes she knew so well. "Gracious, Vic, you scared me half to death."

"Take it easy, honey." Vic took her fist and smoothed it open, lacing his fingers with hers. Claudia's heart skipped. "It's so good to see you," he murmured.

"I didn't know you'd be home. Your car isn't outside."

"I cleaned out the garage Sunday afternoon, so it's in there."

Panic snagged her stomach and she pulled her fingers away from him. "What'd you do with all my stuff?"

"You mean our stuff?"

She rolled her eyes. "Whatever. What'd you do with all of it?"

"Mostly in the attic. I got rid of some." He held up his hand before she could demand to know what he'd thrown out. "Do you know we had three nonworking fans in that garage?"

She bobbed her head, some of that old sass returning. "I would have thrown them out, but you said you'd fix them."

He shrugged, offering a self-deprecating grin. "Well, clearly that didn't work out so well. We can afford new fans. I took a load of stuff like that to the dump."

Again, Claudia frowned her confusion. "But how did you haul it? Your car isn't big enough for anything."

"Casio."

She scowled. "You two are awfully chummy these days."

"At least I didn't go out drinking with him."

"That little tattletale." She gave him a quick glance that she hoped conveyed how beneath him she considered this display of jealousy. "I had a couple of beers."

"That's not how he tells it."

Irritated, she walked around to the table. Stuck her hand inside a box.

"Claude, you shouldn't..."

Too late. She'd already lifted a stack of photographs. Dead, bloody BJ lying there where she'd fallen. Outraged, she stared at Vic. "You're working on this at home?"

He nodded. "It's easiest for Casio and me to piece it all together here. The office is too distracting because I still have to carry my caseload." He dropped his tone and peered closer. "And you weren't here, so what difference did it make?"

Claudia sank into the closest chair; otherwise, her suddenly weak legs would have failed her. She couldn't bear the photos, but in some weird compelling way, she couldn't take her eyes off the images. One after another, the pooling blood, the white shirt BJ had just bought that day. They'd shopped together.

"It was just all so surreal." Her hands shook so hard she barely held on to the photograph.

"Breathe slowly." Vic squatted down beside her chair. His hands, warm and steady, covered hers.

Claudia's head swam and her breathing sped up.

"I'll go get a bag." He started to move, but Claudia clutched at him. She couldn't be left alone with BJ again. All these pictures. BJ's eyes staring at her, asking her to save her, please. "Don't go," Claudia gasped.

"I'm here. Hold on to me. I'm not going anywhere." And he didn't for the next fifteen minutes while Claudia's chest tightened so hard she thought this was the real deal. The time when her panic attack wasn't just a panic attack but her heart getting ready to explode into a million pieces inside her body. She fought for air as pinpricks of darkness swarmed in front of her eyes, threatening to overtake her consciousness. "I don't know how to get over this, Vic."

"Just take it easy and try to breathe in through your nose, out through your mouth."

He thought she meant the panic attack? *Vic! Listen to me. Open your eyes. Hear me.* She held in the cry. She didn't have the strength to rail against him. Victor had always done his best to be there for her. Unfortunately, it had never been enough.

"I want to get my own apartment," she said around short bursts of air.

"What?"

He pulled back, but she grabbed onto his shirt, refusing to let him leave her. Not now. Not until the craziness lifted, breathing slowed, heart stopped exploding. She needed his hands to hold on to. Maybe it was selfish, but she couldn't let him walk away from her just yet.

"Shh." He moved forward and she leaned her head on his shoulder, feeling the calm beginning to settle over her. "Just relax," he said. "We'll talk about it when you're better."

They sat together, Victor speaking gentle, soothing words, encouraging her to breathe. She, focusing on his voice, calming herself. Allowing him to give her his strength even when she knew getting an apartment was the right choice.

He pulled away and kissed her on the forehead. "Better?"

She nodded and gathered in a deep, cleansing breath. "You're going to be late to work."

"I took a vacation day."

"Because of me?"

"Nope." He glanced at the boxes. "You being here is just a happy coincidence. We could spend the day together. You could come upstairs…" He smiled.

"Vic…"

"Please?" He kissed her, slowly, softly, seducing her. And she didn't object again. Upstairs, she let her body tell him good-bye, then snuggled beside him. She gave in to the luxury of lying beside him until he drifted off to sleep.

Later, she dressed while he slept. Carefully, she slid open her dresser drawers, pulled out her clothes, and stuffed them into a duffel bag she'd found in the bottom of her closet. As quietly as possible, she opened the door and took a step into the hallway.

"You were just going to leave without saying good-bye?"

She stopped short and closed her eyes as dread made its way down her back, around her ribs, and into her chest. She turned. Vic lay on his side, propping himself up on his elbow, observing her. Claudia knew that look all too well. Silent accusation hovering just below the surface, ready to attack as soon as she let down her guard. But she wouldn't do that. She had made her decision.

"Well?" he said. "What were you thinking?"

She smiled at him. "I was thinking I just told you good-bye in my own way. Don't tell me you've forgotten already."

"Stop. Don't even try to play that cute little seductress role with me. I thought you were saying, 'Hi, honey, I'm home.' Not 'Good-bye.'"

She set down the bag and walked across the room, sat on the bed at his feet. "Listen. I'm messed up, honey. Too messed up to stay here and dissolve while you and Casio try to solve this murder."

"Then we'll put it back in the vault. I'll stop investigating."

Claudia touched his calf through the sheet. "You already said you've gotten too far in the investigation for that. If you're really so close to maybe finding out who did this, maybe we owe it to Beej and her parents to keep going forward."

"Beej?" His eyes narrowed. "You've never called her that before."

Interesting. She hadn't meant to let it slip out. "She called me Claude, of course, and I called her Beej as long as we weren't at school functions."

Victor sat up and wrapped his arms around her, strong and firm. "Don't leave."

"Let me, please." Tears burned the back of her eyes and clogged her throat. "I have to get away from all of this."

He pulled back so that he could look her in the eye. "And when it's over? When we get the guy who did this and lock him up, then will you come back to me? Or is this for good? Don't keep me hanging on to false hope."

Claudia stared down at her hands. She couldn't face him. Not when she had no idea what the right answer would be. The honest one. "I hope so."

"You hope so?" Vic's voice rose in frustration. "What do you mean you hope so? Claudia, we have a daughter. A life together. You don't just walk away. We said for better or worse. I meant those words."

His anger gave her the push she needed to stand up and face him. Moving out wasn't the only bomb she had to drop today. She swallowed hard. "I want you to keep Emmy. Believe me, my mother will just love helping with her. She lives to sacrifice herself because of my selfishness. It'll give her the moral leg-up. And believe me, she needs one right now."

His expression opened up with incredulity. "Wait. What? You can't abandon her. Emmy needs you. You're her mother."

His blind love washed over her, threatening to force a change of mind. But this wasn't about love. Her head was so messed up, she thought she was going crazy. She didn't want to be around her family when the crash came. "No one needs me right now, least of all our impressionable little girl. Not until I get myself together."

He rubbed his head, and his eyes took on a vacancy as though shock was beginning to set in. "This is wrong. I'm telling you, it's not right."

"I do a lot of things that aren't right." She grabbed the duffel bag.

"Haven't you figured that out by now? I'm not good for you. You'll never be DA with a wife like me falling apart all the time."

"I don't care about that compared to having you in my life."

"I can't let you give up your dream. That's what all this was about, wasn't it? I'd never forgive myself. And neither would you."

"Where are you going to go?"

"I'll rent an apartment for now. I can't stay with my mother. She drives me crazy, and besides, that would be too confusing for Emmy."

"How are you going to pay for an apartment? Don't expect me to fund this little experiment."

His words stung, as he'd meant for them to, but Claudia wasn't going to fight. She knew he was just speaking from hurt, and after all she'd put him through, she had it coming anyway. "Well?" he said. "How do you plan to pay for separate living quarters?"

She had to tell him. Leaving him to discover the bite out of their money wasn't fair. "I took half of our savings. And Daddy asked me to come work for him again."

He stood. Anger flashed in his eyes for a second, and Claudia's defenses soared as he accused her. "Are you serious? You went behind my back and stole money from the account?"

The indignation rolled from him, as contagious as the plague, infecting her before the words completely left his throat. Claudia gave a short laugh, no longer feeling sorry for him. No longer giving a rip about sparing his feelings. "Listen here, you. I have a right to half of what is in our accounts. I didn't touch anything but savings. Period. You make plenty to cover the expenses here. The amount I took will cover my expenses for a couple of months at best."

"Then what? You'll come crawling back, ready to apologize, and move back in?"

"Yeah, sure. I'm planning to go all prodigal son on you. Spend all the money on riotous living and come crawling back asking forgiveness."

He held out his hand. "I want your debit and ATM cards."

"They're already on the table next to you."

He glanced at the table. Then his face lost all color. She had left not only the cards, but her rings as well.

"So this is more than a temporary separation?" His eyes found hers, and she swallowed back the threat of tears.

"I can't say."

"What have I done to make you so unhappy?"

"That's what makes this so much harder, Vic. It's not about what you have or haven't done. It's not about you at all. I married you almost directly out of high school. I need to step into the fresh air and breathe on my own, away from the high school memories. I'm suffocating."

"All right. Go. I won't try to stop you." He turned away.

For just a second, Claudia fought the urge to run to him, wrap her arms around his bare waist, and hold on tight. Part of her knew she was being a fool. But even that part agreed that Vic was too good for her. If she was ever going to get away, she had to do it now.

Fourteen

My mother kneels on one side of me, humming and stroking my hair. And on the other side is sweet Claudia, so much like the little sister I always wished I had. She was right. We were about as close as we could have gotten to being really family. If her mother and my dad had ended up staying together, we might have been stepsisters. But I never told her about our parents' past. It never felt right.

But of course, I can't wish things had been different. My dad leaving would have destroyed Mama. She's stronger now. What will happen to them when I'm gone?

"When this is over," my mother says softly, speaking to Claude, "I hope you'll come to see me from time to time."

Claudia nods against my shoulder. "I will," she whispers. "I think Beej would like that."

"She was supposed to come to my house for dinner Sunday. She said she had something to tell me."

Claudia stiffens. I wonder if she thinks telling Mama about the baby would be a betrayal. She'll find out anyway. They will examine my body for evidence, hoping to identify my killer through DNA, and then they'll discover my tiny secret buried deep inside me. My parents will be notified.

But Claudia stays silent. My heart expands with more love for her. Even now, she won't betray my secret.

My body begins to jerk. Blackness returns. Claudia sits up and screams. "Someone do something!"

Mother places her hands on my arms and starts to pray. "Not yet, Lord. Please. Not yet."

"She's seizing." The voice that speaks is firm and steady. "Hold her down before she hurts herself."

Georgie Newman is still on the bus? She must be looking after Casio. I guess no one wants to move him until the paramedics arrive.

Claudia whimpers. "What do we do?"

"I'm not a doctor, Claudia," Georgie snaps. "It's a seizure. It'll either stop or she will. Her heart will go haywire and she'll die."

Claudia joins in my mother's prayer. "Please, God. If anything my father preaches is true, don't let her go like this. It's too soon."

My legs relax first. And my hips, my arms.

Mama's hand relaxes on mine. Someone checks my pulse. "She's back," Georgie says, her voice rife with relief.

"Thank God."

"Mrs. Remington," she says, "I don't mean to be a downer, but her pulse is superfaint. Don't expect her to make it. She's lost so much blood I can't imagine her coming back from this. At the

least, that seizure could've damaged her brain and her heart. You probably need to start saying good-bye."

How come I didn't realize how grown-up Georgie is? She's only sixteen years old, and yet she's the one taking charge. I suppose being the only child of a widower forced her to grow up, take on more adult responsibilities.

"Get out, you stupid cow!" I hear Claudia scream. "You're just jealous. You wouldn't even be hanging around on our bus if your stupid dad wasn't principal."

"Sorry the truth hurts," Georgie says, unrattled by what must surely be stinging. "But I'm not going anywhere. Casio needs my help. And God knows you're not any help, curled up in a fetal position, covered in blood, whining and crying."

My heart hurts at the way they're insulting each other. Love has poured into my heart. As though the fruits of the Spirit are beginning to truly transform the way I think, feel. If only this had been possible before these final moments between life and death.

"Girls," my mama's sharp voice is filled with such pain I want to cry. "My baby is going away in front of my eyes. I need you to hush or get off the bus."

Claudia drops beside me again. "I'm sorry, Mrs. Remington. I'm so sorry. Don't make me leave her."

"Shh. It's okay." Mama's voice is once again gentle. "Stay with me. We won't let her die alone."

I don't know how I am holding on to life. I think by the sheer force of Claudia's will. Her honest love for me won't let me go until a doctor tells her it's over.

Or perhaps it's Mama. The person who has lived for me every single day of my life. Even when I didn't recognize her sacrifice. Even when I didn't appreciate all she did for me.

Either way, I lie here in some twilight place between death and life, with the realization of one thing I finally know that I've never known before:

I am so loved.

Part Three

While I draw this fleeting breath,
When mine eyes shall close in death,
When I soar to worlds unknown,
See thee on thy judgment throne,
Rock of Ages, cleft for me,
Let me hide myself in thee.

Fifteen

Mama and Claudia are holding hands across my body, joining together in their grief over me.

"Why are you back?" I hear my mama's voice, taut and reserved. Mama will not make a scene. But I can't tell if it's my dad or Pastor. No one else speaks. I feel a hand take mine. Inside, I smile. My dad has returned. I'm glad. Because even as selfish as he is, he would never forgive himself for leaving that way.

"I apologize for being harsh with you earlier," he says and I sense he is speaking to Claudia, "but my wife and I need a little time alone with her before she goes." His voice breaks and inwardly I want to plead with Claudia to step back, for a moment.

"It would just be for a minute, sweetheart," Mama's gentle voice says. "I promise. We just want to say a prayer over her."

"But I don't want…"

"Claudia," Georgie's tone is soft, like a mother's, even though she's the youngest one on the bus. "Come on. Let's allow them their minute with Miss Remington." Claudia is pulled away. Most likely she never would have left my side otherwise.

"Sara, listen," my dad says.

"Save it. This isn't about you. It's about our daughter."

"Don't you think BJ would die more peacefully knowing her parents aren't fighting?" I am disappointed. His tone is manipulative. The dad I know.

"Shh."

"I'm sorry, Sara. I'll do better. Please, forgive me."

"Haven't I always?"

Her answer is cryptic enough to make him wonder if she meant she forgives him this time. But he isn't pathetic enough to press, not now while I lay dying. I should be hurt, angry, that he's using my death for his own purposes, but strangely, I feel compassion. He knows as well as I do that when I'm gone, she will have no other reason to stay with him. Divorce, so tragic, the violent ripping apart of one flesh. I've heard that somewhere.

"Can I come back?" Claudia's tearful plea comes almost as a welcome relief from the tension between my parents.

Something presses against the back of my hand. "I'm going," Daddy says, and I realized he kissed me good-bye.

"You're leaving now?"

"I can't watch this." His voice breaks. "I can't see my daughter and my marriage die the same night."

Poor Daddy. He has no idea how alone he truly is. Selfishness always breeds loneliness.

Mother reaches across me and once again takes hold of Claudia's hand.

It occurs to me that Mama and Daddy never did say a prayer.

Claudia

Claudia sat across from Georgie at Olive Garden. This was their second lunch at the Italian chain, and they'd met for coffee twice since she left Vic to go to her mother's house. At first Claudia dreaded each time Georgie cornered her to go out with her. But the other woman was slowly growing on her, and she was beginning to enjoy the female company.

"Well, you have to stay with me. That's the best solution."

"Stay with you?" She sipped the white wine that went perfectly with a seafood Alfredo sauce. "I don't know, Georgie. I probably ought to go ahead and find a place."

"Oh, please. You'll keep putting it off until you run through all your money at the hotel. My place is much nicer than that Holiday Inn Express you're at. Plus you'll have my fabulous company."

She had already gone through two hundred fifty dollars in three days. Georgie was right. At that rate, her money wouldn't last very long. Plus she truly enjoyed being around Georgie. Claudia barely remembered anything about her from high school, except that she was the mascot—and she gave CPR to BJ. The rest was a blank.

"Come on, Claudia. Just say yes. It'll be fun."

Maybe it was the wine—were they on their second bottle?—or the fact that for the first time since BJ died, Claudia had a friend, but she made a sudden decision. "Okay, I'll do it. And...I can be looking for an apartment." Claudia smiled, feeling relief. "Thank you, Georgie. I really appreciate this."

Georgie's face brightened. "Oh, I'm so happy. Let's go over to your hotel and I'll help you get your things."

Claudia knew neither of them was in any shape to drive, but Georgie waved away her concerns. "Please, I could drink the rest of that bottle and still be sober enough to drive."

"I don't think so." She snatched Georgie's keys from the table. "My husband is the ADA in this town. Just because we're not living together doesn't mean I can humiliate him by being arrested for drunk driving."

"Well, I'm not taking a taxi. Those drivers smell like sweat."

Claudia drank down the last of the wine in her glass and didn't object as Georgie filled her up again. She toyed with the idea of calling Vic to come and get them, but she dismissed the thought almost the second it appeared. Instead, she punched in another number.

"Who are you calling?" Georgie asked.

The phone was ringing. Claudia held up her hand.

"Yeah," the man on the other end of the line said.

"Hey, Casio," she said, wincing at the way her tongue wouldn't quite make the words without slurring. "I need a favor."

Casio

"Why'd you let her drink so much?" Casio asked Georgie as he practically carried Claudia into Georgie's three-bedroom apartment.

"She's just hurting over her marriage. I think it sort of snuck up on her."

"So she's really leaving ol' Vic, huh?"

Georgie shrugged and lifted the covers over Claudia. "She thinks she is. Even says she's going to get her own apartment." She straightened up. "I think she'll go back to him. As a matter of fact, I'd bet money on it. She seems a little lost right now. But she has a hard time keeping her husband and daughter out of our conversations."

Casio had to admit that was smart. She led the way from the guest bedroom back into the living room. "Would you like some coffee or something?" she asked.

"No, I have an appointment in a few minutes."

"A girl?"

"An interview about Miss Remington's murder."

"So you really are working on the case?" She shook her head. "Claudia is a wreck about it. I hope you finally get the guy."

"So do I," Casio said. "You know, Georgie, I never thanked you for keeping pressure on my shoulder that night."

He watched the blood rush to her cheeks. "It's okay. I was happy to do it." She smiled at him. "I had a big crush on you. Helping you not bleed to death seemed like a date to me."

Casio gave a short laugh, appreciating her inappropriate sense of humor. "If you'd looked like this in high school, I'd have taken you out on a real date." The second the flippant words left his mouth, Casio wished he could rein them back in and start over. "Oh, man. I'm such a jerk. I'm sorry, Georgie. That was stupid." He walked over to her. "I was trying to pay you a compliment and instead I insulted you."

To his shock, she laughed. And it seemed genuine. "Casio. I know I was a pudgy, strange girl. In a weird way, Miss Remington's death that night made me realize that life was way too short to live unhappy. That's when I started working on self-improvement. You were gone before the next school year, but I lost all my extra weight over that summer and started off junior year as a size four. It was life-transforming. My first two years of high school were hell, but the last two were every girl's dream."

Casio listened, amazed that anyone had walked away from that experience with anything but invisible wounds. He peered closer at her. "Is that when you decided to go into the medical field too?"

She nodded. "I'd already taken a first-aid class because I was planning to get an after-school job at a day care and it was mandatory. But after that night, I just realized I was meant to save lives."

"That's great."

"So what about you?"

"What do you mean?"

"Well, once you lost your scholarship for football, you could have done anything. Did Miss Remington's death make you decide to be a cop? Like in some way you were determined to bring bad guys to justice?" Her voice was laced with teasing, but her eyes kept a steady gaze.

"I hate to dash your noble dream, but the truth is, I went into law enforcement because my old man was a cop. I just did it to try to get his approval."

Her eyes dimmed a little. Casio narrowed his gaze. Let her be in a noble profession for a noble cause. All he'd ever wanted to be was a ball player. Football was in his blood. The police force had been a fallback plan.

"Well, at least you're honest about it." Georgie jerked her head toward the kitchen. "You sure I can't get you some tea or coffee?"

Casio glanced at his watch. "If I don't get to this appointment on time, Vic's going to blow his stack."

"Claudia's Vic?"

"Used to be." He grinned. "She walked out on him, so I'm not sure she still technically owns him."

Her laugh seemed genuine. "I think he belongs to her until he decides he doesn't want to. ADA Campbell doesn't strike me as the kind of guy who's going to give up very quickly."

Casio glanced at his watch. "You're probably right about that. And let's face it, Claudia's not the kind of girl a guy can forget so easily."

"Do I detect a note of regret in your voice, Officer?"

"Do I regret that we broke up?" He shrugged. "We probably wouldn't have split quite so soon if all that wouldn't have happened. And speaking of splitting, I have to go."

"Let me walk you to the door." Her bare feet padded across the ceramic-tiled foyer, and she reached around him to open the door. "Thanks for coming to the rescue. I was a little too tipsy to drive, and I never really think I am. Good thing Claudia had more sense. At the time, anyway."

"I'm here to protect and serve."

"You know, after all these years, don't you think it's odd that you and Claudia and I have reconnected at the same time you and Claude's husband are reinvestigating the murder?"

"It's a little coincidental."

"Or providential." She smiled as he stepped onto the porch.

"You're religious like Claude?"

She laughed. "Not at all. But I sort of think the universe pulled us together. Maybe it is time to resolve this case so we can all move on with our lives. Get some closure."

"Could be." Casio lifted his hand. "I'll talk to you later. Don't let Claude drink anymore tonight."

"She finished off the bottle at the restaurant, so I imagine she's down for the count." She stepped onto the porch after him and Casio could feel her eyes on his back as he walked toward the car. "Hey, Casio," she called. "Are you guys finished with my dad in regards to the case?"

"We swabbed him." Casio shouldn't discuss the case, but she was his daughter after all, and what were the chances Newman truly had the guts to do anything to Miss Remington, even if she'd rejected him? "Waiting for DNA to come back."

"What sort of DNA could you be looking at?"

"Come on, I can't tell you that. But I can tell you that I know your dad isn't the killer. He's not big enough."

"Not to mention the fact that he could never harm anyone, least of all her."

"So you did know your dad had a thing for her."

Georgie's face darkened. "Yeah, I knew. I just wish he hadn't wasted his time." She shrugged. "Oh well. It's over. Thanks again. Claudia's going to be mortified when she wakes up, but I appreciate the help and so will she."

"It's good of you to keep Claudia here." He reached for his door handle. "She'll come to her senses about Vic soon, I imagine. He's a pretty good guy."

As he drove out of her driveway, it occurred to him that he should have interviewed her while he was there. It might have been awkward to ask her about the bracelet her dad had given the schoolteacher, though. They'd eventually need to ask her since she was on the bus that night, but he didn't like the idea of having to explain to Vic that his wife had to be helped out of Olive Garden dead drunk.

He headed in the familiar direction of Harper's street, hoping to catch a glimpse of her pretty face. Since yesterday, he'd calmed down. He still suspected her true condition had nothing to do with a virus. And if she wasn't going to tell him herself, time always had a way of revealing that sort of truth.

She couldn't hide a pregnancy forever. And the second he could confirm it, he would be able to convince her to come back to him. A baby would connect them eternally.

Sixteen

"Pomp and Circumstance," the song played at graduations around the country, has always made me cry. There's just something about wide-eyed eighteen-year olds dressed in their caps and gowns. The long walk to their seats as the band plays mournfully and parents cry because their child is passing from one season of life to the next. It's the end of childhood, the beginning of something new and wonderful. Maybe that's why I became a teacher. To re-experience that moment over and over. A time for joy and hope, yet sad too.

I can almost hear "Pomp and Circumstance" playing in my head for Claudia and Casio—if he makes it. They'll be graduating at the end of this year. I regret that I won't be there to watch them take that enormous leap from childhood to adulthood with one rite-of-passage ceremony.

My body is beginning to cramp, but there's no real pain. I suppose it's the miscarriage. Even though I know I'll be reunited with my child soon, I still can't help but feel grief. There's so much blood already, I doubt anyone will even notice.

If I could wish for anything right now, I'd wish that I could start the last year over. Stay away from a man who couldn't love me. Let myself love the one who did.

The heart is fickle and imperfect and foolish. If only we could ever truly understand love. This love I feel now as my life ebbs, oh, it's the real thing, filling up my whole body, leaving room for nothing else.

In life, love is complicated. Messy. Filled with jealousy and conditions. In the moments before death, it becomes clear what love was intended to be. Different. Divine. Some humans obtain that Godlike love. The Zoe kind of love. But not many. I think if we were all given the chance just once to be brought to the edge of mortality, the world would not know the pain of unbearable love that is unrequited.

I've been on both sides of human love. I've watched young men fall in love with me, only to be disappointed. And I've been on the other end. Just once. I've given my heart, soul, and body to a man who isn't capable of loving.

"Where is she? Oh my God." I feel myself pulled into strong arms. A familiar embrace that I once thought was all I ever wanted. But now I'm repulsed by his gesture.

"What are you doing?" my mother asks, because, of course, she's never heard anything about our relationship.

"I love her." He buries his face in my neck, his tears burn the cut on my neck where a bullet grazed my flesh. He sobs against me.

Love. His kind of love gave me flowers, stolen moments, secrets. But never kindness, mercy, gentleness, a sense of safety.

Without those things that make a woman feel safe, a man's promise of love is nothing but pomp and circumstance.

Victor

Casio's truck pulled up behind Vic just as he arrived at Jesse's Garage.

"You're here," he said as he waited for Casio to jog up to the door where he stood waiting so they could go in together. "I'm impressed."

"You think I wasn't coming?"

Vic shrugged. "You never can tell with you."

"Sorry, I had to help out a friend."

"Okay. Let's just do this. I have court tomorrow. I need to study tonight."

The smell of gasoline and oil filled up Vic's senses as he stepped inside the garage, making his stomach tight and unsettled.

Blake raised his head from under the hood of a Chevy Impala. "You here for Jesse?" he asked.

"Yeah," Casio said. "He in his office?"

"Nah, just a sec." He turned toward the opposite wall where the sound of air-powered tools shook the room.

"Jesse!" Blake called.

"How do these guys work in a place like this all day?" Casio asked.

"A man has to work where he can get a job."

Casio shrugged, but his reply was cut off as Jesse approached, wiping his hands with an oily rag.

"Thanks for taking the time to see us."

"No problem. Let's go into my office so we can shut out most of the noise."

The quiet came as a relief. Jesse motioned them toward a couple of worn-out chairs, and he took his seat behind a cluttered desk covered in greasy fingerprints.

"Sorry about the mess." He readjusted his filthy cap. "I don't notice how dirty this place is until someone like you pays a visit."

"It's okay." Vic pulled out a notebook. "We'd like to ask you some questions about your involvement with BJ Remington."

He frowned. "Involvement? I didn't have no involvement with her except for fixing her car a couple of times."

Casio snorted. "Dude, don't shine me on. Your dad and brother both said you were dating her. So cut the crap and let's just get to the part where you tell us about your involvement with BJ Remington like the ADA asked you."

Impressed, Vic nodded.

"All right, look. There's something you should know. I wasn't dating her."

"But you wanted to, right?" Vic poised his pen over a clean sheet of paper.

"Well, yeah." Jesse gave a short, sheepish laugh. "I mean, who wouldn't? That girl was different, special. Sexy, but still the kind you think you could marry."

Casio narrowed his gaze. "But you weren't dating."

"I swear." He sighed, leaned back in his chair, stretching his legs out in front of him under his desk. "Okay, here's the deal. I saw her stopped at the side of the road one day, and I pulled over to help her.

Turns out her transmission was no good. On the way back to her place to drop her off, we got to talking about how I didn't graduate from high school but I wanted to get my mechanic's license so I could start my own garage."

"And, what? She wouldn't let you kiss her good-bye?" Casio said.

Jesse frowned. "No, man. It wasn't like that. She never thought about me that way. I think she was seeing someone."

Vic sat forward. "Do you know who?"

He shook his head. "She was pretty hush-hush about it."

Vic looked askance at the detective and then back to Jesse. "Okay, then tell us about your relationship with her. What happened that night?"

"Nothing happened." Jesse shrugged. "I dropped her off and went back to tow her car to my house."

"Why your house?" Vic asked.

"That was before I had this place. I did some part-time jobs from my garage. For extra cash." He sipped from a can of Mountain Dew on his desk, swallowed, and continued. "Anyway, she needed a new transmission. But when I called her and told her how much it would be, she said she couldn't afford it. But I knew she was a teacher so I offered her an exchange. Tutor me so I could pass the GED and the entrance exam into the mechanic's school, and I'd fix her car for nothing."

"You gave her a transmission?" Casio scowled. "That's kind of expensive just for some lessons."

Vic wasn't sure if Casio was playing "bad cop," but Vic wanted to tell him to ease up. Casio might not be the sort of guy that was willing to give up everything for the love of a woman, but Vic understood a little bit about how a guy with a garage might find a transmission for a pretty girl and give it to her on the off chance she might actually date him.

Jesse swallowed hard and adjusted his hat again. "I got a cheap transmission from the salvage yard and made sure it worked good. The owner traded me the transmission for some work. He liked to put cars together and sell them."

"So why did your dad and Blake think Miss Remington used you then dumped you?"

"I guess I kind of let them think we were, you know...together." His face turned two shades of red. "I felt too stupid to tell the truth. When they saw us hanging out so much, they just assumed. They thought I was actually getting some action with the pretty schoolteacher, and I was trying to be a big shot."

"And you never told the truth?" Vic said.

"What a piece of work." Casio gave a humorless laugh. "You know your brother mouthed off to her and got himself a failing grade because of your lie?"

He nodded. "Don't you think I know that? It's my fault Blake lost out on his chance to go to college on a scholarship. After that, she died, and I didn't see the point in clearing it up just for my dad and brother."

Vic cleared his throat. "So you're saying that once Miss Remington was already dead, there was no reason to admit to lying."

Jesse frowned. He nodded hesitantly. "I guess that's right."

This guy was definitely hiding something. Vic pressed him further. "Because if you had admitted that the woman you had a crush on wouldn't give you the time of day, it might have cast suspicion on you. Is that what you meant?"

He averted his gaze to his filthy desk. "I guess."

Casio relaxed his fingers. He squared his gaze at the mechanic. "When did you open this garage?"

"About a year after...you know."

"Miss Remington was murdered." Casio's tone was sharp, like the jagged edge of broken glass.

"Yeah. I got my GED the week after the shooting—kind of like a tribute to all of her hard work with me—then I went to a nine-month school. I came back here and opened the garage."

Vic nodded. He could appreciate the American dream. Who didn't want to come up from nothing and start his own business? That was his story too in a lot of ways. He never really knew his dad because he was so young when he went to prison. He grew up poor and scared in the roughest section of Dallas. His one saving grace was a mama who insisted he study every night and kept him away from the thugs and gangs. The proudest day of his life was moving his mama into a nice condo in a nice neighborhood.

"Impressive." He stood. "One more thing." He pulled the swab kit from his bag. "We'd like permission to take a DNA sample."

Jesse nodded, but swallowed hard. "What do I need to do?"

"Just need to swab the inside of your cheek."

"Okay."

Vic took the sample, thanked Jesse for his time, and he and Casio left the garage.

Casio coughed into his hand. "Man, that place stinks."

Vic shrugged. "I guess you'd get used to it."

"No, thanks." He walked to his truck. Then turned. "Hey Vic, did he seem nervous?"

"Yeah. But that doesn't necessarily mean anything. Some people get nervous around cops even if they didn't do anything wrong."

"I guess." He shook his head, as though trying to put the pieces of something together. Vic understood. He had the same kind of suspicion. But he didn't want to jump to conclusions. "Wait until the DNA comes back," he suggested. "Then we'll see."

"You know he picked up the phone as soon as we walked out of the office?"

Vic frowned. "How do you know that?"

"I looked." Casio reached for his door. "And his eyes were as wide as a kid caught shoplifting. I'm telling you, he's hiding something."

"Interesting." Vic pressed the button to unlock his door. "But like I said, let's wait and see what the DNA says, and then we'll lean on him. Even if he's not responsible, he might know something." He glanced back at the building. Jesse stood in the doorway watching them, phone pressed to his ear. "Let's wait and discuss it someplace else."

Casio shrugged. "Whatever. Where to now?"

"I'm taking this to the lab."

"Good luck with that. You think they'll ever get to them? I called over there this morning. They haven't even looked at them yet."

"Ten-year-old murder cases aren't exactly at the top of their list of priorities. I'm going over there to try to speed things up."

Casio's phone buzzed and he picked it up. "Yeah." He slid his fingers through his hair. "I'll be there in a few minutes."

"Everything okay?"

"My dad again. Burt called."

"A little early in the day, isn't it?"

"Yeah. Lots of early drinking going on today."

"I don't follow."

"I'm just blowing smoke. I have to go." He grinned. "Let me know if the lab gets on that DNA. I'm ready to crack this case."

He wasn't the only one. Vic got into his car and merged into traffic. He hated to go home. Despised the idea. Instead, he turned toward the office. Pulling an all-nighter at work was definitely preferable to going home to a house without Claudia.

Harper

Harper knew she was every kind of fool. She walked inside the dimly lit bar and squinted as her eyes adjusted. Casio had called her, and like an idiot, she had responded to the urgency in his voice. His dad had fallen at Burt's, and Casio couldn't get away from work for a little while. Would she please just go? There was no one else for him to ask.

Burt looked up from the bar and waved. "Hey, haven't seen you here in a while."

She smiled. "I've been busy. Where's Gabe? Casio asked me to come see about him until he can get here."

He jerked his head to the door in the corner. "Passed out in my office. I thought you and Casio were splitsville."

"We are. I'm just doing him a little post-splitsville favor."

He chuckled. "You're a good woman. Casio's an idiot to let you go."

"No more of an idiot than I am." For being here at his beck and call. She lifted her hand. "I'm going to go see Gabe."

There was something nice about the familiarity of this place. Not that she was a drinker. But coming here with Casio after a long day, feeling strong by his side and proud that every woman in the bar knew he had chosen her. Casio was gorgeous with his dark hair and nearly black eyes, and when he'd looked at her, Harper's insides went weak. For some crazy reason, he'd only had eyes for her.

The last three nights she'd dreamed of him. The way he pressed his palm to the small of her back and guided her through a maze of people in any room. The way he kissed her earlobes and pulled her close as though no other woman could possibly exist for him.

Even as morning dawned, the dream ended, and reality battered her—blow after blow like the beating she'd endured, she still ached for him.

And when he had called, because he needed her help, she had responded willingly. She opened the door and stepped inside the little office. It reeked of stale ashtrays and was in dire need of a good dusting as well as a good airing out.

Gabe sat sideways on the couch, definitely not passed out, but with his ankle propped on a couple of sofa pillows. "Look at that ankle. It's swollen up like a softball."

Not only was the ankle swollen, it was beginning to bruise. "It looks pretty bad. What'd you do?"

"Some moron left a purse sitting on the floor by her chair. I tripped."

"I'm surprised Burt didn't get you some ice to get the swelling down."

"He's not a nursemaid." Gabe waved his hand like it didn't matter. He didn't even seem that drunk.

"Well, I'm not a nursemaid either, but I'm going to get some ice for that enormous ankle." She set her purse on the desk and headed for the door.

"Hey, Dolly."

She turned, smiling at his nickname for her. "Yeah?"

"It's good to see you."

"You too, Gabe. I'll be right back."

She walked back to the bar. "Hey, Burt. Can we get a little ice for Gabe's ankle?"

"Sure, help yourself."

She stuffed a gallon-sized plastic bag with ice cubes, snatched a clean towel from a shelf, and headed back into the office. She found Gabe nursing a bottle of Jack Daniel's. "Where'd you get that? You didn't have it five and a half seconds ago."

"I know where Burt keeps his private stash." He grinned like a little boy with a forbidden cookie and Harper couldn't help but smile back. She adjusted his foot back on the pillows. "Keep this elevated and iced. You should probably get it x-rayed."

He made a growly noise and tipped the bottle.

"You might not be hurting right now, but once all that booze wears off, you're going to be crying like a little girl."

A cackle vibrated his throat. "Then I best not let it wear off, eh?" He took another swig, then coughed into his hand.

Harper reached into her purse and pulled out a small bottle of liquid hand sanitizer. She held it out to him. "You have to stop smoking, Gabe. And drinking."

He laughed again, rubbing the gel into his calloused hands. "Should I start going to church too?"

"It certainly wouldn't hurt you any."

"It might." He grinned again, looking so much like Casio, her heart hurt.

"Seriously, Gabe. You have lung cancer. If you don't start taking care of yourself..." She stopped, because she knew there was no point.

The door opened and Casio filled the doorway. His eyes found Harper's. "Hi."

"Hi."

"Well, ain't you two just a mouthful of words."

Casio scowled. "What happened to your foot?"

"I tripped. Your little girlfriend is taking good care of the old man. Ain't you, Dolly?"

"I've done my best." Her heart beat so loudly in her ears she could barely concentrate. She grabbed her purse from the desk and moved toward the door. "Now that you're here, I'm going to go."

"Harper, wait. It's gotten dark. Let me walk you outside."

"Seriously? You think I'd be in danger walking out of a cop bar?"

"Humor me."

Harper had kept her resolve for all these weeks. Now she wanted so badly to have him back. Not the brooding, cruel Casio. The funny, sensitive guy who loved to rub her feet, bring home Chinese, cook a huge breakfast on Saturday mornings and feed her in bed. She missed that man. And she couldn't help but believe he still existed. And that a monster had overtaken the true man.

"Casio. I can make it outside by myself." As much as she wanted him back, he wasn't back yet. Not until he got help for the rage inside of him. If she only had herself to think about, it might be a more difficult decision to make. But deep inside of her, lying in a bed of nourishment, their child was growing.

"Harper, I just want to talk to you. For five minutes. What could it hurt?"

Was he serious? Harper met his gaze, keeping hers fixed and without the hint of softening. "I didn't come here to talk to you, Casio. I came to help your dad. Don't you have any respect for my wishes?"

His jaw tightened, a telltale that he'd clenched his back teeth. She knew that sight well. Her legs trembled. She knew his frustration built from that one little tic.

"I have to go. Don't try to stop me."

"Casio!" Gabe's sharp tone sliced the tension between them. "She don't want anything to do with you. Go on, Dolly. And thanks for the help."

Harper nodded at him and slipped past Casio, holding her breath that he wouldn't try to stop her. Burt was busy with customers as she walked by, so she hurried past the bar and out the door, feeling safer outside than she'd felt inside.

"Harper! Wait."

Oh, God. She turned, trying not to show her fear. "Casio, please. Just let me go."

Casio's eyes took her in, staring at her face, then her body. He frowned as they rested on her new curves, courtesy of the pregnancy hormones.

She drew a sharp breath. "What do you want?"

"I just wanted to let you know I'm ready for counseling."

"Again?"

"I mean it this time."

"You always do, Casio." She gathered a weary breath and leaned heavily on her car. "Have you made an appointment to see someone?"

He stepped closer. With nowhere to back up to, she raised her palm to stop his advance. "Casio. Don't come any closer or I'm leaving."

"Fine. And no, I haven't gotten an appointment yet. I thought you could recommend someone." He didn't bother with the grin. That helped, and gave her hope that maybe this time he truly meant it. She searched his eyes for truth.

"I've made ten appointments for you in the last year. I'm starting to lose credibility." She looked away and then back. "How do I know you'll follow through this time?"

He stuffed his hands inside the front pockets of his jeans. "Because…I hurt you."

"Now you're admitting to it?"

"Do I need to go to jail to prove to you I want to change?" He cleared his throat. "Harper, I miss you. I love you. And I'd do anything to get you back. But this isn't just about you and me."

"What's brought about this change?" If that's what this was and not some new way for him to manipulate her.

"I've been working on this case with ADA Campbell."

"Yes, how is that going?"

He shrugged. "Better than when my dad had it. I don't know how he missed half the evidence he missed."

"I wouldn't mention that to him." She expelled a small laugh.

Casio laughed. "Yeah. He wouldn't be too happy. But all in all, I think he wants the case solved. Anyway, working on the case has shown me how that night messed me up."

Could it really be that easy? Harper couldn't shake the doubt. "All right. I'll set up one more appointment for you with Julia. But if you blow off this appointment, you'd better not call me again."

Somehow, she found the courage to walk around to the driver's side and open the door. But he was there before she could escape, and suddenly she was in his arms.

He pulled her close and she had no strength to resist. God help her, she loved him. "I know I have a lot to prove to you, baby," he murmured against her ear. "But I promise I'm going to make that appointment and every one for as long as it takes for me to get better."

Wordlessly, Harper wrapped her empty arms about his neck and nestled closer as hope in his words lowered her defenses. After all, this was the father of her child. If he got the help he needed, they could be a family. And perhaps if he knew the truth, he would have the incentive to try harder.

"Casio," she whispered just as his head descended. She sighed and gave herself to the familiar feel of his warm mouth taking hers over. His hands finding the curve of her back, her hips, pulling her closer.

"Come home with me," he whispered.

"Casio, I can't…" He pressed his mouth over hers again, harder, more demanding, suffocating her refusal. Her body molded to his, becoming reacquainted with the firmness of his chest and thighs. His hands began to move and she couldn't think. Didn't want to think. Just wanted to feel.

Headlights from a car pulling into the parking lot brought them to their senses. Casio pulled back, staring down at her, passion smoldering in his dark eyes. "You have to come home with me."

"Casio, I can't."

"Don't say no," he whispered, pressing his forehead to hers. "I need you."

"Your dad needs you tonight."

"He'll be passed out in ten minutes if he isn't already." He kissed her on the mouth then pulled away. "Come with me."

Part of her wanted to agree. To shove aside the warning bells sounding inside her skull, to ignore the voice telling her to get out now and not allow herself to be swept into his arms and carried into his bed. Luckily, the door to the bar opened and a couple staggered out into the parking lot. The break in concentration gave Harper the opportunity to back away emotionally.

"I can't. Not yet." She stepped back.

Casio expelled a heavy breath. "I guess I deserve this. I hurt you, so you're punishing me."

Refusing to be sucked into a futile argument, Harper moved behind the still-open door. "Should I still make the appointment?"

He hesitated and she held her breath.

"Make the appointment. I promise I'll show up." He glanced toward the door. "I better get back inside. My dad is probably close to passing out. If I don't help him out to the truck now, I'll be carrying him over my shoulder." He tossed her a rueful grin.

"I'll be in touch."

He nodded, patted the hood of her car and strode away.

Harper got in the car and closed the door. She turned the key and cranked the engine. She sat back, her body shaking as she realized how close she'd been to revealing her secret.

How could she have been so stupid?

Seventeen

"As I lay dying, the woman with the dog's eyes would not close my eyes as I descended into Hades." Homer in The Odyssey.

He is still holding me in his arms, and Homer's words describe how I feel. Like I've suddenly been yanked from the deepest love I've ever known and shoved into evil's arms. If only I could speak, I'd tell him how wrong we were.

"My wife left," he whispers so softly that I barely hear him. "I was going to ask you to marry me on your birthday."

"Please leave her," Mama says. "It isn't right that you be here."

"What do you mean?" he asks, his voice shaking with sudden anger.

Careful, Mama. Careful, you don't know what he's capable of. Please be careful.

"I mean," Mama says in that tone she uses when she pulls her shoulders square and straightens her spine, "that you're needed elsewhere."

"Oh my God." He lowers me gently to the floor and moves away. "Casio."

I feel only relief that he's let me go. Claudia takes my hand once more.

"Are you okay, son?" I hear Gabe ask, his voice shaken in a way I've never heard before. Maybe it would have been okay to tell him about our baby sooner.

I hear Casio's weak response. "I tried to save her, Dad." Tears choke him. "I couldn't get the gun away from him."

"You tried to get the gun away? You idiot. You could have been killed." Gabe berates his wounded son, and suddenly I realize the sort of man I've allowed myself to sin with. In a strange sort of way, I'm relieved it ended this way.

"As I lay dying, the woman with the dog's eyes would not close my eyes as I descended into Hades."

If only I could close my eyes.

SATURDAY

Claudia

Claudia's nerves nearly sent her running back to her Tahoe, but the memory of last night's dream propelled her forward, toward the two-story, red-brick home behind a neat wrought-iron fence. The yard boasted autumn perennials and neatly sculpted shrubs along the front of the house.

She wasn't even sure the Remingtons still lived here. Once, just after BJ's funeral, she'd tried to stop and visit, but the emotions had overtaken her and she'd driven on by. This time, despite the tingling in her jaw that so often signaled an oncoming panic attack, she shoved through the fear, the dread, and took the first step up the brick steps.

Pressing the doorbell took almost superhuman strength. Her arms felt weighted down with ten years of fear, sorrow, regret. But in her dream she remembered her promise to visit. Mrs. Remington's grief pouring from her eyes—a torrent of tears—and knew she could ignore this moment no longer.

The door opened and a slightly older Sara Remington stood. Her eyes narrowed for only the time it took to smile in recognition. "Claudia King! What a beautiful woman you've become."

Her words slid over Claudia like a warm, gentle rain, washing away her fear. In a beat, she found herself wrapped in Mrs. Remington's slightly plumper arms, pressed against a soft breast.

"It's Claudia Campbell now," she said, as the woman pulled back and held her at arm's length.

"Just as pretty as ever."

Claudia shook her head. "Not so much."

"That's a matter of opinion. Come inside," she said, opening the screen door and allowing Claudia to precede her. Predictably, the home smelled like a happy welcome—pumpkin spice, fresh linen, smoke from a fireplace, though there was barely enough chill in the air to warrant the latter.

"Your home is lovely," Claudia said, walking straight into a living area. Wood floors with a round, braided rug seemed old-fashioned, yet homey and inviting. The coffee table was a little cluttered with paper and strewn magazines and needed a good dusting. But the comfort of the atmosphere made up for a little messiness.

Mrs. Remington's cheeks flushed a little as she noted Claudia's perusal. "Please excuse the mess. My son has been home from college, and things always get a little messy when he's home."

Claudia stopped short. She knew BJ had been an only child. She didn't want to pry, but it seemed like an odd thing for Mrs. Remington to say when Claudia knew better. Instead of questioning, she smiled. "Your house is wonderful."

"Would you like to come into the kitchen?"

Realizing she'd been standing in the middle of the room, Claudia's face warmed a little. "Yes ma'am. Thank you."

"Have a seat, please." She walked to the counter and lifted a plate of muffins. "Pumpkin chocolate chip. Just came out of the oven. Will you have one with me?"

"Sure. I'm not turning down anything with chocolate chips."

The older woman smiled brightly. "How about some coffee or tea?"

"Coffee's fine if you already have it brewed."

Claudia watched her. She had to be around sixty, but her face didn't show her age—something Claudia reflected on, considering the grief she'd experienced. Losing her only child. But then...

"Mrs. Remington, I'm confused about something. You mentioned you have a son?" She glanced away, embarrassed to have been so bold. "I don't understand. BJ never said anything about having a younger brother."

"She never knew she had one."

She set the plate of muffins on the table along with two dessert plates, then walked back to the counter. Claudia waited, assuming the older woman would expound.

When she was all settled, with coffee and the fixings and muffins on the table, Mrs. Remington sat in a chair across from her. Her blue-eyed gaze fixed on Claudia, a resigned expression.

She drew in a breath and expelled. "Oh, honey. Life doesn't turn out the way we expect it to, does it?" Her face softened with compassion, and for no good reason, Claudia's eyes filled with tears. Goodness, she had come to comfort a lonely, grieving mother, and instead here she was on the verge of a meltdown.

Mrs. Remington poured cream into her cup and took a sip. Then she smiled. "You want to know about Donnie, my son."

"I'm a little curious."

She nodded. "Mr. Remington and I separated after BJ's murder. There just didn't seem like there was anything left for me to work with anymore."

"You met someone else?" She did the calculations even as she said the words. The boy would only be nine at the oldest. And then there was the age factor—Mrs. Remington's age. It couldn't have happened.

She gave a small laugh. "No. I was too bruised for another man. And I wore the wounds all over me like body armor to keep men away."

Claudia sipped her coffee, savoring the full, sweet flavor and enjoying the warmth in her throat as she swallowed. She couldn't imagine sitting at her mother's kitchen, the living room a mess, and her mother relaxing and having a conversation.

"A year after BJ's murder, Donnie showed up at the door with his mother. She was emaciated, dying from uterine cancer, looking for Nathan, of course. I could see the resemblance between him and

Donnie as soon as I laid eyes on the boy. It was my worst nightmare come true, that some woman would knock on my door holding Nathan's child."

"Donnie is Mr. Remington's son?"

"The product of one of his many affairs."

Claudia opened her mouth to voice her disdain, then snapped her jaw shut. "So the two of you reconciled and raised his son?"

"Oh, no. I wouldn't take him back. I couldn't. He is completely unrepentant." She sipped another sip. "Donnie's mother was in the last stages of her cancer. About to be put on hospice, and she simply couldn't take care of him anymore. She was looking for Nathan because she needed him to be Donnie's father."

"Did he know about Donnie before that day?" Claudia pinched off a bite of the muffin and popped it into her mouth.

"Oh, yes. He knew. As a matter of fact, without me even knowing, he'd been paying child support Donnie's entire life."

"Well, that's something at least."

"I know."

They laughed at the paradox, though it was far from funny.

"Anyway, Nathan met them here. He expressed his regret that she was going to die, but very kindly refused to do anything that would interfere with his bachelor lifestyle. He said he would continue to support Donnie, whoever raised him, but didn't have room in his life for a boy."

"Jerk."

"But then we knew that." She smiled and Claudia smiled back.

"Donnie doted on his mother, and I couldn't bear the fear in his eyes. How could I do anything but offer myself? It just seemed like God had given Donnie to me, and me to Donnie. We needed each other. He and his mother moved in with me a couple of weeks later, and she was dead in six months. By then all her affairs were in order, and I had already been named Donnie's legal guardian. Nathan still pays child support, and I opened a little bakery with my divorce settlement."

"I had no idea." Mrs. Remington had spent the last ten years giving back and building a new life.

"How would you have?"

Claudia's defenses kicked in and she thrust a sharp glance at the older woman.

"No. I'm not scolding you for not coming to see me. I understood how difficult it must have been for you to cope. I saw you at the funeral. You were destroyed. I wanted to take you in my arms and make everything right. But your parents were there, and given some unfortunate circumstances, I didn't feel like I could intrude."

"By unfortunate circumstances, you mean my mother's affair with your husband?"

She nodded. "I wasn't sure how much you really knew."

"I figured it out." She didn't tell her about the letter her mother had written to her "darling."

"I want you to know something." She leaned forward in her chair, folding her arms and resting them on the table. "Your mother came to me a few days after the funeral."

"Did you punch her?"

She chuckled, her slightly plump fingers toying with the pumpkin muffin in front of her. "I like to think I am too dignified to act on my impulses."

"I admire your restraint." Claudia gave a short laugh. "So what did my mother want? Absolution?"

"In a manner of speaking. But don't be too cynical. The affair was short-lived, and she and your father reconciled. But more than that, she reconciled with God. She seemed to have truly repented, and I chose to forgive her."

"But not your husband?"

"He didn't want forgiveness. He wanted a free pass." She sighed and swallowed down a sip of coffee. "True repentance isn't just saying, 'I'm sorry.' It's saying, 'I'm sorry, I'll never, ever do that again because my relationship with you means more to me than anything.'"

Claudia couldn't hold her gaze. She looked down at her fingers. "But my mother didn't want a relationship with you. The two of you..." She glanced up.

"No, we are not friends. But I no longer want to punch her."

Claudia blew out a laugh. "That makes one of us."

Mrs. Remington smiled. Claudia expected a scolding, even a mild one. One of those, "Now Claudia, she's still your mother," sort of scoldings. But the older woman bit into her muffin instead.

Embarrassment heated Claudia's neck. "Anyway, so my mother repented to you, but not because she wanted a relationship with you."

"For her relationship with God." She reached over and laid her hand over Claudia's. "Honey, whatever your relationship with your mother, it's your business. And I'm sure you didn't come over here after ten years to talk about that."

"I just…"

"It's time for healing, isn't it?"

Tears burned and spilled over. This was too much. She'd thought she could be here, but she couldn't. Not yet. "I— Mrs. Remington, I need to go. I'm sorry." She grabbed her purse and stumbled back through the living room.

"Claudia, wait, please."

Claudia stopped just before reaching for the door.

"That night burns in my mind like a fire," Mrs. Remington said. "Every day I see my daughter, lying in her own blood unmoving, her eyes open and staring, and I know she is seeing and hearing everything going on around her."

Claudia took in a lungful of air. Slowly she turned. "Me too," she whispered. "It was like she was trying to communicate but couldn't, and I wanted so badly to hear her."

"You know what I remember most?"

Claudia's brain screamed for her to run away. To not pull up this memory, because every time she allowed herself to think about it, she smelled the blood, heard her own screams, saw herself for the coward she was that night.

"What I remember most," Mrs. Remington said, smoothing Claudia's hair behind her ear. "Is you, staying beside her. Refusing to be moved because you believed she needed you. You were the bravest thing I've ever seen."

As much as she wanted to believe Mrs. Remington, Claudia's mind rejected the words. She shook her head. "I was a coward. A complete idiot. I couldn't do anything but cry."

"Crying doesn't make you weak. It just shows you care."

Suddenly feeling very weary, Claudia sank to the living room floor. Mrs. Remington sat down too. Claudia met her gaze. "After a couple of weeks, I moved on. And I was truly okay for a long time. I didn't have nightmares or anything about that night. I know it wasn't really right for her to be my best friend. But she wasn't that much older than we were, and she was the only person I could talk to."

"When did you stop being okay?" Mrs. Remington asked softly. She sat no more than three feet away, her legs folded, her elbows resting on her knees.

Claudia stretched her legs out and crossed them at the ankle. "I had a miscarriage two years ago." Claudia's hands began to tremble and she laced them together in her lap. "I guess the blood triggered the memories."

"Have you seen a counselor?"

Claudia smiled. "You sound like Vic."

"I take it that's a no?"

"I saw one for a while. I thought the nightmares and panic attacks were because of postpartum depression. When I figured out that I most likely have post traumatic stress disorder from that night, I just didn't feel comfortable talking about it. I felt like I was blaming her for how mixed up I am over that night. As if it were somehow her fault." A twinge of guilt still pressed through her.

"That makes sense." Mrs. Remington paused, then went on. "You were only a girl at the time. Still on the edge between being a child and being an adult. In many ways you teetered more toward the child side, just by virtue of a lack of life experience to that date. It's natural for a girl that age to take the blame for everything."

A knock at the door startled Claudia. She jumped and stood up quickly.

"Looks like you have the only man I know who is right on time," Mrs. Remington said. She stood with a grunt. "I'm too old to be on the floor."

Claudia's stomach curled. "I don't know what you mean. I have the only man who is on time?"

"You didn't know Mr. Campbell had an appointment to see me?"

Claudia felt the blood drain from her face. She shook her head. "We're separated."

"Oh, dear." Mrs. Remington frowned. "I assumed the two of you were meeting here." She opened the door and Vic stepped inside. "Hello, Mrs. Remington," he said extending his hand. Then he saw Claudia. His eyes clouded in confusion and then brightened as his gaze took her in. "Claude? What are you doing here?"

Luckily, Mrs. Remington understood the discomfort of the situation. "She came to visit with me."

Vic's eyes never left Claudia's, and her stomach tightened with dread. "Will you stay while I interview Mrs. Remington?" he asked.

"I'm sorry, Vic. I can't." She swept past him. "Good-bye, Mrs. Remington. Thank you for the coffee and muffin."

Without looking back, Claudia hurried to the Tahoe. Her hands and jaw tingled, her breathing sharpened into quick bursts of air. She didn't bother reaching into the glove box for her bag to breathe into. She needed to get distance between herself and Vic...fast.

SATURDAY AND SUNDAY

Harper

Harper felt the cramps before she was fully awake, and they escalated into heavy pains as clarity dawned. Fear washed over her, and tears formed as she carefully sat up and made her way through her darkened room to the door.

Before she made it down the hall, into the bathroom, blood gushed from her body, and she knew her baby's spirit was gone to heaven.

"Mom!" she called as the tears began to flow. "Mom!" her voice laced with panic, rose to a fever pitch. Her parents came running.

"Oh, no," her mother said, sorrow filling her eyes, her tone understanding loss of a child. "Honey, I'm so sorry."

Her dad stood in the hallway, eyes dark with confusion. "What? What's going on?"

"Sid, please go call an ambulance. She's losing the baby and there's too much blood. We better not drive her."

Harper wept during the quick ride to the hospital. Thank God she hadn't told Casio. Losing the baby would most likely have been too traumatic for him. It could have set his recovery back months or longer. Her parents followed behind in the car. Traffic was practically nothing this time of night. Wee hours of the morning. Wasn't this always the time babies were born? Was it also the time they died?

Grief nearly consumed her as the paramedics wheeled her gurney into the ER and the nurses took charge, pressing absorbent pads against her to soak up the blood flooding out of her. "I'm losing my baby," she whimpered to the white-haired nurse who closed the curtain around her cubicle of a room.

The nurse patted her leg. "Let's just see what's going on."

First she listened for a heartbeat. Her expression softened with compassion and her lips flattened together. Harper didn't have to be told there wasn't one.

Tears of pain and grief poured from Harper as the nurse did a pelvic exam. "Your doctor will be here soon, honey. I'm going to help you get into a gown, and we'll get an IV started."

Harper had no fight. She allowed herself to be led through the motions. Her head swam by the time the doctor arrived. After another internal exam, the doctor turned sharply to the nurse. "Book an OR now. We need to get this hemorrhaging stopped. Did you not see how heavily she was bleeding? She should have gone right in with the doctor on schedule. The fetus hasn't even been expelled yet."

"I'm sorry, doctor, but there was an accident on the highway and everyone is working it."

The formidable Latino woman shook her head. "Ridiculous. Go. Get the OR. Find somewhere for me to take care of this woman, even if you have to kick someone out."

Harper felt herself fading as Dr. Ramirez walked around her bedside. "Stay with me, honey; you'll be okay."

Blackness overcame her like a tunnel. The sound of voices calling her name echoed in her head. And for a while, her grief was gone.

She slowly came to, aware only of the emptiness deep inside, once filled with a mother's heart. Nothing beat there now.

Her sigh beckoned her mother to her bedside.

"Hi, honey." Breathy relief softened her tone. "How are you feeling?"

Harper looked around, frowning. "They kept me in the hospital?"

"Your heart stopped once. Thank God the doctor got here when she did."

"That Ramirez is the only person in this whole hospital with a lick of sense." Her dad took up vigil on the other side of her bed. "You have a lawsuit against those incompetent idiots in the ER. You almost died."

"Come on, Dad," she said, so weary of heartache and disappointment. She closed her eyes, wishing for sleep. "I'm not suing anyone."

"Can we have that in writing?" A youngish doctor entered. He wore scrubs and Nikes and looked like he should be on TV instead of walking into a real-life hospital room. He grinned. "Just kidding. Although we'd appreciate it. Not that I'm admitting to any wrongdoing on our part."

Harper smiled, so grateful for the moment of emotional relief.

Her dad glowered at the doctor. "What are you, some kind of clown? My daughter almost died and you're making smart remarks?"

"Dad!" She glanced at her mother, silently pleading.

"Hon, let's go get some coffee." Thankfully, her mother pulled him out of the room.

Harper cut her eyes at the doctor. "Sorry. He always gets like that when I have a near-death experience."

The doctor's eyebrows went up. Then he gave an appreciative nod and went along with the joke. "I see his kind all the time. We like to call him the overprotective sort."

Harper laughed. "You don't know the half of it."

"So, I'm on call for Dr. Ramirez today. She asked me to check on you especially."

"Super. How am I?"

"Vitals are good. But you did start through the tunnel toward the light, so we'd like to keep you overnight just for observation."

"Was there damage to my heart?"

"We'll keep an eye on you for a while, but you're strong and you were only gone a few seconds. Very doubtful there are long-term damages." He glanced down at her chart. "I'm more concerned with the hysterectomy."

Harper frowned. "I think you have my chart confused. I had a miscarriage."

His face drained of color and emotion. He cleared his throat and pulled up a chair to her bedside. "Miss Abbott."

"My name is Harper." Harper's stomach dropped, her heart pounded in her ears.

"Harper. I wish I didn't have to be the one to tell you this. You were farther along than Dr. Ramirez believed originally. That's why the bleeding was so severe. By the time they got in there for the D and C, the only thing they could do was remove the uterus. The bleeding wouldn't stop otherwise."

Harper nodded. Numb, too numb to reach up and wipe the tears away from her cheeks. She turned her head toward the window. He may as well have killed her.

Casio. All of this was his fault.

The beating, the pregnancy, the miscarriage, mutilation. If only he'd pulled his gun, put it to her head, and pulled the trigger.

Claudia

Claudia knew she couldn't put this off. She sat across from her mother at the kitchen table. Elizabeth seemed nervous. Which was more than unusual. "Mom, I was hard on you about Mr. Remington."

Her mother's jaw dropped. "How did you find out who?"

"Daddy and Mr. Remington exchanged words that night on the bus. I just put two and two together. Then I went to see Mrs. Remington yesterday. She said you went to see her after BJ's funeral."

Mother's eyes filled and she nodded. "That was the worst thing I could have done to your father." She gathered a steadying breath and composed herself. "I regret every moment I spent with Nathan. It took many years to heal the pain in your father. And I don't think it ever fully goes away."

"I'm glad you two were able to work it out so that you kept the ministry and the marriage."

Mother reached across the table and took Claudia's hand. "I didn't deserve his love and forgiveness, but he made the choice to stay. And we've survived for thirty-five years."

Claudia sighed at the thought. "I need to tell you something."

"Something else?" Mother smiled, and Claudia allowed her the attempt at humor in this new phase of their relationship.

She nodded. "I overextended our finances dramatically."

Mother frowned—the concerned sort of frown rather than the scolding one. "Do you need money? We have some savings."

Shaking her head, Claudia waved her hand to dismiss the notion. "No. But I was planning an elaborate anniversary dinner for you and daddy and seventy-five of our closest friends, family, and staff."

"How thoughtful." A gentle smile touched her mother's lips and Claudia went on quickly, knowing her next expression would be disappointment. "Here's the thing. I overextended to the point that I had to call the event planner and cancel the dinner." Claudia held her breath, waiting for her mother's reply.

"I'm proud of you, Claudia."

Claudia couldn't help but expel an ironic laugh. "How could you be?"

"Because you took a hard look at what you could do and made the right choice. Even if it meant disappointing a few people."

"So what about your anniversary? The staff deserves some sort of celebration of ministry."

"We'll figure it out. You did the right thing."

She and her mother hugged before she left. It was a small start, but at least they were moving toward healing.

Victor

Vic and Casio sat across from the retired forensic pathologist. Sweat beaded James Farraday's brow, and Vic had a feeling they were about to hit pay dirt. The autopsy report sat on the table in front of Dr. Farraday, whose mouth moved while reading the words.

"I remember this case," Dr. Farraday finally said. "It wasn't solved, was it?"

Casio snorted. Clearly he had no problem playing bad cop again. "I'm not in the mood to play patty-cake with you, Farraday. We know you suppressed evidence about Miss Remington's pregnancy. What we don't know is why."

Farraday's face blanched. "I don't know what you're talking about and I resent the accusation."

"Spare me the outrage," Casio shot back.

Vic raised his hand to silence the argument brewing between the two men. "Dr. Farraday, we don't want to accuse you of anything. We've reopened the case because evidence has surfaced that Miss Remington was pregnant when she died. We couldn't find anything about a pregnancy in your autopsy report."

"Then how did you find out?" The man's question proved Vic knew the truth. He only needed to ask the right questions and it would come out.

"There's no question that you suppressed the file. We found the pages you left out of your final report."

Farraday released a slow breath. "I want immunity."

"You're not under arrest, Dr. Farraday," Vic said, although the man most certainly would be.

"And I plan to keep it that way." His face had turned to stone and Vic knew the man had him. There was no way to prove he had suppressed the information.

After a call to the DA to confirm the deal, Vic waited for Izzy to type up the agreement. Thirty-five minutes later, they were back in business. This time with a video camera to record the confession.

"Okay, Dr. Farraday," he said. "You're on."

The retired pathologist nodded. "It's true. I handed over the file—with the pages that later went missing—to Detective Hightower. Afterward, when I found out they had not been included in the report, I assumed he'd shredded them."

"Hightower is my dad." Casio's gaze narrowed as he stared at the man. "Why would you give him those pages?"

"He didn't tell me why he wanted the information to go away, but my son was about to go to Berkeley."

"He paid you?" Vic asked, frowning.

Shaking his head, Farraday fingered the report still on the table in front of him. "My son was something of a partier during those days. The department was investigating a drug ring and he was part of it. The detective made a deal to leave my son alone if I handed him the part of the report that mentioned the girl was pregnant." He met Vic's gaze for the first time. "I never knew why he wanted the information suppressed. I just knew that if my son was arrested and convicted of a felony, he'd lose his chance to go to college."

Casio's face was red with anger. When Farraday left the room, he practically exploded. "So my dad was a crooked cop!"

"Looks that way." Vic steadied his gaze on the officer.

"He couldn't have killed her. I saw the guy, I tried to tackle him right before he shot me. It wasn't my dad."

"In light of this new information, I think we're going to have to have a chat with your dad."

Casio expelled a breath and slicked back his hair. "Let me talk to him alone, okay?"

Despite his misgivings, Vic nodded. After all, this was Casio's dad. He couldn't blame him.

"Get to it quick and let me know."

Eighteen

I believe in miracles. I always have. Even during the lean years of no spiritual input from anyone in my world, I had faith that God was there, was bigger and smarter, and most of all, that He was pulling for me. Perfection wasn't the requirement for His attention. He knew my heart.

In these last few minutes, I realize that miracles aren't always the blind seeing, or the deaf hearing, or the lame walking—Jesus kind of miracles.

I find it miraculous to know Gabe is a foot away, and I have no desperate need to feel him holding me. Twenty minutes ago, I'd have taken a bullet for him. Ironically, I no longer would.

A miracle.

Grace.

If I were going to live, I would break things off with him and immediately surrender my life to God in such a way that everyone would see that I am changed. That's the problem with living for yourself. Sometimes miracles come too late to save the body. We have to be content to save the soul.

*So, in this moment, while I lie where I've fallen, blood stain-
ing my new white shirt, Mama on one side, sweet Claudia on the
other, angels nodding to each other in their respective corners of the
bus, I don't just see a miracle. I'm about to experience one.*

Life to death to eternity.

SUNDAY

Casio

If he got her voice mail one more time today, Casio was going to go
ballistic. Harper was supposed to call him today and confirm his
appointment with the counselor. He jammed the phone in his pocket
and downed the last of his beer. She made him act like a total idiot.
All she had to do was answer the phone. Women loved to play mind
games.

He nodded at Burt for another beer.

Gabe flicked the ashes from his cigarette into the glass ashtray on
the counter, took another puff. "What's your problem?"

"That's my business."

Burt set another draft in front of him.

Gabe shook his head and gave a low chuckle. "She left you, boy.
What does she have to do to convince you she wants to be left alone?"

"I'm not talking about Harper with you of all people." He just
needed to get the guts to tell his dad what that stupid file he'd given
to Casio had opened up. The old man wasn't as smart as he thought
he was.

"Well, just listen then. I might be off the force, but I still have my contacts there. You beat her up bad. You'd be in jail right now if you weren't a cop."

Casio slammed his fist on the bar. "Shut up."

"You watch how you talk to me, boy."

Casio sneered. "Considering what I know about you, I suggest *you* watch how you talk to *me*."

Gabe yanked the oxygen tubing from his nose and, in a fluid movement, stood, grabbed Casio's shirt, and hauled him from the bar stool through the bar and out the front door. The night had turned fall-crisp, and cars lined the parking lot, but that didn't stop Gabe from taking the upper hand and slamming Casio against a blue Ford Focus. "Listen to me, kid. I don't know what you think you know, but don't ever threaten me again. You got that?" His breath, labored and heavy, reeking of booze, slithered across Casio's face, threatening to make his stomach turn over.

Casio wouldn't be bullied. Not by anyone, and especially not by his drunk dad. He leveled his gaze. "You know we're looking into who the father of Miss Remington's baby was. I remember you rushing to her side that night, Pop. Maybe I'm sick of protecting you."

"You were in shock that night. Your memory's playing tricks on you. I was off duty, but a police officer is always ready to do his duty. I was just doin' my job and trying to keep her alive until the EMTs got there."

Even in his half-drunken state, Casio could appreciate the desperation his father must be feeling. "Believe me, I remember perfectly. It was touching. You gathering your pregnant mistress in your arms. I guess that explains why Mom left."

"Your mom left because she had better things to do."

"Yeah, right. It had nothing to do with Miss Remington and the little bun you two had in the oven." Casio hadn't seen his mother in years. She'd left one day, without warning, and had never contacted him or Gabe in ten years.

"You shut your mouth. Hear me?"

"Or what, Dad? You going to kill me too?"

The belligerence dropped from Gabe's face so fast that Casio thought maybe he'd been wrong about his father: maybe his dad cared more about him than he'd thought.

"You think I killed BJ?" He unclenched his fist around Casio's shirt as though he'd lost strength. "You think I shot the bus driver in cold blood, shot BJ, and then shot my own son?" His voice rose with bewilderment. "All these years...that's what you thought? That I was the one who shot you?"

The door opened and a couple staggered past them. Casio waited until they got into a pickup and started groping each other before he turned back to his dad.

"No. I don't think you held the gun." He hesitated then just decided to go for it. "But Vic has some questions about that autopsy report, Pop."

Gabe clenched his fist and Casio thought for a second his dad might be about to punch him. "What's that ADA have to do with this? What did you do? You told about the file?"

"No, Pop. I didn't tell him you gave me the file. He thinks you hid it in the evidence room, and I found it while I was cleaning."

"Then what are you talking about?"

"We interviewed James Farraday."

"The forensic pathologist?"

"He gave you up, Pop. Told us about his son's drug problem and the deal you made with him."

Gabe's shoulders slumped. "It ain't what you think, son."

"You know what?" Casio shook his head as headlights flashed into the parking lot, making Gabe squint against the glare. "I'm too drunk to think about it tonight. But you best get your story straight. If you have any defense at all, start pulling it together because Vic is going to want to talk to you tomorrow. And I'd be ready to give up a DNA sample if I were you."

"Not without a court order."

"Well, that pretty much says it all, doesn't it Pop?"

Gabe shook his head and walked away, his shoulders rounded as though all the fight had left his body. He opened the door and walked back into Burt's. Casio watched him go, his gut churning.

He leaned against the nearest car, fighting off the effects of sucking down six drafts in an hour. He definitely didn't like this feeling of not being in control. Folding his arms across his chest, he closed his eyes and the images of that night flooded back over him, relentless, threatening to drown him once more in fear and shock.

The bus could have easily made it over the tracks before the train arrived. The guys needled Mr. Montrose, the bus driver, for being such a weasel. Any one of the football players would have gunned it and made the train, if they'd been driving.

It had been a cloudy, dark night, sprinkled with drops of rain. Just enough so that hardly anyone else in town had ventured out—

not like home games when the town lit up afterward, restaurants filled with game attendees. Miss Remington's murder aboard the bus that night would have been impossible if the game had been played on their home field. But then the killer must have known the game schedule, known when BJ would be on the bus.

The train whistle blew from a block away. The crossing lights flashed as the bells signaled the train's imminent arrival. The door of the bus swished open, but the action was barely even registered. The bus door—something kids are conditioned to ignore. And then two shots were fired. Screaming followed. Casio looked up from his portable CD player and yanked off his headphones as some of his teammates hit the deck.

The killer carried a pistol and turned down the aisle. He wore a mask and seemed to be searching the seats—it had not been a random killing. "Leave her alone!" Casio yelled. His voice cracked like a twelve-year-old. He'd been so ashamed.

The gunman turned toward Miss Remington and shot once, twice, three times, and four. Without thinking, Casio rushed forward, charging the guy. The gun went off. Pain seared his shoulder and the man stood over him. "You okay, kid?"

Casio tried to place the voice. His stomach tightened. He knew those eyes. The voice. He pressed his fist against his forehead. Who?

He shoved out a deep breath and walked back into Burt's. He found Gabe back at the bar, a bottle of Jack Daniels in front of him. Gabe tensed as he straddled the stool he'd vacated a few minutes before.

"I'm surprised you want to sit next to a killer. A woman-killer at that." He tipped the shot. Wrapping his fingers around the base of the bottle, he poured himself another glass.

Burt slid a drink to the guy at the end of the counter, then turned to Casio. "You want another beer?"

"No, thanks."

The bartender scowled. "If you ain't drinkin', don't be sittin' at my bar."

"Fine, give me another beer then." He turned to Gabe. "Look, Dad. I know you didn't shoot anyone on that bus. Vic's determined to find the killer and he's looking to find the father of Miss Remington's baby, who, shock or no shock, I think is you. And this autopsy thing makes you look even worse." He was afraid to ask outright. Wasn't sure he wanted to know if his father was capable of orchestrating a murder to rid himself of a mistress and baby.

"So, the ADA is lookin' to finger the father as the killer?"

"It's a lead. And not a bad one. If you were investigating a case like this, wouldn't you suspect the baby's father?"

"Yeah. Why do you think I tried to bury the examiner's report?"

"Anyway, what do you say we get you home so you can sleep this off and tomorrow we'll go see Vic and fess up about the baby?"

"It's a thought." A fit of coughing overcame him for the next minute. Casio helped him reattach the tubing. He took a wheezing breath. "Do you have anything else? Any other DNA evidence?"

Surprised to feel such concern as his dad obviously declined physically, Casio took a swallow of his beer and gathered his composure. "A couple of things. We're interviewing witnesses. We're trying to find a missing bracelet she was wearing earlier that night but didn't make any of the photos in the file. A couple of days ago we talked to Jesse Simpson."

Gabe nodded, clearing his throat. "The garage guy? Why are you questioning him?"

"We thought he might have had a motive, but it didn't pan out."

"Easy come, easy go."

"Yeah."

"Tell you what. I'll be a man about it. I don't got anything to hide. So I was her baby's father, we had a fling for a while. That don't mean I killed her."

Casio eyed Gabe from the corner of his eye. He remembered that night. It was more than just a fling his dad had carried on with Miss Remington.

His mother had left a month before the murder. It could only have been that she found out about Miss Remington. That didn't explain why she would have left Casio, but he had come to terms with the loss years ago. Maybe it had been too painful.

"There's something else you should know, Dad." He swallowed hard, because he knew he had no right to judge.

"What's that?"

"The medical examiner's report also showed Miss Remington had bruises on her body."

Gabe kept his gaze straight ahead as he slowly brought the glass to his lips, his expression never changing.

"They'll be looking at you since you two had a relationship." Still no response. "The report said the bruises were consistent with ongoing physical abuse."

He downed his drink and turned to Gabe. "Take me home. We'll go down to the station tomorrow."

Casio knew he couldn't safely drive after so much to drink. He was a lot of things, but a drunk driver wasn't one of them.

"Sorry, Dad. I'm in no position to drive myself right now."

"Fine." Gabe staggered from the bar. "I'll take a cab."

"It's a long way home. That's going to cost a mint."

"That's my business."

Casio rolled his eyes and watched his dad stagger toward the door. It opened before he could reach for the handle. Claudia entered, followed by Georgie. But it was Claudia that Casio zoned in on. She nearly bumped into Gabe, then she slowly looked up. Her eyes widened, and even in the dim lights of the bar, he could see panic wash over her face.

Casio slid from his bar stool and went to her. He slid his arm around her shoulders and leaned in close to her ear. "Breathe. It's okay."

"Hey, Casio!" Georgie's pep rally voice sang, oblivious to Claudia's impending meltdown.

He nodded to her. "Let's get a table," he said. He turned to Georgie. "Get her a drink."

"Do I get to get me one too?" she asked with a pretty pout.

"Yeah. Whatever."

He led Claudia to a corner table. "H-he was there that night. I didn't remember that."

"Yes. He got there toward the end."

Her hands shook. He took hold of them. Holding tightly. She

looked into his eyes, speaking slowly as though remembering for the first time. "Your dad and Beej were seeing each other." He could see the understanding dawning in her eyes. "She was having a baby...*his* baby."

"Yes. That's one of the things we've been focusing on in the investigation, finding the baby's dad."

"But you knew. Why didn't you tell Vic? He's been spinning his wheels on this investigation."

"I wasn't sure. The pieces are just coming together for me too."

Georgie arrived with two martinis. She slid one to Claudia and sat across from her. "Okay, dense me, I didn't realize something was wrong. What's going on?"

Her frown seemed sincere. Casio nodded toward the spot where they'd run into Gabe. "My dad."

"What about him?"

Claudia sipped her drink and stared into Georgie's face. "He was having an affair with BJ."

The expression on Georgie's face went from laughter to a frown in a beat. "Wait. You're serious? Of course she was having an affair. We knew that." She made an imaginary circle with her index finger. "The three of us were there together. We saw him come onto the bus..."

Claudia squinted. "He grabbed her away from me and he was crying."

"Yes," Georgie said. Then she sucked in a breath. "Are you telling me you've had this blocked out for ten years?"

A shrug lifted Claude's shoulders. "I don't know. I must have. All

I remembered was the blood. A couple of days ago, I remembered my dad in there with me, and then the Remingtons. But until I practically ran into Detective Hightower just now I didn't remember him at all." She turned to Casio. "Did he do it?"

Casio shook his head, but Georgie once again spoke up. "He couldn't have."

Claudia sipped her drink again. "What do you mean?"

Georgie broke in. "He's bigger, stockier than the guy who killed her."

"You've got a good memory," Casio said.

Georgie shrugged. "I notice things. And...I have a good memory."

Claudia's gaze turned glassy as she stared into what must have been the awakening memories. Tears glistened in her eyes.

The speakers blasted out a country love song, and Casio stood. "Come here, Claude. Dance with me."

She frowned and shook her head.

"I'll do it," Georgie offered.

"Next song, Georgie." Casio kept his gaze on Claudia. "Come on, Claude. For old times' sake."

Gathering in a surrendered breath, she nodded. "One dance."

The dance floor was mostly empty as Claudia slipped into his arms. "Just like all those old dances we went to in high school."

She smiled. "Except we're not making out in your car later, so forget that right now."

"Darn it." Casio grinned. "Crossing that off the list of things to do later."

Claudia moved her hands over his shoulders and clasped them behind his neck. "You're awfully tense, Casio. Everything okay?"

He shook his head. "Harper. She won't answer my calls."

"Harper?"

"My girlfriend. Ex-girlfriend, I guess."

Claudia pulled back and faced him. "What?" She said, then looked away again. "I didn't realize you had recently broken up with someone."

"I know, but we are sort of reconciling." He moved slowly with the music, remembering Claudia's curves, wishing she were Harper. "I'm going to counseling with someone she knows."

He peered at her more closely. She seemed distracted.

"So…do you think you'll be going back to Vic?"

"I hope so. Do you think he'll find out who killed BJ?"

Casio frowned. "We're trying to find out who took that bracelet."

"Which bracelet?"

"The love knot one she always wore."

She drew a sharp breath.

"What?"

"Casio, I hate to tell you this, but if your investigation is hinging on that bracelet, you're at a dead end."

His gut tightened. "What do you mean?"

"I have it. The clasp broke when we were getting on the bus to come home after Pizza Hut. BJ asked me to stick it in my pocket. I kept it."

Her words hit him like a punch. "You better let Vic know."

Georgie tapped her on the shoulder. "My turn."

Claudia smiled. "He's all yours."

Georgie must have been drinking several martinis because she stumbled a little as she took Claudia's place. Casio hated drunken women. "Oh, hey, Claude. I meant to tell you. Remember that woman who came into the ER the other night, thinking she was miscarrying?"

Claudia's face drained of color and she shook her head.

Georgie frowned. "What? You're the one asking about her at lunch the next day. Remember how I said she didn't have a miscarriage?"

"We can talk about it later." She laughed. "Casio isn't in the mood to hear girl stories."

Georgie shrugged. "Okay." Georgie wrapped her arms around him and they swayed to the music.

Something about the way Claudia acted when he mentioned Harper...

"Tell me about the woman in the ER, Georgie."

Harper

Harper felt the warmth of a body standing over her as she slowly became conscious. Hospital beds and rooms in general were not the place for proper rest, but with the nurses coming in every couple of hours to take vitals, it went from difficult to impossible.

She waited for the blood pressure cuff to squeeze her arm and the nurse to slide the thermostat into her ear for a quick read. But it didn't happen. She opened her eyes, and as her vision slowly cleared, a hand covered her mouth.

Casio...

"Can I trust you not to scream?"

She nodded and he removed his hand.

Casio leaned over her, his face so close she felt his breath as he spoke. "Good morning, sunshine."

Every nerve in her body stood at alert. She knew that tone. No matter what words were spoken in it, she knew she was in danger. "What are you doing here?"

She reached for the nurse caller and found only empty space where it had been all day.

"Looking for this?" Casio asked holding it up, disconnected from the bed. "I didn't think we needed the interruption."

Harper's heart sped up and pounded in her ears. Her head grew dizzy. "What did you want to talk about? I'm sorry I didn't have a chance to get back with you yesterday. Obviously, I was busy almost dying."

The smile he gave her was not a reward for her witty comment. Rather, he grabbed her wrist, squeezing hard until she let out a yelp. "You think this is funny?" He leaned over the rail again, loosening his grip marginally.

"No, of course not."

"Shut up," he commanded, his lips curled into a snarl.

He stood, dropped her wrist, and began pacing the floor. She knew the move. He paced and allowed his mind to work, processing his twisted view of whatever she had done to wrong him. The pacing was a prelude to the punishment. Fear rose to her throat and she glanced toward the door, for the first time sorry that her dad had insisted that the hospital, as compensation for their negligence, upgrade her to a private room at no extra fee. Grateful he wouldn't sue, the hospital had been eager to comply.

She was so tired of being afraid. If she made it out of this alive, she would leave Texas, get as far away from Casio as she possibly could—Seattle, maybe. As much as it would break her heart to leave her parents, she had to find a place where she wasn't terrified every second of every day.

Her eyes followed his movements back and forth in the small area in front of her bed. He raked his fingers through his black hair. "I don't know what to do anymore, Harper," he said. "I can't even grieve because you didn't tell me about my kid."

"I'm sorry, Casio. You had every right to know I was pregnant." *Forgive my lie, Lord.*

"Don't say that," he snarled. "Don't act like you regret keeping it from me."

Unsure how to soothe him, distract him, she kept silent, holding her breath and hoping silence wouldn't make things worse. She could never be sure of the response he wanted.

"So what happened?" he asked. "You did too many aerobics? Took some kind of pill to induce an abortion? Why? Why did you kill my baby?"

Shock burst through her throat and out of her mouth. "No. Casio. That's not what happened."

Tears streamed down his handsome, tanned face. The face she had fallen in love with instantly. "Don't lie to me! You never wanted my baby. You got rid of it. Admit it!"

"I had a miscarriage." If they were a normal couple, a loving, mutually respectful couple, they would be holding each other, weeping together, consoling one another, and he would be assuring her that maybe they could adopt a baby someday, after they healed from the pain of the hysterectomy. But they weren't. And Harper saw now that Casio was too damaged to be the man she needed. She would never be able to forgive him for invading her moments of grief with accusation. "Casio, look at me. It wasn't an abortion. I lost the baby during the night."

"No. You didn't." The look in his eyes no longer held any affection for her. Pure disdain darkened his brown eyes to nearly black, and Harper began to shake. "You never wanted the baby because he was mine. Did you? Admit it!"

"Casio, that's not true. I was trying to find a way to tell you. I just didn't know how. You said you didn't want kids."

He stopped and looked at her for a long moment, studying her, trying to gauge her honesty. Harper hoped she was keeping her eyes open enough, her mouth soft enough. He needed to believe her. She needed him to.

Slowly, deliberately, he reached behind him, pulled out his gun.

A gasp escaped. "Casio," she breathed. "What are you doing?"

"I have to know the truth," he said. "Were you ever really coming back to me?"

Oh, dear Lord. Help me.

"Answer me!" he raised his voice.

The door opened, and a nurse walked in. She saw the gun. "Oh my God."

Casio didn't hesitate. He lifted the gun and fired. In horror,

Harper watched as the twenty-five-year-old mother of two dropped to the ground.

Without a second of hesitation, he pivoted back around to Harper. "Answer me. Were you coming back to me?"

Harper knew she wasn't making it out of this room alive. The gun was already pointed at her heart. She looked him in the eyes and determined that the last words from her lips would not be a lie. "I love you… But no, I would never have brought my baby into your home."

The gun fired. Pain seared her chest and she lost the ability to breathe. She knew this was the last moment of her life. Another shot fired, but Harper Abbott felt no more pain.

After all the months of living in terror, suddenly she felt utter calm. There was no fear. She closed her eyes and breathed her last breath.

Nineteen

There is no fear in this death. Though it is soon to overtake me, I finally know that nothing in this world, neither height nor depth, nor anything else in all creation, will be able to separate me from the love of God that is in Christ Jesus my Lord.

Funny how it took death to remove my fear of death. I come naked, alone, and completely without excuse, plunging into grace I don't deserve.

I want so much to grab Claudia's hand and say, "My blood is nothing. It's His blood that has power to save." I'm sensing the fleetingness of earth. All the cares that seemed monstrous just hours ago have vanished as I observe the cross. I'm filled with the awareness that every second since the beginning, when God spoke, "Let there be…" has led up to this one breath, the last one for me.

The beginning of eternity.

I long to be released from this flesh and yet something holds me.

I hear mother singing, Claudia crying—softly now.

The train is winding down. Outside the bus, people begin to cheer. The caboose must be in sight.

"Oh, thank God," my mother breathes.

"Hang on, Beej," Claudia whispers. "They're almost here."

"Who?" I ask, but of course she doesn't hear.

All I can hear is the sound of singing. Cheering, a different sort of cheering than that of the people milling around outside the bus. It's like the sound at a marathon. There's a finish line in sight. My race is run.

And I suddenly realize, heaven is cheering me on, bidding me come.

I feel my mother's soft, warm lips on my forehead. "It's okay, sweetheart. You can go."

"No!" Claudia's voice echoes, tunnel-like.

I'm floating above my body.

"Georgie!" she screams. "Do something."

I look down. Claudia is frantic. Mother silently weeps.

But nothing is holding me this time.

I am filled with such unspeakable joy as I rise.

I know I will soon see His face.

MONDAY

Victor

The call came at 9 a.m. The news of the shootings numbed Vic. Even though he'd faced a great deal of inhumanity in his line of work, he'd never been closely involved with the victims before. His heavy heart barely allowed for the drive to work.

Harper's murder the night before, followed by Casio's suicide. A young nurse caught in the crossfire. Vic should have taken the day off. He let the intercom button flash and buzz, in no mood to speak with anyone who didn't know him personally enough to call on his cell. But as Isobel stepped into his office, he knew something was about to break.

"You're going to want to take that call," she said, nodding toward the phone. "It's the lab."

Vic's heart nearly stopped as he picked up the line. "ADA Campbell."

"Yeah, this is Sherwood at the lab. Slattery asked us to expedite some samples for you."

"What do you have?"

"Of the four swabs you sent over, only one matches any of the DNA found at the crime scene."

Vic's mind went back over the last couple of weeks. He'd sent principal Newman's, Blake Simpson, Jesse Simpson, and their dad's. If the killer was stupid enough to leave behind evidence, why wasn't he caught earlier?

"Whose?" he asked, finding himself barely able to breathe.

"The DNA matches a hair we found at the scene. Three, actually. One on the bus driver—the perp must've leaned over him for some reason—one randomly on the floor of the bus, and one on Miss Remington."

Impatience built within Vic. Did he really need to know all that? He just needed a name. "And the winner is?"

"Jesse Simpson."

Vic sat back, unable to respond for a couple of seconds. His mind replayed the interview.

"Mr. Campbell?" the voice on the other end of the line sounded hesitant. "You still there?"

"Yes. Thanks, Sherwood. Fax me over that report, will you?"

He picked up his phone to call Casio...then remembered.

Within an hour, the warrant was issued and four cop cars drove up to Jesse's Garage. Vic, along with two officers, walked into the place. Blake met them at the door. "What's going on?"

"We're here for Jesse. His DNA placed him at the crime scene for BJ Remington's murder. Is he here?"

Blake's face blanched. "As God is my witness, Mr. Campbell, he's been gone for two days. Just checked out and never said a word. Dad's been trying to reach him, but he's not answering his phone or anything."

Vic's stomach dropped. "We'll have to search the place anyway."

Blake nodded. "I understand." He frowned. "The thing is, it doesn't make sense. We just got a new contract to service all the sanitation trucks. It was a huge contract, and we went out and celebrated Friday night, then come Saturday, he was gone and we haven't seen him since."

The search of the garage was futile. Wherever Jesse was hiding, this wasn't it. They'd put out an APB and hope Jesse turned up.

As he drove away, Vic's cell phone rang. His heart picked up a beat as caller ID identified Claudia as the caller. "Hi," he said.

"Hey," her breathy voice sent a wave of calm through him. "I heard the sirens. What's going on?"

"The lab matched some hair to Jesse Simpson's DNA swab."

"Jesse?" Claudia remained silent for a few seconds as he had, digesting the information. "I wonder why he would have wanted to hurt BJ."

"Obsession? Maybe he cared a little more about her than he admitted."

"Beej never mentioned him except that she was helping him with some test."

"That's what he told us too. We never really thought he'd turn out to be the killer."

"Did you arrest him?"

"No. He took off two days ago. His family doesn't know where he is."

"You believe them?"

A fair question. "Yes."

"Are you going to the funeral day after tomorrow?"

"Which one?" The thought of the senseless murder-suicide weighed down his heart.

"Casio's dad isn't doing a regular service, and he can't have a cop funeral considering the circumstances." She sighed.

"How did you find out?"

"My dad went to see Gabe. In a ministerial capacity. Gabe's just going to cremate him without a service. Which is probably what the town needs while it's healing over Harper anyway."

"So Harper's funeral is Wednesday?"

"Yes. My dad is preaching the funeral and there will be a dinner afterward in the hall."

"I'll be there, but I might be late."

"Will you meet me in the church sanctuary after the service? Say one o'clock?"

Vic's heart picked up. *Please God, let this be her first step toward coming home.* "I'll be there."

WEDNESDAY

Claudia

Vic hadn't arrived by the time Claudia stepped inside the cavernous building at 12:55 p.m. She'd had to force herself to wait that long so as not to appear too eager.

She made her way to the sanctuary. Only the large, lighted cross on the wall behind the pulpit cast any glow on the darkened room.

Daddy said God had shown him that cross in a vision before the church was built. And it was a nonnegotiable element during construction.

A sense of reverence enveloped her, and she bent down, slipped off her heels, and left them on the end of the last pew. This place had been her playground growing up. Suddenly she wished to be eight years old again, sliding along the floor on her belly under the pews. Mama fussing at her for getting dirty. She smiled.

Slowly she moved in and out of the rows of pews, like she had as a child, running her fingertips along the smooth wood finish. She continued the maze as she very deliberately made her way to the front of the church. Silence engulfed her and even her breath seemed to echo off the stained glass.

She was glad her dad had remained firm and kept the traditional church look, even as the church itself moved forward with the times, adding media and contemporary music, the arts and video announcements.

Finding her way to the front pew, on the far right of the building, she sat, staring at the fifteen-foot cross, beaming light onto the ceiling, a mirror image. She looked up, wondering if Casio had found peace at last. The events of the past few days still felt unreal. She would never have guessed Casio would kill his girlfriend and then himself. Those sorts of things do not happen to people you love.

It had taken ten years to get to this place, and the answers still eluded them. Vic admitted there was no place to go with the investigation unless Jesse turned up. But everyone figured he was probably in Mexico by now.

But for Claudia, her closure was tight. At least knowing who had killed BJ was enough. She would move forward now, working toward her own cure. She only wished she could have come to this place so much sooner.

Her chest tightened with remorse as she replayed the last two years. The pain she'd caused Vic with her absence from their marriage. But more than that, her absence from a real relationship with God.

She was ready to go back to him. She only prayed that all the changes hadn't ruined everything. What if he didn't want her back?

The back doors opened. "Claude?"

"Up at the front." Her voice shook.

"Want me to turn on a light?"

"I like it this way, if you don't mind. Your eyes will adjust in a second. The cross is pretty."

She heard his steps coming to the front and felt his hand on her shoulder. She reached across her body and covered his hand with hers, leaning her head into his arm.

"It's been quite a day, hasn't it?" Vic said softly, stroking her hair.

"Yeah. Surreal. Harper's parents are alone now." She lifted her head. "I wish Mr. Hightower hadn't cremated Casio. I know he did a terrible thing. But I wish he'd been given a burial."

"I know. Me too."

"Thank you for meeting me here," she said, sliding over so he could sit down next to her.

"It's just us?"

"Mama and Daddy are at the hall still helping with the funeral guests. When I left, Daddy was praying with someone. Mama was organizing the food."

Vic took her hand, lacing their fingers. Claudia made no objection, enjoying the warmth of his closeness.

A soft breath escaped between her lips.

Vic turned his body to face her. "Your mom said you didn't sleep last night. You must be exhausted."

Once she'd made up her mind to go back to Vic, Claudia had spent the last two nights at her parents' home. She knew Vic deserved to hear the truth in her heart, but she felt like they both would do better to wait until after the funeral. "I am exhausted," she said. "I feel like I could sleep for a week."

Vic's gentle hand massaged her shoulder. How could she have

ever left this man? Why hadn't she known how much she needed him? How God had shown her such mercy when He touched Vic's heart with love for the likes of her?

"I'm glad you called me here."

"I was so scared we were over."

Gathering in a breath, Claudia knew she had the opening she needed. She took his hand, pressed it to her lips, and then held it against her. "I do want to move on. And I truly feel like I'm ready to do that. Yesterday I made an appointment with a Christian counselor at Cornerstone counseling in Dallas. I'll be starting next week."

He smiled, his eyes lighting up against the backdrop of the glowing cross. "Are you nervous?"

She shrugged, aware that only someone who knows you well would ask the right question. "Some. But I know it's what I need to do."

"Why did you want to see me here, Claude? To tell me that?"

It was now or never. Her eyes misted over with unshed tears. "I want to say that I'm sorry I left the marriage like I did. Mama said the cruelest thing a spouse can do is leave the one who loves you. You were trying to cover me by solving BJ's murder, but all I could see was the pain I felt every time a memory surfaced."

"I wasn't sensitive enough to your feelings, Claudia." He shook his head.

Claudia raised her palm to his cheek. "You did the right thing by letting me go." Tears dripped down her face. "But...now all I want is to come home. If you'll have me back."

Turning his head, he pressed his lips into her palm. "I didn't let you go, honey. I just knew I couldn't make the choice for you. If I gave in to all the panic I was feeling about you leaving, I could have ended up like Casio. Crazy and jealous. I just couldn't let that happen between us."

He slipped his arms around her, drawing her close. He took a breath and said, "I need to tell you something too."

She froze, praying he didn't have bad news.

"I shouldn't have opened the Remington case the way I did."

"What do you mean?" Claudia frowned. "I thought we just established it was a good thing. You solved the murder, freed me to move forward. Et cetera, et cetera."

"And that's the good part. The best part. But what wasn't good was the other part of my underlying motive."

"And what was that?" She'd thought it was for her.

"I wouldn't have admitted it before, but I wanted to look good to take Slattery's place. Everyone in the office was starting to insinuate I should run for the position and it went to my head a little."

"So what are you saying?"

"That I don't think I am ready to run for the job just yet."

"Oh, come on, Vic. Don't punish yourself."

He chuckled and kissed her forehead. "I'm not. Right now I want to be able to support you while you get counseling. And I think we need to work on building back our relationship."

Peace washed over Claudia at his words. They sat together under the shadow of the lighted cross and started over.

Epilogue

SIX MONTHS LATER

Claudia

Claudia tasted the spaghetti sauce one more time and glanced at the clock. Vic would be home any minute. She would have preferred a nice piece of salmon or shrimp scampi for tonight's special meal. Spaghetti wasn't exactly the most romantic dinner—unless one considered Disney's *Lady and the Tramp,* but it was Vic's favorite and she hadn't made it in several months.

She opened the oven and smiled at the golden-brown rolls. Perfection, if she did say so herself. She lifted out the pan with a potholder and set them on the rack to cool.

Something was missing. Glancing about, she placed her hands on hips that had gotten a bit curvier during the past six months. Not much, but Vic seemed to like her with a bit more padding. And as long as her clothes fit, she refused to stress. He could have her any way he wanted her. She was just so grateful God had given Vic the grace to take her back and love her as passionately as ever.

Emmy was staying with Mother and Daddy tonight. The dining table was set beautifully with her best china settings and candles. Everything had to be just right.

Salad! That's what was missing. Flustered, she glanced at the clock again as she hurried to the fridge. Vic said he'd be home no later than six tonight and it was ten till. Darn it. She'd wanted everything to be laid out and ready for him. Upstairs, in the bathroom, she had laid out his favorite comfortable clothes for him to slip right into after his shower.

She'd been working all day to make this night special for her husband. And it all came down to a salad. How frustrating. She'd never liked salad anyway. But Victor did. Especially with pasta, so there was no way she was leaving it out.

She chopped quickly, tossed the vegetables, and breathed a sigh of relief as she wiped down the counter just as the phone rang. Vic's caller ID showed up. She smiled, her heart picking up speed at the thought of how happy he would be in just a little while.

"Vic! Where are you? You were supposed to be home two minutes ago." She laughed. "I have a surprise for you."

"Sweetheart." His voice was sullen, and Claudia sobered instantly.

"What's happened?"

"Turn on the TV. I'm pulling into the drive right now. I'll be inside in a second."

"Okay." Claudia stayed on the line as she walked barefoot across the kitchen, through the hallway, and into the living room where the TV sat. She grabbed the remote and switched it on. *SpongeBob*

SquarePants belted out at her since Emmy had been watching TV earlier that day. "What channel?"

"Six."

As soon as she switched it over, the banner across the top of the screen flashed BREAKING NEWS. The familiar news reporter stood against the backdrop of a nondescript, fifty-year-old brick home. In a corner of the screen, a scene from what looked to be earlier today showed the same house, only during a rainstorm, and this time with an ambulance and two police cars flashing blue-and-red lights. Yellow tape was draped around the edge of the yard to keep curious onlookers at a proper distance.

Paramedics wheeled out a covered body. Claudia frowned, her gut clenched tight. "Who was it, Vic?" she asked into the phone.

The front door opened and closed. She glanced over her shoulder as he entered the living room and tossed his briefcase and keys on the coffee table. He came to her and wrapped his arms around her from behind. She clutched his forearms.

The reporter answered her question. "Retired Detective Hightower was found dead earlier today from complications due to advanced lung cancer. We are awaiting a news conference with Police Chief Braverman and DA Slattery, which should happen any minute."

Claudia gave a snort. "Slattery? What's he doing conducting a news conference about a dead guy?"

"You'll see." He kissed the curve of her neck and Claudia's knees went weak. "Hey, you look even prettier than usual." He lifted his head and sniffed into the air. "And is that spaghetti?"

She flushed and grinned. "Thank you, and yes."

"Oh, here's the news conference."

The police chief wore his blues and, even with a beer belly, looked official and distinguished. "Thank you all for coming. I am going to read a brief statement and then we'll take a few questions."

He cleared his throat and glanced down at the podium that had been set up in front of city hall.

"Today we have sobering news about one of Conch Springs's most decorated and honored retired police detectives, Gabriel Hightower. He had been battling lung cancer for the past several months, and during his bedridden stage, he wrote a confession that implicates him in three murders."

Claudia's eyes widened, and she pressed her fingertips to her mouth.

"Mrs. Hightower, the former detective's wife, was killed and discarded in the rock quarry southwest of town."

The left corner of the screen showed the quarry, where it appeared workers were dragging the water.

Claudia's phone rang, and she moved out of Vic's arms, picked up the device from the coffee table and answered absently.

"Are you seeing this?" Georgie's voice screeched in her ear.

"Yeah." She sank to the couch.

"Is Vic there with you? You shouldn't be alone."

"He's here. Are you alone?"

"No. Well, yes, but I'm okay."

"Are you sure?"

"Oh, please. You know I am."

Her eyes were fixed on the screen and she only half heard Georgie. "Thanks for checking on me. I'm going to hang up so I can hear this, okay?"

"Of course. Call me tomorrow and let me know how you are."

"I missed something," she said to Vic.

"Gabe killed both his wife and Jesse and dumped them in the quarry."

"Jesse Simpson? But why?" Claudia's eyes went wide as the square in the corner switched from a view of the quarry to a school photo of BJ.

The chief had relinquished the microphone to DA Slattery. "The note from Detective Hightower stated that he hired Mr. Simpson to scare the former schoolteacher, Miss BJ Remington, due to personal reasons we will not reveal at this time. We'll open up for some questions now."

Claudia turned to Vic. "So Jesse really did kill BJ, but Gabe's the one who set the whole thing up?"

Vic nodded. "We got word a few hours ago, but I couldn't get away to tell you."

"I'm glad you waited. I'd rather see it after everything is already figured out than sit here all day glued to the news. Did you get to read the note?"

"Yes." His expression remained sober, and he sat next to her, scrubbing his palm across his five o'clock shadow.

"Well?" Claudia raised her eyebrow as if to say, *You will not keep this information from me.* She had gone through hell because of this man and she deserved to know the truth.

He slipped an arm around her shoulders and pulled her close against him as he slouched, propping his legs on the coffee table. "He knew a month before the shooting that BJ was having a baby. His wife had suspected about the affair and one day she saw BJ coming out of her ob-gyn's office and just assumed she was pregnant. She went ballistic."

"But she couldn't have known if BJ was definitely pregnant or not."

"Exactly. The whole thing was a stupid fight based on no real evidence—even though she was right."

"The wife usually is."

Vic gave a small smile. "Anyway, they fought and he killed her in a rage. To cover his tracks, he told his cop buddies she found out about the affair and no one ever questioned his word. He was a decorated cop. A favorite on the force. No one had a reason to suspect him."

Claudia shook her head. "Poor Casio. All those years he thought his mother didn't love him anymore." She leaned up and looked at Vic. "But why kill BJ if everyone believed him?"

"To throw off suspicion about his wife. The news of their affair would have eventually come out. And when that happened, people would have naturally begun to wonder why his wife never came back to see her son. Especially her friends."

"So he hired Jesse, who probably did it for the money." Claudia clenched her fist, feeling the bite of her newly manicured nails. She would definitely need a meeting with her counselor tomorrow.

"Right," Vic said, uncurling her fist. He lifted her palm to his lips and kissed the nail marks. "After we questioned Jesse, he wanted to confess everything. But first he met with Gabe and got himself killed."

Claudia glanced at the TV. The news conference was over and the scenes were looping back to the beginning of the story. "Do you mind if we turn it off?" she asked.

Vic shook his head and pointed the remote. The screen went blissfully dark. "So, thank you for my surprise. I've been craving your spaghetti."

Claudia smiled. "Well, mister. That's not your surprise."

His eyebrows went up and he pulled her back to him. "Oh?"

She laughed. "And *that's* not it either."

"What then?"

"Later." She pressed a kiss to his cheek and stood. "Will you go shower and change while I finish up in the kitchen?"

He frowned just for a split second, his eyes flashing worry. "Will you be okay alone?"

"Don't worry, this didn't set me back," she said. "But I do need a few minutes alone to pray and process. Okay?"

"Sure."

She went to the kitchen, stirred the sauce and began to ladle it into a sauce bowl. "Jesus," she whispered, finding comfort in that name. The last thing she wanted was to ever, *ever* go back to the pain that once surrounded her, like a bubble.

She closed her eyes and remembered that day in the sanctuary as they sat in silence beneath the cross, each ready to move on. Even though it hadn't been easy, and she had endured months of painful counseling, it had all been worth it. And she was changed. A smile touched her lips as she moved around her kitchen, praying, surrendering, and getting her meal ready.

By the time Vic came back smelling of fresh soap and warm

water, she was ready to shove aside the newscast and concentrate on why she had prepared all day. As they sat together, she poured him a glass of red wine, herself a glass of water from a pitcher.

Vic frowned. "Not drinking wine tonight?" He absently set his napkin in his lap.

She shook her head and gave as nonchalant a shrug as she could pull off without grinning. "The doctor says I can't."

His chin jerked up and concern darkened his beautiful eyes. "Are you sick?"

She looked up at him beneath hooded eyes. "Only in the morning."

"Only in the..." His eyes widened. "Are you trying to tell me something?"

Claudia couldn't hold back anymore. She nodded and pressed her palm to the spot just below her navel, where deep inside of her God already knew their yet-to-be-born child. Joy such as she had never felt before welled up and came out in the song of laughter. Sharing the smile in Vic's eyes, the pride and joy as he stood and lifted her with him, she felt a contentment she never knew existed.

He drew her into his arms. "Claude..." He kissed her and then grabbed her to him again. "I'm beyond words."

Somehow she had weathered a storm of pain and death, and just when it seemed like loss would win, grace had stepped in.

Claudia held on to her husband, wrapped her arms around his neck, and allowed herself to be loved.

For More Information on PTSD

U.S. Department of Veterans Affairs
The National Center for PTSD
www.ptsd.va.gov or e-mail: ncptsd@va.gov or call (802) 296-6300

U.S. Department of Health and Human Services
National Institute of Mental Health
www.nimh.nih.gov

Centers for Disease Control and Prevention
www.cdc.gov or www.bt.cdc.gov/masscasualties/copingpub.asp

American Psychological Association
www.apa.org

American Association of Christian Counselors
www.aacc.net

The National Suicide Prevention Lifeline
www.suicidepreventionlifeline.org

If you are experiencing emotional distress or contemplating harming
yourself or attempting suicide, seek immediate assistance:
- Call your doctor's office.
- Call 911 for emergency services.
- Go to the nearest hospital emergency room.
- Call the toll-free, 24-hour hotline of the National Suicide
  Prevention Lifeline at **1-800-273-TALK (1-800-273-8255)**
  to be connected to a trained counselor at a suicide crisis
  center nearest you.

God's Leading Ladies
Life Enrichment Program

If you're a woman who's experiencing the freedom of Christian living and you're ready to enhance your life, Mrs. Serita A. Jakes invites you to join the God's Leading Ladies Life Enrichment Program (GLL). This widely celebrated international program is strategically designed to position and propel Christian women to move beyond their comfort zones by stepping out of the shadows and into the light!

With powerful and provoking topics delivered by a stellar platform of internationally acclaimed speakers, the nine-week curriculum is anchored in conference lectures and interactive workshops. Sessions provide life-changing instruction that encourage Christian women to lead exemplary personal, professional and spiritual lifestyles.

GLL culminates with an elegant celebration. This majestic graduation night, renowned for its breathtaking regalia, splendid theater, and famous celebrity attraction, is held in the fall of the year. Since its 2003 inception, thousands of women from all walks of life have grown immensely through phenomenal instruction and impactful experiences. In 2011, the program was introduced internationally, and has given women from around the world the unique opportunity to participate in GLL.

If you would like more information about GLL visit www.godsleadingladies.com